Praise for the previous no

Praise for *Kee*

"A baby born less than perfect in the world's eyes, a mother persuaded that giving up her child is for the best, a lingering bond that pulls and tugs yet will not break. *Keeping Lucy* follows a mother willing to give up everything to save the child she's been told she must forget. This story will have readers not only rooting for Ginny and Lucy, but thinking about them long after the last page is turned." —Lisa Wingate, *New York Times* bestselling author of *Before We Were Yours*

"In T. Greenwood's latest page-turner, a betrayed mother discovers just how much she is willing to sacrifice for the safety of her child, deemed unwanted by even those most trusted. *Keeping Lucy* is a wholly absorbing tale in which the bonds of marriage, friendship, and family are pushed to the ultimate limit. A heartrending yet inspiring novel that kept me reading late into the night." —Kristina McMorris, *New York Times* bestselling author of *Sold on a Monday* and *The Edge of Lost*

"With *Keeping Lucy*, Greenwood once again mines emotional depths that have become the hallmark of her writing. In fighting for the right to raise her daughter with Down Syndrome, a mother in the late 1960s harnesses the courage and confidence she didn't know she'd possessed. Readers can't help but be drawn into her heartbreaking and uplifting journey." —Mandy Mikulencak, author of *Forgiveness Road* and *The Last Suppers*

"How much would you be willing to sacrifice for a child you didn't know? This is the question posed in T. Greenwood's *Keeping Lucy*, the story of a young mother betrayed by those who claim to know best—including her husband—and the harrowing journey she must take to find her voice and take a stand—even if taking a stand means losing everything. Compassionate, clear-eyed, and often wrenching, *Keeping Lucy* is the kind of story that's meant to be read with the heart, and one that will resonate long after the reading is done." —Barbara Davis, bestselling author of *When Never Comes*

"Greenwood's heart-wrenching, emotional roller coaster of a read also seamlessly captures the transformation of women's roles in the early 1970s. A heartfelt tale of true friendship, a mother's unstoppable love, and the immeasurable fortitude of women." —*Booklist*

". . . An unabashed heart-tugger . . . a moving depiction of the primal power of a mother's love." —*Publishers Weekly*

Praise for *Two Rivers*

"*Two Rivers* is a dark and lovely elegy, filled with heartbreak that turns itself into hope and forgiveness. I felt so moved by this luminous novel." —Luanne Rice, *New York Times* bestselling author

"*Two Rivers* is a convergence of tales, a reminder that the past never washes away, and yet, in T. Greenwood's delicate handling of time gone and time to come, love and forgiveness wait on the other side of what life does to us and what we do to it. This novel is a sensitive and suspenseful portrayal of family and the ties that bind."
—Lee Martin, author of *The Bright Forever* and *River of Heaven*

"The premise of *Two Rivers* is alluring: the very morning a deadly train derailment upsets the balance of a sleepy Vermont town, a mysterious girl shows up on Harper Montgomery's doorstep, forcing him to dredge up a lifetime of memories—from his blissful, indelible childhood to his lonely, contemporary existence. Most of all, he must look long and hard at that terrible night twelve years ago, when everything he held dear was taken from him, and he, in turn, took back. T. Greenwood's novel is full of love, betrayal, lost hopes, and a burning question: is it ever too late to find redemption?"
—Miranda Beverly-Whittemore, author of *The Effects of Light* and the Janet Heidinger Kafka Prize–winning *Set Me Free*

"From the moment the train derails in the town of Two Rivers, I was hooked. Who is this mysterious young stranger named Maggie, and what is she running from? In *Two Rivers*, T. Greenwood weaves a haunting story in which the sins of the past threaten to destroy the fragile equilibrium of the present. Ripe with surprising twists and heartbreakingly real characters, *Two Rivers* is a remarkable and complex look at race and forgiveness in small-town America."
—Michelle Richmond, *New York Times* bestselling author of *The Year of Fog* and *No One You Know*

"*Two Rivers* is a stark, haunting story of redemption and salvation. T. Greenwood portrays a world of beauty and peace that, once disturbed, reverberates with searing pain and inescapable consequences; this is a story of a man who struggles with the deepest, darkest parts of his soul, and is able to fight his way to the surface to breathe again. But also—maybe more so—it is the story of a man who learns the true meaning of family: When I am with you, I am home. A memorable, powerful work." —Garth Stein, *New York Times* bestselling author of *The Art of Racing in the Rain*

Praise for *Grace*

"*Grace* is a poetic, compelling story that glows in its subtle, yet searing examination of how we attempt to fill the potentially devastating fissures in our lives. Each character is masterfully drawn; each struggles in their own way to find peace amid tumultuous circumstance. With her always crisp imagery and fearless language, Greenwood doesn't back down from the hard issues or the darker sides of human psyche, managing to create astounding empathy and a balanced view of each player along the way. The story expertly builds to a breathtaking climax, leaving the reader with a clear understanding of how sometimes, only a moment of grace can save us." —Amy Hatvany, author of *Best Kept Secret*

"*Grace* is at once heartbreaking, thrilling, and painfully beautiful. From the opening page to the breathless conclusion, T. Greenwood again shows why she is one of our most gifted and lyrical storytellers." —Jim Kokoris, author of *The Pursuit of Other Interests*

"Greenwood has given us a family we are all fearful of becoming— creeping toward scandal, flirting with financial disaster, and hovering on the verge of dissolution. *Grace* is a masterpiece of small-town realism that is as harrowing as it is heartfelt." —Jim Ruland, author of *Big Lonesome*

"*Grace* amazes. Harrowing, heartfelt, and ultimately so realistically human in its terror and beauty that it may haunt you for days after you finish it. T. Greenwood has another gem here. Greenwood's mastery of character and her deep empathy for the human condition make you care what happens, especially in the book's furious final one hundred pages." —*The San Diego Union-Tribune*

"Exceptionally well-observed. Readers who enjoy insightful and sensitive family drama (Lionel Shriver's *We Need to Talk About Kevin*; Rosellen Brown's *Before and After*) will appreciate discovering Greenwood." —*Library Journal*

Praise for *Bodies of Water*

"A complex and compelling portrait of the painful intricacies of love and loyalty. Book clubs will find much to discuss in T. Greenwood's insightful story of two women caught between their hearts and their families." —Eleanor Brown, *New York Times* bestselling author of *The Weird Sisters*

"*Bodies of Water* is no ordinary love story, but a book of astonishing precision, lyrically told, raw in its honesty and gentle in its unfolding. What I find myself reveling in, pondering, savoring, really, is more than this book's uncommon beauty, though there is much

beauty to be found within these pages . . . A luminous, fearless, heart-wrenching story about the power of true love."
—Ilie Ruby, author of *The Salt God's Daughter*

"T. Greenwood's *Bodies of Water* is a lyrical novel about the inexplicable nature of love, and the power a forbidden affair has to transform one woman's entire life. By turns beautiful and tragic, haunting and healing, I was captivated from the very first line. And Greenwood's moving story of love and loss, hope and redemption has stayed with me, long after I turned the last page."
—Jillian Cantor, author of *Margot*

Praise for *Breathing Water*

"A poignant, clear-eyed first novel . . . filled with careful poetic description . . . the story is woven skillfully." —*The New York Times Book Review*

"A poignant debut . . . Greenwood sensitively and painstakingly unravels her protagonist's self-loathing and replaces it with a graceful dignity." —*Publishers Weekly*

"A vivid, somberly engaging first book." —Larry McMurtry

"With its strong characters, dramatic storytelling, and heartfelt narration, *Breathing Water* should establish T. Greenwood as an important young novelist who has the great gift of telling a serious and sometimes tragic story in an entertaining and pleasing way."
—Howard Frank Mosher, author of *Walking to Gatlinburg*

"An impressive first novel."
—*Booklist*

"*Breathing Water* is startling and fresh . . . Greenwood's novel is ripe with originality."
—*The San Diego Union-Tribune*

Praise for *Undressing the Moon*

"This beautiful story, eloquently told, demands attention."
—*Library Journal* (starred review)

"Greenwood has skillfully managed to create a novel with unforgettable characters, finely honed descriptions, and beautiful imagery."
—*Book Street USA*

"A lyrical, delicately affecting tale."
—*Publishers Weekly*

"Rarely has a writer rendered such highly charged topics . . . to so wrenching, yet so beautifully understated, an effect . . . T. Greenwood takes on risky subject matter, handling her volatile topics with admirable restraint . . . Ultimately more about life than death, *Undressing the Moon* beautifully elucidates the human capacity to maintain grace under unrelenting fire."
—*The Los Angeles Times*

Also by T. Greenwood

Such A Pretty Girl

T. Greenwood

KENSINGTON
PUBLISHING CORP.

www.kensingtonbooks.com

A photograph is a secret about a secret.
The more it tells you the less you know.

—Diane Arbus

Lost River, Vermont
August 2019

It is Sunday morning, early. Mist hovers over the river outside the window, insinuates itself through the trees. Sasha is still out on the sunporch daybed where she has been sleeping all summer, but I've been up since my phone started buzzing at six a.m. with text after text from Gilly. **Call me**. Gilly should not be awake this early on a Sunday. Sundays in the city are for sleeping until noon, and then La Bonbonniere for salami omelets. **Ry, you up? Please. Call me.** Only bad news comes before noon on Sundays.

And so instead of calling him back, I take the extra time required to make coffee with the French press, stepping outside to grind the beans, so as not to wake Sasha. Boiling water in the kettle on the stovetop, removing it before it begins to scream. I ignore the phone as I wait for the coffee to steep.

It's Sasha's birthday today. *Eighteen*. I promised her we'll go raspberry picking to make a birthday pie for her party tonight. I gather the tools for the crust from the pantry: sifter, mixing bowls, rolling pin. I study the glass jars in the cupboard: flour, salt, sugar. I make sure there is butter and that it's cold.

My phone buzzes again, and my shoulders tense. I slowly pour myself a cup of coffee, then sit down at the kitchen table and look at the screen. This time, there's another entreaty—**READ**—and below it, a link to a *Times* article. I scowl. Usually, Gilly reads the paper, the actual physical paper, from cover to cover, and he never forwards links to anything.

I click.

Mother or Monster?

The headline asks a question, but the implication is clear. The conclusion foregone. They have always questioned my mother's motives; this is nothing new. But I'm confused. It's been years since anyone has written about us, my mother and me. Thirty years since my last film, and nearly as many since I left the business and came home to Lost River. I am no stranger to this vitriol, but it has been decades since a journalist posed this particular rhetorical question.

I remember them, the reporters and talk show hosts, with their Aqua Net hair and hungry smiles. A lifetime later, I can still feel my hands clasped between my knees, ankles crossed, as we sat on their couches, bright lights in our eyes. My mother's body was warm next to mine, an arm around my shoulder or hand on my quaking thigh. *They say you're a* stage *mother*, one of them would, inevitably, say. *That you're living out your unfulfilled dreams through your daughter.* Then the word that made me think of a snake, its V-shaped tongue, flicking, followed by a dangerous hiss: *vicarious.* It was meant to incite, but she would not humor them. Her sharp laughter was quick and purposeful, the squeeze of my shoulder or knee meant to punctuate her answer. *Ryan is a child, and I am her mother. I am her protector. That's all there is.* After the interviews, we would walk hand in hand off set, and she would lean in close and whisper, *It doesn't hurt me, you know.* Somehow, she knew my only concern was how their speculations and accusations might upset *her.* Because even as she claimed to be my protector, we both knew I was hers, too.

I hear Sasha stir, and through the closed French doors to the porch, I see the soft lump of her comforter move, hear her morning grumbles. She'll be up soon.

I look at the screen and quickly scroll up. Below the headline is an image. A black-and-white photo of me as a little girl. Eleven years old.

Blackout, 1977, by Henri Dubois.

How did they get this?

The article explains that this never-before-seen photo of the young actress, Ryan Flannigan, was found during the raid on billionaire Zev Brenner's Paris apartment. And now, apparently, leaked to the press. This man, Brenner, has been in all the newspapers for weeks. But now, this photo—*my* photo—is somehow evidence, historical *proof*, of the depth and breadth of his unspeakable crimes?

I have no idea how Zev Brenner, this horrible man, this *pedophile* and trafficker of girls, came to possess *my* photograph. I haven't even seen it since the day we made it, Henri and me. Since I watched the image emerge from the paper, like magic, in his darkroom at Westbeth, as I sat on the rickety blue step stool I thought of as my own, his large hands awash in red light. Of course, I had known even then that it was a powerful picture, a dangerous one, from the way Henri's face had changed. *My god*, he'd said and shaken his head, his expression not one of wonder but of fear.

They have only posted a portion of the portrait, of course, the photo cropped to reveal just my face, eliminating the offending imagery below. How foolish. They don't seem to understand it is *the face* that offends, that has always offended. I remember the words they used to describe me also felt like beestings: *precocious, preternatural.* The face of a woman on a child's body, the contradiction that launched my career and, in the end, destroyed it.

Mother or monster?

I imagine this ambitious journalist's smug self-righteousness as she writes, this millennial with her black-and-white life, her black-and-white type. Unlike those prickly talk show hosts, she sits safely at her laptop and is not forced to address what she goes on to refer to as my "arresting" face. I imagine the tingle of pride she feels at her byline, unaware or indifferent to the wound she has just clawed open with her words.

I scroll up again, scanning the obligatory recap of my *brief but prolific* career, and my mother's dubious role in it, to get to the final paragraph.

But more disturbing than the discovery of this photo, taken of the preadolescent actress and displayed by the accused sex offender, is the inscription, ostensibly signed by Ryan Flannigan's mother. "For Zev, Remember, darling: les loups ne se mangent pas entre eux—wolves do not eat each other. —Fi."

My heart stutters, sputters, and stops.

Neither Fiona nor Ryan Flannigan was available for comment.

I think of the three *Unknown* calls last week from a New Jersey number. I hadn't even bothered to listen to the voicemails.

My phone shudders in my hand, but it's not my mother. I'm certain she's read the article by now, too, but what could she possibly say to make this untrue? She gifted a private photo of me to this man, a *true* monster. For what? How did she even know him? I feel sick.

The French doors creak open; Sasha yawns and pads softly into the kitchen in a pair of bear-claw slippers and a thrift store cashmere robe riddled with moth holes. "Morning, Mama."

"Happy birthday," I say and smile, pretending that the earth has not just dropped out from under me. She comes and hugs me from behind, her face warm with sleep. The phone persists.

"Coffee's ready," I say.

"You should get that," she says, glancing over my shoulder at the screen. "It's Gilly."

I nod and click Accept, press the phone to my ear.

"Ry?" he says, and at the sound of his voice, the shell begins to crack, that delicate thing I have made to hold my heart.

Sasha blows on her coffee and sips.

"Hi, Gilly!" she says, leaning toward the phone.

"Happy birthday, Sashimi!" he says.

Sasha returns to the porch and nestles into the daybed, the steam from her coffee curling into the crisp air of the porch. A ghost.

"Come home," Gilly says softly.

"I *am* home," I say, looking around at the house where I was born and to which I returned almost thirty years ago. The home Andy and I shared before he left, where we began raising our daughter together, and where I have finished raising her alone. The one place I have always felt safe.

"I mean to Westbeth," he says. "Your mother needs you right now."

"*She* needs *me*? You read the article, right? What on earth would I have to say to her?"

"She wants to explain," he says. "*Please* come home."

It's not Gilly's fault; he only knows part of the story. He was there, of course, but what they always said is true. I *was* a "gifted" actress. But what most people don't realize is that she was, too.

Lost River, Vermont
August 1976

This memory is made of sunlight and mud. Before the city, before Westbeth.

I was ten years old, playing at the river's edge with the other Lost River kids.

"You can do it!" Gilly said from the opposite bank, the river between us. "Come on, Ry! Don't be afraid."

It was August, the end of the season at the Lost River Playhouse. Lost River was the summer home of about thirty people, but my mother and I lived there all year long. The Lost River compound was built on the site of an abandoned motel, with a big main house and a dozen tiny cabins all perched on the edge of a lazy river. A large barn, converted into a theater, sat high on the hill above. Serafina, the proprietor, had been a stage actress in New York when she fell in love with a director who had dreams of starting a summer stock theater in Vermont. Together, they built Lost River, a summer respite for actors who worked in the city and a place for aspiring actors to apprentice themselves. Serafina said she quickly learned she was a better teacher than actor, finding her calling in Lost River. And so, when her husband became bored with rural life and returned to the city, Serafina stayed at Lost River, where she mentored season after season of hopefuls. My mother first came to Lost River in 1965, having just graduated high school, leaving her small hometown near the

Canadian border to play the role of the nurse in *A Streetcar Named Desire*. But at the end of the summer, she didn't want to go home to her sad mother and angry father, and Serafina invited her to stay. Seven months later, on Valentine's Day of 1966, she had me. I was born here and had never lived anywhere else.

Over the next few days, most of the kids would return to the city with their parents, our summer family shrinking again. But I wasn't sad. People came and went from Lost River like the seasons in Vermont. It was no different than the way I felt at the first cold snap of fall, or the first below-zero morning when the wooden floors in our cabin felt like slabs of ice. Or when the last bit of snow in the woods where we played disappeared into the earth.

Besides, we still had time. For now, there was nothing but cold water and mud, the kaleidoscopic green of leaves over our heads, and the burn of the rope in our palms as we each swung out over the water.

"Just grab on tight and run!" Gilly instructed.

All summer, I'd been gathering up my courage to swing across to the other side, but I was afraid. I had studied the others, watched the way they got a running start and then flew. I'd spent months gathering my courage, only to be paralyzed once the thick rope was in my hands. "It's okay," Gilly would say, slinging his skinny arm across my shoulders. "Next time." But after today, there would be no more *next times*, not until the following summer, anyway. Today was my last chance, the last day before Angelica, Joaquin, and Gilly piled into their parents' converted school bus and returned to the city where their mother, Liliana, taught art and their father, Guillermo, was an actor.

Most of the actors and actresses who came to work at Lost River in the summers were on stage or in movies or on TV the rest of the year. This was my mother's dream, too, her longing something I could practically touch. I watched her as the other actors talked about their lives—grumbling about auditions or reminiscing about being on location—saw her eyes widen, and paid attention to how she held her breath. She was hungry for their stories, and they offered them to her in little bits, tiny morsels that she savored. Once, when we all went into Quimby to go to the movies and her friend, Cheri, appeared on the screen, a sound escaped her lips like the first bit of steam escaping from a teakettle, quiet but dangerous. She'd squeezed my arm so hard, her nails made half-moons that lingered there for hours. That was the first time I realized her wanting could be a violent thing.

She never got the lead roles in the Lost River productions, though; she was always at the edges, in the wings. The highlighted characters in the worn Samuel French scripts she carried in the back pocket of her faded bell-bottoms never had names: *Pretty girl* (her favorite); *Matron* (her least); *Waitress*; *Passerby*. But whether she had one line or ten, she took on each role as if it were the lead. She was the only one who, despite having been up late drinking with the cast around the fire behind the big house, or dancing with the handsome actors in the barn until she got slivers in her bare feet, was up at dawn to practice not only her lines, but the lines of every actress in the show.

"Always be ready. People get sick. Hurt," she said. "Shirley MacLaine was just an understudy in *The Pajama Game* on Broadway. When Carol Haney got injured, Shirley stepped in, and within a year, she had a contract with *Paramount*." This legend was as familiar to me as any bedtime tale. She loved stories like this. Of how stars were discovered. Marilyn Monroe was discovered by a photographer while working in a munitions factory. Lana Turner was discovered at sixteen at a soda fountain, where she was skipping class. All these stories felt like magic to me, too: regular people being plucked from their ordinary lives. There were rumors of directors who came to Lost River to scout for their films. Agents who were searching for models. Producers looking for their next project. My mother was convinced that all it took was being in the right place at the right time. Though now it seemed another summer had passed, and my mother remained *un*discovered, like a shimmering bit of quartz just under the surface of the water, waiting for a chance to sparkle in the sunlight.

This summer, they had put on *Streetcar* again, and *again* she had been cast as the nurse, though she knew every single one of Blanche's lines. I could hear her whispering them as the early morning light spilled through the window into our cabin: *I can smell the sea air. The rest of my time I'm going to spend on the sea. And when I die, I'm going to die on the sea. You know what I shall die of? I shall die of eating an unwashed grape one day out on the ocean.* During performances, I watched her struggle not to say the words aloud along with Cheri in that scene, the *want* wild in her eyes.

Now, as I stood looking across the river at Gilly, I understood how it felt to want something just out of reach.

The sun was high overhead, which meant it was almost noon. Time for lunch. Serafina would be expecting us at the big house soon. And after lunch, everyone was supposed to pack up their belongings, clean their cabins. We were running out of time. I was getting so close. At least today I had tried, though I'd had two failed attempts so far. The first time, I managed to leave the bank but chickened out halfway and swung slowly back, dangling over the cold water; Joaquin, who was only ten but already bigger and stronger than his brother Gilly, had to yank on the rope to pull me back to shore. The second time, I swung out far enough, but when it was time to drop the rope, my hands would not loosen their grip, and I wound up back where I'd started.

Gilly, who was twelve, stood on the opposite riverbank waiting for me, the way he had every day since I'd announced my plan. He, like his brother, was shirtless and filthy with mud, shielding his eyes from the sun.

"Come on, Ryan! You can do it," he said again. "Get a running start, hold on, don't let go until you see the ground."

I nodded, gripped the rope, and backed up, grass tickling my ankles. I held tight to the rope as I ran full tilt toward the water, held on as the earth fell away from my feet, and then I was flying across the river below. I felt my bare left foot drag into the cold river and then the earth was coming toward me again. Instinctively, I pulled my knees upward, curling up like a pill bug inside its shell, and I could see Gilly beaming at me.

"Don't let go yet! Hang on!" he said. "Woohoo!"

I shut my eyes tightly, felt the air rushing against my face.

"Now! Drop it!"

I hesitated.

"Now!" he said again, more urgently this time, but already I was a pendulum, reaching the end and beginning to swing back toward where I'd started.

"Wait! Hold on!" he said. "Don't drop it now! It's too late!"

But I was determined, and I released the rope.

I saw the ground rising to meet me, but it wasn't the grassy slope where Gilly stood; rather, the rocky riverbank below. I hit the bank hard and then fell, landing on my back. I felt my chest freeze, my breath seize. I tried to cry out at the pain in my spine, but there was no air in my lungs. I shook my head as Gilly scrambled down the rocky wall.

I sucked in air, but still, nothing came out. When sounds finally did come, I didn't recognize my voice. The moan was deep and raw and hurt, like a wounded animal's.

"It's okay. You just knocked the wind out," he said. "It'll come back."

He helped me up and hugged me, and I felt his heart beating scared in that hollowed-out part of his chest that he didn't like to talk about.

We pulled apart, and his eyes sparked with sunlight. "You *did* it," he said, but I felt almost sick with disappointment.

"Let's *go*! It's time for lunch! We're gonna be late!" Joaquin hollered. He, unlike Gilly, was impatient. He hopped from one leg to the other as if he had to pee.

"I'm starving to *deaf*," Angelica said dramatically, as if *she* were Blanche Dubois.

Gilly and I walked along the opposite shore to the little foot-bridge that traversed the river and then made our way with his siblings back up the steep grassy bank to the main house. The sun had dipped behind the clouds, which were moving dramatically across the sky. I shivered. I'd forgotten to bring my towel, and the mud from the riverbank was wet and cold on my skin.

At the side of the house, we hosed the mud off our feet and legs, screeching when the initial warm bursts of water turned suddenly and bitingly cold. We were filthy, wild children when we were on our own, but we knew we would not be fed (never mind allowed inside) until we cleaned up. We took turns, helping each other and then toweling off (towels yanked from their pins on the long line strung from the house to the big maple tree in the yard) before climbing up the steps and entering through the screen door into the kitchen.

When Serafina was on lunch duty, we had sourdough bread still warm from the oven. Tabbouleh with fresh mint, tomatoes, and cucumbers from the garden. She made sweet sesame-seed cookies and chamomile sun tea with honey. My mother's lunches were less inspired: day-old sourdough bread, a hunk of sharp cheddar cheese, and mealy apple slices. It made me feel bad when the kids accepted their disappointing meals and mumbled their thanks. I always made sure to hug her extra tightly and tell her how delicious it all looked.

Today was no different, and I mustered delight at the pallid green grapes and disc of canned Boston brown bread. "Thanks, Mama! We're starving!"

But as the others plodded back outside with their sorry lunches, she set my plate down and then helped me up onto the counter so we were eye to eye.

"I have a proposition," she said.

My mother always had *propositions*. A proposition, she had explained, meant that I got to help make the decision. We were in this together, she said. *Partners in crime*: Butch Cassidy and the Sundance Kid; Bonnie and Clyde.

"How would you feel about going to the city with Gilly's family?"

"By myself?" I asked.

She laughed that sharp short laugh of hers and shook her head. "No, of course not! I meant how would you feel if *we* went to the city with Gilly's family? To Westbeth."

Westbeth. Gilly had told me about his apartment in New York, of course. Westbeth was a complex of old factory buildings where hundreds of people lived, and everyone who lived there was an artist. Actors, like at Lost River, but all different kinds of artists, too. There were painters and puppeteers. Photographers and dancers and musicians. He told me his neighbor played the French horn for the New York Philharmonic, and the lady down the hall made sculptures out of junk she fished out of the Hudson River. There was even a dance studio in the building; their ceiling thumped as the dancers leaped.

Still, I had never been to the city. I had never even left Lost River. The only cities I knew were from TV and movies. Earlier that summer, we'd all piled in the bus to go to the drive-in movies, a double feature. When *Rosemary's Baby* came on, the grown-ups sent us all to the back. Told us to go to sleep, but Gilly and I had peeked out from our sleeping bags to watch. When I thought of New York, it was of Mia Farrow's character, pregnant and desperate, wandering the streets. The dark apartment, the horrifying chanting in the walls of her building.

"You mean go for a visit?" I asked.

My mother tilted her head, smiling. "Actually, I was thinking more about giving it a try."

Giving it a try was the phrase my mother used whenever she wanted me to do something new that I might not be very happy about: trying a new food, or trying to wash my own hair, or trying to sleep alone in my bed while she took a walk to clear her head.

"You mean leave Lost River?" I asked; the realization of the enormity of her *proposition* was starting to hit. I couldn't swallow, and I wondered if I had lost my breath again.

"Gilly's dad is going to be on location in LA from the beginning of November through May. He doesn't want Liliana all by herself with the kids, and Liliana said she'd love to have us. If we like it there, then we'd jump to the top of the waiting list when a new apartment opens up."

She was saying words, but they were disappearing into the air like puffs of smoke. I was trying so hard to hold on, to make sense of what she was saying.

"And if we hate it, we can always come back here. Serafina said we'll always have a place to come home to."

"But what if I don't want to go?" I said.

She frowned.

"Ryan," she said, and her voice felt like a balloon about to pop. "Where will we sleep?"

"The apartment is big, much bigger than our cabin. We'll have our own sleeping loft."

I thought of our cabin, just two rooms with a big lumpy bed. A narrow bathroom and a tiny kitchenette, a small potbelly woodstove to keep us warm. I thought of the barn cats that snuck into our cabin and snuggled under the covers. I thought of the little mint-green fridge, where my mother kept ice-cold bottles of Tab for her and Orange Crush for me. I thought of the way the sun streamed through the sheer curtains onto our faces in the morning, the sound of the river below, and the rain on our roof. *Home.*

I shook my head. I couldn't breathe.

She backed away from me and grabbed the empty can of brown bread. "I'm never going to get anywhere if I keep playing these bit roles here every summer. Guillermo knows people in the city. On Broadway. Casting directors. Agents. He promised he'd line up auditions before he leaves for LA."

She walked to the sink to rinse the can. When she turned around, she looked at me almost angrily.

"This wasn't supposed to be forever," she said, but I knew she wasn't talking to me. Not really. It was as if she were only reciting someone else's lines.

And then I felt myself release, the earth fall away beneath my feet. I closed my eyes tight, my only solace that Gilly would be there on the other side.

Lost River, Vermont
August 2019

"What did Gilly want?" Sasha asks, as we walk from the house down to the riverbank. "He never calls that early."

I pretend not to hear her over the rushing of the river and a hermit thrush's song.

The mist has lifted, and the sun is burning brightly. I can hardly believe that summer is almost over. Just two more weeks until Sasha leaves and I'm alone here.

Sasha leads the way. She knows Lost River as well as I do. Better, even. She has spent eighteen years roaming these pastures, memorizing this land. It is a part of her as much as she is a part of it. I can't picture Lost River without her. I can't imagine *myself* without her. All summer, I have been hoping she might change her mind and stay a little longer.

We walk down the well-worn trail to the river, dead grass and flattened leaves beneath our feet. They call these trails *desire lines*—nature eroded by human impatience. Even here, ten miles from civilization, we are still looking for shortcuts, minimizing the distance between ourselves and that for which we yearn.

There are raspberry bushes all over the property, but the ones along the river's edge are the first to ripen. Sasha carries an old, white enamel colander for our birthday harvest. I watch her as I have always watched her, with a sort of reverent fascination. The fact that she is my daughter, that she came from me, is something I still cannot entirely understand. My own mother and I had shared so many physical traits: honeyed skin, molasses hair, and maple eyes. But Sasha's skin is milk, her hair shimmery corn silk, with eyes lighter than the blue of the sky. Eighteen years, and it still stuns me to think that my body created something, *someone* so very different from myself. When she was born, I remember looking at her in baffled wonderment that she could be so profoundly *herself*, and no longer a part of me.

This summer, she has taken to braiding her blond curls into a sort of Pre-Raphaelite crown, into which she threads whatever wildflowers are blooming. Lilacs in the spring. Later, dandelions and daisies and forget-me-nots. Today, she has woven black-eyed Susans and purple thistles through her curls. She wears a faded gingham frock she found at the thrift store in Quimby—a sort of 1950s housedress with a Peter Pan collar and pearly snaps down the front. It is too big, and she has altered it to fit with safety pins and a few stitches. She wears worn lace-up boots and the same men's tube socks she wore yesterday and slept in last night, the heels likely black from walking in stocking feet outside. She has dressed herself since she was two years old; she was never a doll to me, as I had been to my mother.

When she turns back to me and catches me wondering at her, she smiles. Summer freckles speckle her upturned nose, a nose that is also neither mine nor her father's. Her elfin features are, perhaps, the greatest mystery. Perhaps some distant Celtic ancestor is making herself known in Sasha's face. She has none of my darkness, and none of her father's clumsy oversized features, either.

"Did you hear me?" she demands, stopping on the footpath and resting the colander against her hip. "What did Gilly want?"

"Oh," I say, shrugging. "He was just checking in." The tempered truth.

It would be foolish to think that the news of the raid, the photograph, won't reach her. By the time we left the house this morning, at least a dozen of my friends had texted, emailed, and messaged me a link to the article, which by nine a.m. had been syndicated across all news outlets, from the local ABC to TMZ.

And even if no one has shared it with her yet, she could still stumble upon it, like the buzzing hornets' nest she found in the barn when she was seven. Curious, she'd lifted it out of the eaves like plucking an apple from a tree. She was stung fourteen times that day, and she had looked at me as I applied a poultice of bread soaked in milk, searching not for comfort but an explanation. "Why?" she kept repeating. As if I knew the secrets behind a hornet's rage. She has always come to me for answers to impossible questions.

"What happened?" I ask, distracting, pointing to the large Band-Aid on her bare knee.

She looks at it, mystified, as though she's forgotten it was there. "Oh, I fell," she says and shrugs. "At silks the other day."

All summer, she has been learning how to climb into the sky using only slippery swaths of fabric. Ascension, suspension, cocooning herself in the silky chrysalis before unfurling into flight. I was nervous, of course, when she said she wanted lessons, but I made a promise to myself the day she was born that I would not allow *my* crippling fear to become hers. As a result, she lives a thrilling life. A dangerous life. Roller coasters, skydiving, trapeze lessons, and now, aerial silks. Parenting Sasha has always been an exercise in relinquishing control.

But now, she's embarking on her next adventure, leaving Lost River, driving cross-country alone to LA, where her father lives. She wants to be a photographer, and her plan is to take a gap year and work on her portfolio to apply to art schools. This spring, she got the idea that she'd like to document in photographs what it means for a young woman to travel alone across the United States. I have spent most of the summer trying to dissuade her, offering to fly her to LA, suggesting that the project sounds amazing but that it is just too risky. There is no harness or safety net for this challenge. She's never left Lost River, and as savvy as she might appear, she's still so naïve. Her father hasn't helped things. He dismisses my worries the way he always has. "She'll be *fine*," he says. "It's two weeks on the road. And then she'll be with me."

When we reach the river's edge, I pull my sleeves from my elbows down to my wrists. To reach the berries requires navigating a tangle of sharp brambles. We pick in silence under the hot late-summer sun. Perspiration rolls down my back as the colander slowly fills with fruit.

"What does it mean?" she asks after a long time, and I study her face for clues. She could be four years old again: *Why is the river cold? Who put the stones there? Do birds ever sleep?*

"What does what mean?" I ask, spotting a bright red burst amidst all the green.

"*Wolves don't eat each other.*"

The brambles are sharp. I feel them scratching the exposed skin of my hands and wrists as I reach into a crimson cluster. I gently pinch the berry, coaxing it off its stem. It is ripe and falls easily into my palm; it's ready to let go. Gently cradling it there, I reach for the second berry in the cluster. When my palm is full, I gingerly withdraw my hand.

"Mom?"

She is looking to me again for answers. She's grown now, but I'm still her mother, and she still believes I can explain every mystery.

"That photo?" she asks. "Henri took it?"

I nod.

"The paper makes it sound like it's . . . like kiddie porn or something. But it's art, right?"

I close my eyes and breathe. On the insides of my eyes, I see the image. I remember the night of the blackout, when we took it. "Yes," I say. "Of course. It was innocent. I was a little girl."

Sasha looks at me, hard, as if gauging whether I am telling her the whole story. She will make a terrific photographer one day; her gaze is relentless and demanding.

"It was a different time," I say. "And Henri was like a father to me. He didn't do anything wrong. Fiona is the one who did something wrong."

"How did she even know that guy Brenner?" she asks. "Have you read about what he did? He recruited girls, girls younger than *me* . . . what a sick—"

"I think we have enough for a pie," I say, peering into her colander. The berries are bloodred against the chipped white enamel. "You can help me with the crust."

"Are you going to talk to her?" she asks softly.

"No," I say, shaking my head.

"Why not?"

Sasha has only met her grandmother a handful of times. I've never taken her to the city. Everything she knows about my life before her birth is from what I have told her and, I imagine, what she's been able to glean from the Internet. From the films themselves, too, of course, those odd little time capsules: VHS tapes and scratched DVDs from yard sales and thrift stores. Occasionally, we'll catch one playing late at night on TV or streaming on Netflix. She's seen them all. Read the articles, I'm sure. I've only forbidden her from reading my mother's autobiography; I don't keep a copy in the house. But she's eighteen now; she will do what she wants. What she must.

"Wait," I caution as she starts to walk back up the trodden path. "Hold still."

"Why?" she asks, turning to me.

There's a hornet buzzing about the flowers in her hair.

"Just don't move," I say, and gently wave my hand over her head. I watch as the hornet lands on my thumb, barely wince as the stinger enters my flesh. *This*, I think, is a mother's job. To take on your child's pain.

"Make a wish," I say to Sasha. "Close your eyes."

The candles melt into the hot crust of the pie. Eighteen of them, ablaze.

Sasha's friends have gathered in our barn to help her celebrate:

the girls and boys that she's grown up with. Her best friends, Pia and Josephine. Arthur. Sweet Luca, who insisted on coming, though I know she has been slowly breaking his heart all summer. These people are her pack, these beautiful, feral children.

Luca's band plays "Happy Birthday" on the stage, a projector flashing a dreamy slideshow of photos she and Pia made this summer onto an old sheet behind them, their hazy images cast against a sea of faded rosebuds.

Tonight, Sasha wears a pair of paint-splattered men's Levi's, cinched with a thick leather belt, and a cropped red tank top that reveals her pale, tiny waist. Red lipstick to match, false eyelashes, and heavy liquid liner. It's chilly in the barn, and she is wearing a white angora sweater I don't recognize. The girls share everything: clothes, secrets, boys. The flowers have wilted in her hair. She closes her eyes, makes a wish, and then leans over the flames.

At midnight, I leave them, walking through the cold grass down the hill from the barn with an armload of dirty plates. The music sounds far away by the time I am in the house again. I have told them all they can stay the night, spoken to their parents, who are our neighbors and friends. The cabins are crumbling but warm and dry, and I know they have likely snuck in beer or strawberry wine. Josephine's dad grows weed; I have smelled it on all of them. They're good kids, just bored. I never planned to be one of those parents who says, *If she's going to drink, I'd rather she do it safely at home than be out on the roads,* but now here I am. I am so many things I never expected to be.

My thumb is swollen where the stinger went in. A red rash is spreading up my wrist. The skin of my whole hand feels tight. I need a Benadryl. I change into my pajamas and go to the bathroom, catching a glimmer of my face in the beveled mirror.

My throat constricts as I think of the photo in the article. Of that little girl. I search for her now, leaning toward my reflection. My face: heart-shaped still, sun-kissed skin from a summer spent in my garden. The deep dimple under one sleepy amber eye remains. But over the decades, my face has aged and changed. It's no longer extraordinary; it's simply a face now fitting its body, which, too, is a casualty of time.

As the drowsy effects of the antihistamine take hold, I curl up in my bed, the window fan set to low. The breeze blows across my skin. The music quavers in the distance.

It feels like only moments later that I wake with a buzz and a jolt. Something is wrong. My thoughts go immediately to the barn, to the kids. I jump out of bed and rush to the window, expecting catastrophe. Half-dreaming disaster. But the barn is not on fire. It's quiet outside, other than a bit of distant laughter. Confused, I return to the bed. Then the phone vibrates.

Gilly. Again.

"Gilly," I say, my throat froggy.

"Oh, *Ry*," he says, his voice strange.

I close my eyes, wonder what has happened now, how things could possibly be worse. I feel the sickening thud of my heart, and suddenly I know, even before he speaks, what he's going to say. Somehow, I'm able to intuit everything from his ragged breath. Gilly and I have always communicated in this way.

"It's Henri," he says. "Fiona found him tonight. In his bathroom. Hanging from the pipes."

My throat aches. *Henri.*

"Because of the photo?" I ask Gilly, though what I mean, what Gilly knows I mean, is *Because of me?*

He doesn't answer, because, unlike my mother, Gilly has never been able to lie.

"Come home," he says.

"I can't," I say, tears filling my eyes. "I don't think I can face Fiona right now."

There is a pause, and I worry the call was dropped. The reception here is spotty at best. "Gilly?"

"Please, Ry," Gilly says. "Never mind Fiona. *I* need you here."

Lost River, Vermont
August 1976

W e brought only the things we needed or loved. Serafina said to leave anything we couldn't fit in the bus behind. That it would all be here waiting for us. Even if we didn't return until the following summer, Lost River would always be our home.

Before we left, Serafina held onto my mother for a long time, cradling her face in her veiny hands as she whispered something to her, as if she were her mother. They stood, foreheads tipped and pressed together, fingers locked into knots as they said their good-byes.

Angelica and Joaquin had already staked claim to the back of the bus, where the seats had been removed and a bed installed. Gilly took my hand and showed me where to store my small backpack of treasures (a red leather copy of *Grimm's Fairy Tales;* my collection of butterfly wings; my Sunshine Family dolls—though I had lost both the gray-haired grandmother in her calico dress and the tiny plastic family dog). We took seats at the opposite sides of a dinette booth, which, he explained, also folded open into a bed.

"Are you hungry?" Gilly asked. "There's lots of food in here."

Serafina had sent us off with a wooden apple crate full of snacks, as if we were driving across the country rather than the six hours it would take to get to New York. Gilly pulled out sandwiches wrapped in brown butcher paper, labeled in waxy grease pencil with our names. Red and green Jersey Macs, picked from the tree just that morning, and cellophane packets with the sweet sesame cookies I loved inside. Cold bottles of root beer for us kids and real beer for the adults.

I shook my head. "I'm not hungry," I said.

"You wanna play war?" he asked.

He had a worn pack of cards he'd pilfered from one of the actors. It had photos of naked ladies on the back, ten different ones. Over the summer, we had studied them all. I was fascinated by them, by their pouty smiles and cartoonish breasts. Of course, I saw women naked all the time at Lost River. I spent many nights playing with my dolls in the actresses' dressing room, and clothing was optional when swimming in the river. But the playing-card ladies were otherworldly. Beautiful and strange.

When Gilly had first shown them to me, I'd felt prickly, ashamed, but he'd just shrugged and shuffled through like it was any old deck of Bicycle cards. "We're missing the two of spades, but I found one from another pack." And luckily, it didn't matter in war, which was the only game we both knew.

Gilly was shirtless as always, birdlike shoulder blades and knobby shoulders. He sat cross-legged on the bench seat across from me.

"*War . . . huh!*" Gilly sang now, as we settled into the little booth and he shuffled. "*What is it good for?*"

This was our usual call and response. But today, I couldn't summon it.

"Come *on*, Ry, *what is it good for?*" He tilted his head at me, waiting.

"Absolutely nothin'," I managed, as my mother and Liliana climbed aboard, and Guillermo positioned himself in the driver's seat. When he reached to the bar and pulled the folding door shut, it felt like we were sealing ourselves into a space capsule. My ears rang, and my heartbeat pattered like heavy rain on the roof of our cabin. I held onto the edge of the bench seat and felt like I might throw up. Gilly was dealing the cards, and each time, a different naked lady looked up at me.

Sweat broke out across my forehead, and I wiped at it with my wrist, as Guillermo turned the ignition and the bus roared to life.

"You okay?" Gilly asked.

My mother and Liliana were in the row of seats behind Guillermo, chatting. Angelica and Joaquin were laughing in the back; I could hear the claps and slaps of their hands as they played Miss Mary Mack.

Nobody besides Gilly knew I was having one of my attacks.

I shook my head and leaned forward, putting my head between my knees, as the bus lurched forward and the gasoline fumes made my empty stomach turn.

"Come down here," he said softly as he ducked under the table.

Shaking, I followed his lead. He sat on the floor, splayed his legs out into a V, and I sat in the crook he'd made, my back to his chest. We'd had to do this before.

My mother's sharp laughter filled the bus, and the smell of Liliana's cigarette made my stomach flip again.

"Cross your arms," he whispered, putting his arms around me and holding on. I closed my eyes as the earth rumbled beneath us, focusing only on Gilly's words. "Now breathe in," he said. I took a deep breath through my nose, focusing on the smell of grass that he carried in his skin. He smelled like Lost River, and I knew—somehow—that as long as I had Gilly, I still had home, and after a few minutes, I could breathe again.

New York City abruptly came into view through the bus windows. It felt like the opposite of Dorothy's arrival in Oz, as if the bus had hurtled through the technicolor landscape of Vermont only to land in a black-and-white world, absent of color or life. It was a painting created using a palette of gray: asphalt, concrete, sky. Even the river was a leaden swath.

My mother turned to me and caught my eye, her face filled with wonder and delight. I mustered a smile, but looked out the window

at the looming monochrome skyline and felt as if we'd been swallowed into the belly of a whale.

Guillermo dropped us off on Bank Street, unloaded our things
onto the sidewalk, and then gave a little honk of the horn before he
took off to park the bus across the river in New Jersey, where he
stored it during the year. Angelica and Joaquin raced across a concrete courtyard toward the front doors, and my mother and Liliana
gathered our boxes and bags, our backpacks, and one giant terra-cotta
pot with peachy-colored begonias that Serafina insisted my mother
take to remind her of home. I was grateful for the orange blooms
now, so hopeful and bright in this strange world of shadows.

The neighborhood was eerily quiet, not at all how I had imagined New York would be. I'd expected streets packed with cars and
yellow taxicabs, a million people bustling about. But the sidewalks
here were empty, and the only vehicles on the streets were big trucks
bending around the corners, hissing and sighing. The smells were
dizzying, though: hot asphalt, nauseating diesel, and the wet dog
smell of the river. The sidewalk was strewn with cigarette butts and
candy wrappers. Black garbage bags lay stacked in small heaps with fat
flies hovering over them. I stepped over an open Styrofoam con-
tainer, what I thought to be grains of rice suddenly wiggling. *Maggots.*
A ship horn blasted in the distance.

"You kids got the rest?" Liliana asked. "And don't dillydally out
here." She and my mother also disappeared into the building.

Gilly shouldered a duffel bag, then helped me put a backpack on.
He grabbed my mother's wicker basket filled with our clothes, and I
picked up the begonias.

"Hey there," someone said, and we turned around.

The woman was tall, wearing the highest pair of platform shoes I
had ever seen, her muscled legs encased in fishnet stockings. She was
wearing a sparkly green dress and a shiny black wig.

"Little G!" she said huskily, clapping her hands together.

"Hi, Jackie!" he said, smiling.

"I missed you this summer!" she said, pouty with bee-stung lips.

"And who's this gorgeous little creature?" she asked, putting her large hands on her knees, bending down to look at me. Her green eyes were sparkling under heavy blue lids.

"This is my friend, Ryan. She lives here now."

"Well then, little beauty," she said, "welcome home."

"Who's that?" I asked as Jackie walked away, teetering on her impossible heels, the smoke from her cigarette circling her like a wraith. "Is she an *actress?*"

"No. That's just my friend, Jackie-O," he said, shrugging. "*Come on.*" He waved for me to follow him.

We walked into the building. After passing through a long hallway, he gestured for me to join him outside again, in another courtyard this time: an interior one, surrounded on all sides by towering buildings. My eyes sought the sky. Up, up, I looked. The building surrounding us made me think of the M.C. Escher drawing that hung by three red thumbtacks in Serafina's bathroom. The curved balconies jutted out from every other window like winding stairsteps to the sky above. I squinted at the sun, which was fighting through the gloom.

"Which one is yours?" I asked.

"Almost all the way up," he said, pointing.

Unlike the streets outside, the inner courtyard was full of people. Men and women were reading and eating. An elderly gentleman was painting at an easel; the image on the canvas held a few vibrant slashes of blue. A group of kids of all different ages were playing some sort of game, racing and screaming through the courtyard. I stepped back as a boy in roller skates zoomed past me, close enough to touch, the Bazooka scent of him lingering. I smiled. Maybe this wouldn't be so bad.

"Is that hide-and-seek?" I asked, looking at the kids. We played hide-and-seek at Lost River, too, though the game always scared me a little. I didn't like to hide, because all the best spots were in the dark and shadowy places I usually avoided (the empty horse stalls, the dark woods, the damp root cellar under the heavy bulkhead). And I didn't like to be It, because the quiet hush of people trying not to be found always made me uneasy.

"Manhunt," Gilly said. "It's fun. I promise."

Liliana and my mother had stopped to talk to a woman wearing a fuchsia scarf wrapped around her head. "We'll meet you upstairs," Liliana said as we approached them.

Standing near the elevator was a tall, thin man in a uniform. His skin was pale, and his cheeks were sunken. He reminded me of Ichabod Crane from "The Legend of Sleepy Hollow." He was so lanky, it seemed there was nothing but bones inside his uniform. He nodded at us as we pressed the button to go up.

When the doors closed, Gilly said, "That's Raymond. He's the head security guy. They say he has a wooden paddle he uses when he finds kids running around after curfew."

"A paddle?"

"Yeah, if he catches you outside your apartment after ten o'clock, he'll come after you with the paddle for a spanking. He keeps it in his apartment in the basement. My friend, Ricky, got caught once. He couldn't sit down for a week."

My stomach plummeted as the elevator jerked us skyward. I had never been on an elevator before. Gilly reached out and squeezed my hand as we ascended to the ninth floor.

The corridor leading to their apartment was narrow and dimly lit, eerie despite the white walls and ceilings. It was like the hospital, a place I had only been once, when I broke my arm. The linoleum floors were polished and made our sneakers squeak.

I could hear the distant sound of music playing. It made me think of the tin can telephones we made at Lost River, the sound shivering along our stretched string. The whole building seemed to be humming, in fact: voices and music, the clattering of dishes, and the muffled sounds of fans whirring against the late summer heat. A clear mellow sort of sound pulsed from behind a closed door.

I remembered *Rosemary's Baby* and took a deep breath.

"French horn," Gilly explained. "There's an opera singer down the hall, too. Mrs. Lake. She's always singing when Angelica's trying to sleep. Also, just so you know, Mom thinks she's a *witch*."

At the end of the hall was an open door.

"Here we are!" Gilly said.

Inside was a small room, with a double bed and Liliana's easel and artwork stacked against the wall. Where would we sleep? Where was the kitchen? The bathroom? My mother had said it was a big apartment, but this room was smaller than our cabin at Lost River.

"This is just my mom and dad's room and Mom's studio," Gilly said. "Come!"

He then led me around the corner to a steep staircase, and I could hear Angelica and Joaquin arguing above us.

Walking up the steep stairs to the main floor of the apartment, I was first struck by how cheery it was, how bright. Tall white walls, white ceilings, curtainless paned windows on either side. The ceilings had to be a dozen feet tall. The glossy parquet floors were slippery, and I almost fell as Gilly grabbed my hand and we ran toward the far end of the apartment where the kids slept and where, as promised, there was a loft bed for me and my mother. A row of windows looked out at the city below.

"That's the World Trade Center," Gilly said, pointing at two tall towers far in the distance. "I watched them get built from here. They're the tallest buildings in the whole city. If you ever get lost, just look for the Towers, and they'll help you find your way home."

I nodded, but planned never to get lost here.

Back at home, my mother had pulled out Serafina's atlas to show me where we would be living, but maps to me felt like riddles. It didn't seem to make sense that you could flatten the world like this. But now, from way up here, I could almost relate those grids in the tattered book with the streets I saw below.

"What happens if there's a fire?" I asked when I realized there was no door to the main building on this floor. I felt a familiar slither of panic.

"Fire escape!" he said, and moved across the room to where

there was a small kitchen and dining area flooded with golden light. He went to a tall window and shoved it open, revealing one of the half-moon balconies we had seen from the courtyard below.

"You just climb out here and go over to Mrs. Lake's apartment," he explained. The very thought of climbing out onto that precarious perch, while a fire raged below, made me dizzy.

"Don't worry," he said. "We're safe here."

The building felt like the wooden puzzle box I'd gotten for my tenth birthday: all sorts of moving pieces and hidden compartments. It was magical and scary all at once.

There was a knocking sound, and it took me a few moments to realize that it was coming from the door downstairs. Gilly pulled me again by the hand, and we raced back down the steps. I assumed it was my mother and Liliana, needing us to open the door for them since their arms were full. But when Gilly swung the door open, there was a man standing in the hallway.

He was older than our parents, but not *old man* old. He had a round belly and wore a chambray shirt with red suspenders and faded blue jeans. He had a beard and droopy sort of mustache and big, kind eyes. "Well, *allo!*" he said.

"Henri!" Gilly said, and threw himself into the man's arms. The man hugged him back. When he caught my eye, he smiled at me.

"Henri, this is Ryan!" Gilly said excitedly. "I told you about her, right? She's from Lost River. My best friend."

"Well," Henri said, laughing. "How lucky you are."

But I didn't know if he meant Gilly or me.

Lost River, Vermont
August 2019

Henri is dead. I feel the weight of this in the center of me, an extra, aching bone. He was an old man, of course. Nearly eighty. But the violence of his death stuns me.

"I'll go with you," Sasha says when she finds me crying in the kitchen. "To New York."

"That's okay," I say, shaking my head. I press a tissue against my nose and wipe away the tears that are hot on my cheeks. "It's your last couple of weeks at home. You should be here with your friends."

Outside, the world is made of fog. Usually, this enclosure makes me feel safe. But today, it is suffocating. I look out the window, down the hill, to the tidy, quiet row of cottages along the river. The kids are all sleeping still, except for Sasha and Luca, who had to leave early to go work at his parents' diner in town. He and Sasha walked up to the house together earlier, and I watched him lingering in the driveway, waiting for something from her. But she'd just stood there, arms wrapped around her own waist, kicking at rocks with her slippered foot.

"How are things, with Luca?" I ask.

"*Done*," she says. "At least for me. I haven't told him that yet."

"I'm sorry."

She shrugs. "I'm just over it. He's so . . . agh . . ."

"Needy?"

"That's an understatement," she says. "It's more like he's *hungry.* And I'm like this delicious piece of chocolate cake. But really, he's just looking at the frosting. For all he knows, I could be plain old vanilla on the inside. Or like spice cake. With *raisins.* But he just sits there *salivating.*"

I smile. "I *like* spice cake."

"Not my point," she says, and sighs. "I think he's more interested in my frosting than my cake. You know what I mean?"

I do know what she means. I remember exactly how it felt for everyone to look at my face and think they knew what was inside my head, my heart. I remember that hunger for what people thought I was, for what people wanted me to be.

But not Henri. Henri *saw* me. He used to joke that his camera gave him superpowers, that he could see *inside* people with his Rolleiflex. It was true; when I looked at his photos of me, it felt like he was the only one besides Gilly who understood who I really was.

I think of the photo, of the night of the blackout, and the ache in my chest returns.

"So, the memorial is on Wednesday," I say. "At Westbeth. I figure I'll head down Tuesday and come home on Thursday."

Before Sasha and Luca came up to the house earlier, I was searching for last-minute plane tickets online. It will be faster to just drive. We're two hours from the closest airport, and the train takes all day. I hate driving in the city, though.

"I can drive!" Sasha says, reading my mind. "It'll be good practice for LA."

"Aren't you planning to see Zu-Zu this week?" I ask. Sasha has been soaking up every last minute of her time here with her friends before they are scattered like so much dandelion fluff. Every weekend on the calendar is marked up, her tiny handwriting filling the hours with her friends' names and various destinations. This weekend is a stay with her friend Zu-Zu and her family at their house on Lake Gormlaith. Next weekend is the county fair in Quimby. Only two weekends left before she's gone.

"She's actually still down in the city. Her intensive is over, but she stayed on for a one-week *pas de deux* program. We could bring her back up with us!" she says. "Her mom and dad just went down for her performance last week; I'm sure they'd be psyched not to have to drive back down again."

Zu-Zu has been living in New York since she was sixteen, training to be a ballet dancer, seeing her family only on holidays and at the end of each summer. I don't know how Effie and Devin do it. I suppose it's easier since they still have one daughter at home, their nest only half-empty.

Our two families have been close since the girls met in elementary school. Effie is one of my best friends. Sasha is right; she would be very grateful not to have to make another trip to the city. She drives the library's bookmobile and is literally always on the road.

"Come here," I say, and Sasha sits down on a barstool at the kitchen island. I pull the withered flowers from her hair, the stems limp, the petals curled in on themselves or brittle at the edges. I make a pile on the counter next to my laptop.

"Is there any pie left?" Sasha asks.

"Of course," I say. "I saved you the last piece."

She pours a cup of coffee, and I serve her the generous slice of pie. We are quiet. When there is nothing but the little bit of pie crust left, she says, "Mom, let me go with you. You shouldn't have to do this alone. Plus, I'd love to see Gilly."

"Remember?" I say, pointing to the crust. "You used to call that the 'rind.'"

"I've never been before, you know," she persists. "To Westbeth."

I would like to say that it won't be what she thinks it is—this magical place of my childhood—that she, too, is looking only at the *frosting*. But it is partly my fault. In recounting those years at Westbeth, I have been an impeccable curator. Like my mother's "autobiography," my account of my childhood has been its own fictional rendering.

Tears well in my eyes again.

"You *loved* him, Mama, right? Henri?"

I blink hard and nod. "I did."

On Tuesday morning, we load up the trunk of my car with our one shared suitcase. I have packed some snacks; I put these in the back seat along with Sasha's camera bag, which accompanies her everywhere these days. I called Effie and told her we would grab Zu-Zu on our way home on Friday. "You are my *hero*," she said.

The sky is dark. Ominous and brooding. I'm still skeptical that this is a good idea, and the dusky sky seems like a warning.

Sasha takes her spot behind the wheel and scooches the seat forward a good six inches. While I am tall, she is tiny. She turns on the windshield wipers, which smear the bugs and summer dust across the glass. I don't remember the last time I drove anywhere. I am the consummate homebody. This trip to New York is contrary to every instinct I have.

New York City
August 2019

Things have changed since I was last here.

For one, the Towers that Gilly promised would guide the way if I were ever lost are gone now. In a few weeks, they'll appear as two ghostly columns of light on the anniversary of their demise. Of the day we *all* lost so much. Gilly's sister, Angelica, had been working that day—she'd finally gotten clean, and had started a new job waitressing at Windows on the World. It was only her second day.

I couldn't go to New York for her funeral. Sasha was a newborn, and I was still recovering from complications from her birth. Instead, Gilly came to Lost River and lived with us that winter. He helped me take care of Sasha while Andy was in LA working, and I took care of him.

At that point, I hadn't returned to the city since I left at twenty-three, and vowed that I never would. *Let the world come to me*, I had joked. And it did. We always seemed to have company visiting. Gilly and Henri knew the city did nothing but break my heart again and again. I'd made a single trip down since then, when Guillermo died. I did that for Gilly and Liliana. For Joaquin. Even then, I'd been there only long enough for the service in Queens, and then I came straight home again. I haven't been to Manhattan in decades.

The New York of my memory is usually obfuscated by a sepia haze, but as we drive along the West Side Highway, it is not the rust-colored landscape of my recollection. The rain has stopped, and it is so *clean*. Green and pristine. The raised West Side Highway, where we roller skated and made mischief, is gone; the dilapidated piers have been replaced with bike paths and cheerful parks; even the river beyond *glistens*. It is a dreamscape, somehow both deeply familiar and entirely strange.

We get off the West Side Highway onto 14th Street, Sasha navigating traffic on the brick streets like a pro, as I use my map app to guide her.

"Here," I say, and she turns onto Washington and then eventually onto Horatio, where we locate the Jane Street Garage.

As Sasha grabs our suitcase and camera bag from the trunk and locks up the car, I text Gilly: **Meet at the apartment?**

Gilly no longer lives at Westbeth, but Liliana still does, in the same duplex on the ninth and tenth floors. She and Guillermo, like so many of the aging residents, had always said they wouldn't leave unless it was in a body bag. Their grim joke pains me now.

I suggested to Gilly that Sasha and I get a room at The Standard, the hotel that hovers above the High Line. But Gilly insisted we stay with Liliana at Westbeth. That he would, too. "It'll be like old times," he said, and then added, "Besides, the only people who stay at The Standard are pervs who want people to see them screwing in the windows."

I haven't told my mother I'm coming, though I suspect she's heard by now. I try to rehearse what I will say to her but come up blank. Maybe I should just let her do the talking. She's the one who owes me an explanation. She can't give one to Henri, but perhaps she will have one for me.

My phone dings. **How about lunch at Chelsea Market? The noodle place,** he suggests, as if we are tourists and he wants to show us around. I realize that this is at least half right. We put the suitcase back in the trunk to pick up after lunch, but Sasha makes sure to bring her camera. As we exit the dark garage into the city, her jaw has come unhinged, and she walks gazing upward, gawking.

"Look straight ahead," I caution. "Otherwise, you're asking to have your purse snatched."

I realize these were my mother's words to me the first time we went out walking together in the city, her hand clutching mine as we walked past a man crouched in a doorway dressed in rags, licking his crusty lips. *Hey, baby girl. Hey, sweet baby.*

I swallow hard and reach for Sasha's hand. She looks concerned.

"You okay, Mama?"

I nod. "Yeah. Everything's fine."

We get to Chelsea Market, and I am once again stunned by this city's beautification. Its gentrification. Its Disney-fication. Sasha leads the way down the industrial innards of the old Nabisco factory, while I attempt to locate the noodle place on my phone. I am studying the floor plan when I am suddenly blinded, bony fingers over my eyes, stealing the light. I cover his hands with my own and then stay there for a moment. Smelling the familiar grassy scent of him.

"Guess *who*," he sings.

When Gilly lifts his hands, I turn and lean into him as he encloses me. I will myself not to fall apart in his arms.

"It's okay, Ry. It's okay now. I'm here."

We order giant bowls of noodles and sit at a high table as Gilly riddles Sasha with questions about her move to Los Angeles, about her photo project. He looks good. Healthy. I worry about him, though not as much as I used to. I am grateful for the medicines that allow him to be here while so many of his friends, *our* friends, have died. His face is still boyish, despite his salt-and-pepper hair, the deep lines at the edges of his eyes.

"How's Howard?" I ask.

Gilly rolls his eyes but smiles. Howard and he have been together for ten years, married for five. The wedding was at Lost River. It was the last time I saw many of our New York friends, the last time I saw Henri, who had taken the wedding photos.

Gilly and Howard live in an apartment above a funeral home on Bleecker Street, not too far from Westbeth. *Quiet neighbors*, Howard always jokes. Gilly left Westbeth, but he's never left the Village. Like native Vermonters, lifelong New Yorkers' roots run deep. He and Howard met at the Village Community School where they both teach: Gilly, kindergarten and Howard, eighth grade science. I love Howard and his dry sense of humor. He's good for Gilly. He's good *to* Gilly.

"Oh, he's *fine*," he says. "Curmudgeonly as usual."

"Will he be at the memorial?"

"Of course," he says. "He's bringing his famous *tarte de citron*. Any excuse to show off his baking skills."

Gilly had said that the memorial would be small and private, mostly former and current Westbeth residents, friends of Henri's. There would be a display of his work in the Westbeth gallery, a reception, and an opportunity for people to share their memories of him. I try to imagine where I would begin, what I could possibly say.

Sasha slurps a super long noodle from her chopsticks. Her hair is in two high knobs on either side of her head today, like Minnie Mouse. Her dangling chandelier earrings almost dip into her bowl.

"I need to take *you* to MoMA," Gilly says brightly to Sasha. "Do you like Cindy Sherman?"

"Oh my god, yes! Her Instagram self-portraits are amazing. Can we go?" she asks me. "And the Met? I have *always* wanted to go to the Met."

"Can we talk about it later?" I ask. "I think this is going to be kind of a crazy couple of days. Liliana will want to spend time with you. Fiona, too."

At the mention of my mother, I watch Gilly's mouth twitch. Just a bit.

"You know," I say, nodding, "it's actually not too late for us to get a hotel room. Maybe that would be better. We're parked right near The Jane. It's been renovated, right?" In the seventies, there was a theater in the basement of the hotel. We went to see a play there, about a field trip to the Natural History Museum; one of Angelica's friends, who lived at Westbeth, played a little boy in it.

Gilly's expression is unreadable.

"*No!* I want to stay at Westbeth," Sasha pleads. "You promised."

"I just think the focus should be on remembering Henri," I say. "Not on Fiona, or me. With everything going on, it might be distracting." I have not stopped thinking about the *Times*'s article. About the photo. About what it all means: the cryptic inscription, the fact that Zev Brenner somehow *knew* my mother. It has been a very long time since the media had any interest in me. Before the Internet, even. My fame is ancient history. But I don't know what this news will mean for me. For my mother. I also have no idea if Henri's suicide has anything to do with my portrait, and if anyone has made this connection. The last thing I want, that anyone at Westbeth would want, is the media lurking around, trying to dig up dirt.

Gilly takes a deep breath and glances around the room, as if he is looking for someone.

"She's not coming *here*, is she?" I ask.

He shakes his head tersely.

"Actually . . ." He's struggling, and for a brief moment, I worry that he's going to deliver more horrific news. As if Henri was only the first card in a whole precarious house of them.

"What's the matter?" I ask. "What did she do *now*?"

Sasha stops slurping.

"I'm sure it's nothing. But she's sort of . . . um . . . disappeared."

I feel a strange amalgam of anger and relief.

"She's gone?" I ask, remembering all the other times she's fled. I feel an old, familiar feeling, a sort of childlike sense of helplessness and rage. It's in my shoulders. My neck.

"She probably just needed to get away," he says. "Clear her head? This has all been so horrible. She's really devastated."

"I'm sure she'll be back in time for the memorial. To make her dramatic entrance," I say, and force a laugh. "Did you call her?"

"Straight to voice mail," he says. "Mom was worried. So, she let herself into Fiona's place."

"And?"

He reaches into his pocket, pulls out an envelope, and sets it on the table in front of me. I recognize the handwriting immediately. My mother's loopy script. *Ryan*, it says.

"Well, are you going to open it?" Sasha asks.

I look at the envelope and feel breathless. I am eleven years old again. Both here and somewhere else. I grip the edge of my stool, as I feel the world upending.

New York City
August 1976

I woke the first morning at Westbeth staring at the ceilings, which undulated like waves over our loft bed. Guillermo had told us that this building, like most in the neighborhood, used to be a factory; the wave design made the ceilings strong enough to bear the weight of heavy equipment. Westbeth had once belonged to Bell Labs; it was the place where TVs were first made. "The first talkies," he'd said.

"What are *talkies*?" Angelica had asked.

"*Movies*," my mother said, the word like something sweet in her mouth. "Sounds like kismet to me."

"What's kiss-mitt?" Angelica asked.

"You know, serendipity!" My mother's eyes sparked.

"Seren-dip . . . ?"

"Serendipity." She turned to me and smiled. "It means it was *meant to be*."

Now, I stared up at the ceilings and felt a little seasick. Gilly explained there was a dance studio above us on the eleventh floor. He said sometimes you could hear the dancers when they were jumping, the sound of their movements rippling across those waves.

I rolled over, and my mother's side of the bed was still warm, but she was gone. I was accustomed to her getting up early at Lost River. She liked to wake up before the sun rose and walk along the river with her coffee to practice her lines. *Performing for the bees and the trees,* she said. There was a river here, too, but it wasn't the same. It was murky and dark and expansive. The rotten wooden piers and polluted water smelled fusty and fetid. Liliana had said that we should never, ever go out walking alone. "Nothing but junkies and gypsies and thieves out there," she said.

My mother had told me she had an audition today, our first full day in the city, but that she would be home by the afternoon. That we'd go out for ice cream later to celebrate. Liliana had wanted Guillermo to go along with her, but she'd insisted she'd be fine. *He'd* insisted on slipping her two crisp five-dollar bills and told her to take a taxi rather than the subway.

The idea of the subway system running under the city like some sort of subterranean kingdom was almost unfathomable to me. The day before, we'd taken a walk around the neighborhood, and when we passed steaming grates on the street, I imagined dragons beneath the asphalt, breathing their hot breath into the air. Maybe that was why it was so hot and smelly here, I thought. I wouldn't have to take the subway to school, at least.

School wasn't starting for another couple of weeks. I would be in the fifth grade at PS-3, the local public school. Gilly and his siblings went to the Village Community School, where Liliana taught art. I was terrified of going to a brand-new school, where I didn't know anybody, but my mother had explained that private schools cost a lot of money, and Liliana's kids had scholarships. Besides, my school was right around the corner from Gilly's, so he, Joaquin, and Angelica would all walk me there and then come pick me up after school, as well.

While we were touring the neighborhood, we walked by my school and stopped at Duane Reade, where my mother bought me a bunch of colorful notebooks and pencils and a box of sixty-four crayons with a built-in sharpener in the back. She had squirreled away all the money Serafina had paid her for the work she did at Lost River: cooking, cleaning, and the small stipend she was paid to perform. But Serafina must have known it wouldn't last long in the city, and so she'd ordered two pairs of Toughskins dungarees from the Sears Catalog and had them sent to me at Westbeth. All my pants were high-water; I'd grown almost three inches since last year.

My mother needed to find work, but for me, for the next couple of weeks until school started, there was nothing to do but settle into our new home. Today, Gilly was excited to show me around Westbeth, which felt like a maze, a dimly lit labyrinth with endless hallways. A city within a city.

"It'll be fun!" he promised, but a pit had settled into my stomach and stayed there, taking root, I thought. I was homesick already.

I could hear Liliana shuffling around in the kitchen and the low hum of her and Guillermo's voices. Threaded through their conversation was the radio, turned low. Opera music. Liliana listened to opera at Lost River, too, and the familiar sounds of *La Bohème* softened the hard pit in my belly. I could smell something delicious, as well; Guillermo was a renowned cook at Lost River, and when I climbed down the ladder from the loft, I could see that he was making banana pancakes, the jug of maple syrup he'd brought from our neighbors' farm in Lost River on the table.

I was the only kid awake, but I was used to being the only kid around grown-ups, and Liliana and Guillermo were like family.

"Good morning, sunshine!" Liliana said. She was sitting at the little oak table with a steaming cup of tea. She wore a loose terry cloth robe that gaped open a bit. I could see she was naked underneath, just a little gold cross at her cleavage. Liliana was curvy and soft, while my mother was angular. Sharp.

"Your mother said to give you a big wet kiss," she said, and stood up, coming to me and kissing the top of my head. "Did you sleep okay?"

I shrugged. I had woken at least twenty times. The loft bed felt like a little nest, with soft, worn sheets, but it was hot in the apartment, so we'd kept the window open, and outside, the city was suddenly louder than it had been when we arrived. Voices, cars honking, and the distant sounds of the ships' horns. Every time I started to slip into sleep, something would jar me awake again.

"You'll get used to the noise," Liliana said. "Just like the cicadas and peepers in Vermont. After a while, you'll hardly hear them any-more."

Guillermo stood at the tiny stove, flipping pancakes. He was wearing a ladies' red gingham-checked apron with white rickrack on the edges.

"Come have some breakfast," he said, gesturing to an empty seat at the table. "I'll wake Gilly up."

Gilly gave me a tour of the ninth floor; he seemed to know everybody who lived behind the doors, if not by name, then by oc-cupation.

"Painter," he said, pointing. "Acrobat. Flute. Mime. *Composer.*" He said that in a fancy voice and waved his arms like a conductor.

I tried to remember what he told me, as if he were a teacher and I was memorizing something for a test. When we got to the eleva-tors, he stopped. "Let's see what Henri is doing."

Henri was the man who had come to the door the day before. He hadn't stayed long, but had introduced himself to my mother and me, and told her that if she needed headshots to bring to her audi-tions that he was more than happy to take them for her. She had nod-ded, grateful, and penciled the appointment in her planner, where she scribbled down all the cattle call auditions she could find in the back of *Backstage.*

The only photo she had to bring to the audition today was over three years old and wasn't really a headshot at all, just a black-and-white picture of her sitting on the riverbank at Lost River. In the photo, she looked like she was far away, a look that always made me feel sort of sad and scared. Like she was somehow both there and not there at the same time.

We took the elevator down to the second floor.

Henri answered the door and clapped his hands together at the sight of us. *"Allo!"* he said, grinning. "Come in, come in!"

Henri's apartment had a long, narrow foyer that opened into a large open space. I followed Gilly and Henri, who led us into the room and then stood there, arms outstretched, like the ringmaster of a circus.

The parquet floor was the same as the one in Gilly's apartment, but in the center of the room were heaps of what looked like bear skins, a furry sea surrounding a pale green velvet sofa, a large console TV, and a lumpy red armchair patched with black electrical tape. Along the left wall was a giant card catalog, like I'd seen at the Quimby Athenaeum back at home, and on the right were floor-to-ceiling shelves stuffed with books, and piles of them on the floor, as well.

"Bienvenue!" he said, bowed at the waist, and made a flourish with his left hand before gesturing as if to say, *Feast your eyes!*

Every inch of the remaining walls was covered with framed art and photos and posters, including a life-sized circus sideshow poster: STRANGE GIRLS, it said. WHY WERE THEY BORN? The brightly colored poster featured illustrations of girls with long necks, mermaid tails instead of legs, or no legs at all. My mother had taken me to the circus once, set up at the fairgrounds in Quimby. But she had not allowed me to enter the tents advertising the Lobster Boy and Bearded Lady. "They'll give you nightmares," she said. Nothing upset my mother more than when I woke up screaming and sweating, delirious with whatever monster had invaded my dreams.

There was a desk at the opposite side of the apartment, with shelves almost all the way to the top of the high ceiling littered with more books and old-fashioned toys: a rusty jack-in-the-box, and a threadbare monkey with cymbals attached to his hands.

"Would you like something to drink?" he asked, moving to a small kitchenette and opening the fridge.

"Yes, please," I said, leaning close to study a shadow box filled with butterfly wings hanging at eye level. I thought of my own collection I had brought from Vermont.

"I collect butterflies, too," I announced. "Mostly swallowtails. But I found a mourning cloak this summer."

"Oh, you are a lepidopterist, eh? A collector?"

I nodded. I thought of the delicate dusky wings of the butterflies: the buttery yellow and impossible blue of the mourning cloak.

He popped the tops off two glass bottles of Coke and handed one to me and one to Gilly, who drained it in a few long swallows, then wiped his mouth with the back of his hand and burped loudly. I sipped on mine, the sweetness flooding my mouth.

"Henri took these," Gilly explained, as my eyes found the wall of photographs again. The photos were street scenes mostly, pictures of people. A lady with a plastic rain bonnet and a deep frown, a hairy mole on her chin. A little boy whose lip was deformed, connected to his nostril. There was a photo of a little girl, as well, probably about my age, staring defiantly at the camera, hand on her bony hip, which jutted out. She was wearing a bathing suit, and a swim cap with plastic flowers. The freckles on her cheeks stood in high relief, and despite her defiant stance, her eyes were brimming with tears.

"Come," Henri said, and led us through the little kitchen to another hallway, which opened to a large room filled with photographic equipment. There was a brick wall and two windows that spilled light across the floor. An antique-looking camera was propped up on a tripod, and a single blue stool sat before a gray paper backdrop. Big white umbrellas stood on either side, and hanging on a heavy wooden door was a handwritten sign that said, GARDE LA PORTE FERMEE!!!

"Your *maman*, she will come to get her photo taken?"

I nodded.

"*Elle est très belle*. Very beautiful."

He looked at me thoughtfully.

"Do you like cats?" he asked.

I *loved* cats. I had hated saying goodbye to the barn cats at Lost River. There were at least a dozen of them, and nobody could tell them apart except for me and Angelica. We had named them all, mostly after Saturday morning cartoon characters. Her favorite was a jet-black kitty she called Bamm-Bamm, but mine was a little tiger I'd named Daphne. I had pleaded with my mother to bring Daphne with us to Westbeth, but she had said that she was a country cat, not a city cat, and wouldn't be happy in Manhattan. I had worried after that— I was a country kid; how would I fare in the city?

"Come," Henri said, and motioned for us to follow him. He grabbed a camera from the coffee table in the living room and strung it around his neck.

We took the elevator up and then trailed behind him through another dimly lit hallway. He pulled a key from his pocket; it had a tattered red ribbon strung through the hole. "It is magic, this key. It unlocks every door in this building." I marveled at this. One key that could fit into every lock?

He opened the door, but instead of entering another apartment, we found ourselves outside, on a rooftop looking out over the city. I gasped with delight and turned in a complete circle, marveling at the three-hundred-sixty-degree aerial view of the city skyline. I could see the Towers in the distance and felt an odd sense of comfort. Just like Gilly had promised, I knew where I was.

"Come," Henri said again, and led us to a little shadowy alcove, where I heard a sort of humming, rustling sound. *Purring!*

We knelt on the crumbling asphalt ground, and there, in a cardboard box lined with a striped beach towel, was a big fat gray cat with six or seven squirming kittens suckling on her.

"Can I hold one?" I asked.

"Of course," he said, and reached into the box, plucking one nursing kitten from her mother. I held out my hands with the wriggling little ball of fur. Its warm body squirmed in my palms, its eyes still sealed shut.

"She's brand new!" I said. I knew from the barn cats' litters back at home that their eyes remained closed for the first week or two after they were born.

"*Oui*. Born just last week."

Instinctively, I held the kitten against me, felt the tiny little motor-like purr as she tried to find her mother's milk.

I heard the shutter click, and I looked up at Henri. Was he taking my photo?

"I am sorry," he said. "I should have asked. It is okay?"

My mouth twitched, and the kitten burrowed its hard little skull against my beating heart. I nodded.

He clicked again, and I felt the trapdoor feeling I sometimes had. Like those dreams where you start to fall but are jerked awake again.

"She needs her mother," I said. I leaned over the box and carefully placed the kitten at her mother's belly, relieved when the kitten latched onto the one free, angry, pink nipple, and I heard the quiet motoring hum under its ribs.

As Gilly and I returned to the apartment, we could hear voices coming from upstairs. Liliana's was clear and high.

Gilly and I looked at each other. When I moved to go toward the doorway, he put out a hand to stop me.

Liliana kept talking. "Where the hell is she? The audition was hours ago. I told her not to take the subway."

"You know these things can run all day," Guillermo said. "The longer, the better—that means she wasn't cut right off the bat. It's probably good news. You're just being paranoid."

"It's getting *dark*. You know what happened to Marcy. And that happened in broad daylight, Gill."

"Who's Marcy?" I whispered, scared.

Gilly shrugged. "I think she's a painter my mom knows?"

Golden sunlight streamed through the western-facing window, the sort of afternoon light that came through our own window in the cabin, gilding the edges of everything. But instead of bringing comfort, it made everything worse. The last golden minutes of the day meant that it would be dark soon. It wasn't safe in the city in the dark.

"I think we should go find her," Liliana said. "Where did she say the audition was?"

Tears filled my eyes at the thought that something terrible had happened to my mother on our very first day in New York City. Gilly and I walked toward the open door. Just then, I heard the jangle of their phone. It rattled and echoed down the hallway. Was it the police?

Liliana had picked up the phone and wandered into the kitchen, the long cord trailing behind her like a venomous snake.

When Gilly and I got to the top of the stairs, Guillermo stood up from the chair where he was sitting. His face went sort of blank at the sight of me.

"Where's my mom?" I asked, trying not to blink. Once the tears started, I knew they might not stop.

"I'm right *here*."

I heard the door shut and turned to see my mother climbing the stairs.

She was wearing the tall, caramel-colored suede boots I loved and a denim miniskirt. A red floral blouse that revealed her tiny waist. Her hair was parted in the middle in two low pigtails. I had never been so happy to see her in my life.

"Where were you?" I asked, choking now on the sob that had gathered in my throat.

She lifted the strap of her fringy purse off her shoulder and set it down on the kitchen table.

"What do you mean?" she said. "I told you I had an audition."

I shook my head and clung to her, the familiarity of her body the only thing keeping me grounded. She smelled like cigarettes, and when she bent down, I could smell it stronger on her breath, with something sort of cloying underneath. Wine, maybe?

"Jesus H. Christ," Liliana said when she came back into the main room. "Where *were* you?"

"Oh my god, it's like the Spanish Inquisition here," my mother said, putting up hands like she was under arrest. "I had the audition I told you about. And then a *callback* . . . and then a few drinks with a new friend I made while we were waiting in line."

"Wait," Liliana said, her face softening. "A callback?"

"Yes. I mean, it could be nothing, but I made the first cut. And they said the second callbacks will be on Friday. I gave them the number here."

My mother unpeeled me from her waist. "I also stopped by Times Square to pick up a little gift for you," she said, and reached for her purse. "Oh, shit," she said as she lifted the snow globe from her pocketbook. It had cracked, and all the liquid was gone. There were sparkles all over her hand, and her fringy leather purse was soaked.

But I didn't care. She was home.

I take the envelope from Gilly, fold it up, and put it in my pocket, unopened. I will not do this. I will not read her sorry excuses, her insincere apologies. I am a grown woman, a mother myself. A mother who would never leave her daughter alone to fend for herself when life got hard.

"She'll come back," I say, and sigh. "She always comes back."

Gilly looks troubled.

"She *will*," I insist. I feel like I am ten years old again. Stubbornly defending my mother. I think of the freckled girl, the one in Henri's photo, the one with swim cap and tear-filled eyes.

I pull my phone out and send my mother a text. Why can't she just communicate like a normal person?

We're here

We stop at the garage and get the suitcase, which Gilly insists on taking. I'd forgotten what a fast walker he is; Sasha and I have to hustle to keep up with his fast clip, the suitcase rolling behind him down Hudson Street, before we turn onto Bethune. My heart flutters in my throat when I spy the river in the distance and spot Westbeth at the end of the street.

The air is thick with late summer heat and humidity. I can feel the hairs at the nape of my neck beginning to curl. I swipe my hand under my hair and lift it up, twisting it into a loose knot. The relief is momentary and small. I fan the back of my neck futilely with my hand.

The city has changed, but the smell is the same: the rotten, hot scent of my childhood summers. The first summer in the city had been an assault on my senses. I never thought I'd get used to it, but then one day, I did. I suppose that's like a lot of things.

We walk in silence for a couple of blocks until we get to the Bethune Street entrance of Westbeth.

Gilly turns to look at me, a smile on his face.

Despite my cautions, Sasha is still looking up. This time, she has her camera out, and she is taking pictures. "Are those train tracks?" she asks, shielding her eyes from the sun.

I follow her gaze, though of course I know what is up there already: the defunct tracks running above the first floor along Washington Street.

"Your mother and I used to go up there to smoke cigarettes," Gilly says.

Sasha gawks. "You *smoked*, Mom?"

I laugh. *"Once,"* I say. "Literally one time." Though I can still remember the feel of the rope ladder as we climbed down onto the tracks, the crinkle of cellophane, the pack stolen from my mother's purse, and the way my knees melted with the first puff. That dizzying rush of nicotine. I remember how Gilly's bare chest was white in the moonlight. And how I had walked along the tracks and then lay down across the ties, pretending I was one of those silent-movie ladies, a damsel in distress. It had felt like this that night: the world rushing to meet me, and me, powerless. But what I remember most vividly was wishing Henri were there, to capture this. Midnight, shivery moon, and the glowing end of that stolen cigarette, and me, at the edge of everything.

The High Line tracks north of Westbeth were turned into a walking path about ten years ago; Gilly pointed them out on our way back from Chelsea Market. So much green. New York City had been a perilous playground when I was a girl, but now it feels like an amusement park.

As we reach the entrance, I see a new, ornate sign noting the address.

"How long has it been since you were here? Thirty years?" Sasha asks as we walk up the ramp toward the door. Her voice feels far away. "Is it weird, Mom?"

I didn't have a name for this feeling the last time I was in this building. I had only thought of it as quicksand. The sucking, desperate feeling. Drowning, not in water but in the heavy, suffocating grit. Of course, now I have labels for my sense of helplessness and overwhelming anxiety. Labels and tools. And so, I breathe.

"Ryan!" I hear my name, and realize I have closed my eyes. Like a child, jumping into the deep end of the pool.

When I open them, Liliana is reaching for me. The last time I saw her was at Guillermo's funeral two years ago. I'd skipped the Westbeth memorial, citing an upset stomach (not a lie), and had met everyone at the graveside in Queens, where Guillermo had grown up. She'd been racked with grief that day; it had left me feeling anxious. Gilly and Joaquin had held her up through the service. My mother had been there, too. Liliana had clung to her; I'd watched her shuddering and my mother's firm embrace. I observed as my mother held her face in her hands, reassuring her that she would be okay. I remember feeling a sick pinch of jealousy and then self-loathing for it. My mother had always been there for Liliana. First, when she lost Angelica, and later, when Guillermo passed. She was sturdy, reliable. Available. Everything she had never been for me. I felt like a little girl then instead of a grown woman. A *hurt* child. I'd made up some excuse to Liliana, who was too consumed with her sorrow to notice, and I'd gotten on the next train back to Vermont.

"Ryan," Liliana says again, her voice breaking on my name. As she embraces me, I smell the old familiar scent of her herbal shampoo, and I am sinking again.

She pulls away and looks out the door behind us. "Is he gone?"

"Who?" I ask, confused.

"That goddamn *photographer*," she says.

I am lost. Why would a photographer be here? I think of Henri, the *click, click* of the shutter. I think of the other men behind their cameras, every one of them searching for something, wanting something from me. Always with their *give me, give me*. Then I realize, what she means is the paparazzi.

New York City
September 1976

Henri took my mother's headshots that weekend. She had spent most of the morning trying to pick out what to wear. She'd slept with empty orange juice cans in her hair to tame her frizz into smooth, silky waves. All night long, I'd bumped into them when I tried to snuggle her. I don't think she slept at all. In the morning, she had looked at her reflection and moaned at the dark half-moons under her sleepy eyes.

"I look like death," she said.

"You look pretty, Mama."

She ignored me and began to rifle through the clothes she had brought.

In the end, she borrowed a dress from Liliana; it was a black wrap dress that revealed the rows of bone at her chest, the ones that always made me think of old-timey washboards. She brought a change of clothes "to show a different side of herself": one of Guillermo's white button-down shirts, a loose silk tie. She tried it on and then added a black beret to complete the look. I thought she should wear something colorful, until she explained that the photos would be in black-and-white, anyway.

She hadn't been called back for that first audition, but it hadn't deterred her. She'd simply crossed it out in her planner with a bright red pen and moved on to the next one. And then the next one. The way she figured it, a professional headshot was exactly what was holding her back. Once she had a headshot and a resume, there would be no reason why she wouldn't be on the stage or on set by January.

After she was dressed, and she'd covered the shadows under her eyes with thick, creamy concealer, she studied herself in the giant ornately framed mirror that leaned against the wall by Gilly's front door. I could see myself behind her. I was wearing a pair of threadbare silky track shorts and my favorite T-shirt that said, ANYTHING BOYS CAN DO GIRLS CAN DO BETTER! with a little girl swinging a bat at a ball. I had mismatched tube socks on (one with yellow stripes and one with red) and mud-splattered sneakers. Two braids I'd been sleeping in for a week.

She caught my eye in the mirror and smiled at me.

I led the way to Henri's apartment. Gilly and I had been back at least half a dozen times since that first visit two weeks ago. Henri had the key to the rooftop, and so anytime we wanted to visit the kittens, we had to see him first. He told us he wasn't allowed to give us the magic key to use ourselves—he'd be in big trouble with the security man, Raymond, if he did that—but he was also almost never too busy to come with us.

It was a weekend, and it seemed like everyone was home. Doors were wide open, and as we walked down the long corridor, I peeked into each apartment, hoping to catch a glimpse of the neighbors Gilly had told me about. But the people inside didn't look extraordinary. Even the acrobat wore a ratty old robe and drank coffee. Only Mrs. Lake's door was shut; I wondered what a witch's apartment might look like.

We got in the elevator, but instead of heading down to take us to Henri on the second floor, it lurched upward. "Shit," my mother said.

On the eleventh floor, the doors opened, and a man stepped into the elevator. He had curly hair with wild eyebrows and a sharp jaw. He was wearing a red shirt, unbuttoned enough to reveal more curly hair on his chest, and a pair of ragged knit tights. Ballet shoes.

My mother seemed to be holding her breath. I looked at her questioningly, but she refused to meet my gaze.

When the elevator stopped at the second floor, he moved to let us out, and then pressed his hand against the door to hold it open.

"You should put her in dance classes," he said softly.

My mother cocked her head.

"Her legs are *made* for ballet," he clarified.

I realized he was talking about me. About *my* legs.

"Who was that?" I whispered after the elevator door had closed and we were making our way down the hallway toward Henri's.

"*That* is Merce Cunningham," she said. "His dance company's studios are upstairs. I've been thinking about taking a class or two. You never know when a director is going to need someone who can dance."

"Oh," I said.

"But apparently, you're the one with the *legs for ballet*," she said, and her words stung a little bit. It made me think of the barn cats, the way you could sometimes be stroking them gently when they'd suddenly take a sharp bite at your hand.

"Can I take ballet?" I asked.

I knew Angelica took ballet classes. Lots of the Lost River kids took ballet and tap dance. I had had no interest in it before, but I'd also never had someone tell me I should try it, either. But we were in New York City now. Where anything was possible, I thought. Where my mother could be a movie star. I, too, could be anything I wanted to be.

"You're too clumsy for ballet," she said. "I mean, that was flattering. Of course. Sweet of him to say. But grace is really not your forte."

She was right, I thought. I'd broken my arm falling out of a tree at Lost River. I always had bumps and bruises and cuts. But her words still felt like a prickly burr; they stuck to me, and I couldn't seem to pluck them off.

"Come in, come in," Henri said, ushering us into his apartment.

I felt sort of proprietary about his house, and I acted as a tour guide for my mother as he told us to make ourselves at home while he got his studio ready for her session.

"This is a card catalog from the New York Public Library. Henri had to hire piano movers to get it into the apartment. Now he uses it to store his film," I said. He had shown me the compartments filled with unused film, and the ones with film waiting to be developed. "I shoot faster than I can print," he had explained.

My mother nodded and sat uncomfortably on the edge of the velvet sofa. The skirt of the wrap dress was short, revealing her own long, pretty legs. As I rattled on and on, I caught her pinching the edge of her thighs. My mother was skinny, but she was always complaining about her weight. Always dieting. For breakfast that morning, she'd eaten a half a grapefruit sprinkled with a packet of Sweet'N Low, while I scarfed down two bowls of Liliana's homemade oatmeal with chunks of melty brown sugar, plump raisins, and apples. My mother skipped dinner most nights, and sometimes I could hear her belly rumbling as I fell asleep.

"Okay!" Henri said, clapping his hands together and beckoning us into the studio.

Henri situated my mother on the blue stool I had noticed the first day I'd come to his apartment, but she couldn't seem to get comfortable. No matter how he positioned her, she looked *stiff*. Self-conscious. She didn't seem to know what to do with her hands, and her eyes kept darting around the room—looking for something to focus on.

Finally, he said, "Perhaps a glass of wine would help?"

My mother accepted, and she and Henri chatted as she drank not one but three glasses of the deep red cabernet he offered her. Looser now, she seemed to relax, and soon he was clicking away.

"Should I change into my second outfit?" she asked after he'd taken a whole roll of film. I noticed that the wine had stained her lips and that her teeth were tinged gray. The wine had also brought a blush to her cheeks. I could always tell when she'd been drinking by how pink her cheeks were. At Lost River, she got silly after she'd been drinking wine. She made everyone laugh with her stories, which she acted out as if she were the lead in a play.

"Of course," he said, gesturing to his bathroom. "*Les toilettes.*"

She disappeared into his bathroom with her other outfit under her arm. When she was gone, Henri turned to me.

"Do *you* want to make a picture?"

I tilted my head, wondering what he meant.

"A photo?" he explained, and held up his camera.

I shrugged. My mother had dropped and broken her camera a couple summers ago, when we were on a hike, and so there were few photos of me. It was always strange when someone at Lost River showed me a picture of myself. I was fascinated by the way my image on paper wasn't at all how I imagined myself. Or even what I saw in the mirror. It was almost as if the camera *changed* me. Made me look older. More serious. The way I looked in photos never matched how I felt inside.

"Come," he said. "Sit here." He ushered me to the little blue stool where my mother had been. I sat down, and my mouth twitched. I had never *posed* for a photograph before other than for annual school photos. Like my mom, I also didn't know what to do with my hands. I felt awkward just sitting there. When Henri wiggled his eyebrows at me, I felt my hands go to my face, my knuckles pushing into my cheeks as if to keep myself from laughing.

Click.

"No, no! No laughing. Absolutely no laughing," he teased. "You must not move an inch. Not one centimeter!"

I was aware of an old bug bite on my knee that suddenly itched. I tried to focus on not smiling, not scratching.

"I have an itch!" I said finally, laughing, feeling as if I might crawl out of my skin.

Click.

My mother came out of the bathroom then, wearing nothing but the men's shirt and tie, the beret in her hand.

"I wasn't sure if I should wear the beret or not," she said, and then spied me on the stool.

"Oh," she said.

I scurried to my feet, still scratching the bug bite. Henri lowered the camera and studied my mother.

"*Avec le chapeau*," Henri said, nodding. "Yes, yes. With the hat."

My mother was quiet as we made our way back to the apartment. I tried playing tour guide again, repeating all the information Gilly had given me about our new neighbors.

"The lady in that apartment was a photographer, too," I said as we passed #945. "She killed herself! In the *bathtub*," I whispered. I had been mortified when Gilly told me about this poor lady, Diane. I couldn't imagine what would make someone sad enough to do that.

"Maybe she was onto something," my mother mumbled, taking the beret off her head.

"*On something*?" I asked. I knew that probably meant she thought she was on drugs. Drugs could make people act crazy. I had overheard Guillermo say that an actor he knew had taken angel dust and leapt from the top of a building on Fifth Avenue. I imagined angel dust like glitter, like light.

"No," she said, stopping and enunciating. "I said, maybe she was *onto* something. Maybe she was smarter than the rest of us. Just quit while you're ahead."

There was real anger in my mother's eyes then, and I knew she was angry at *me*, although I didn't understand why.

That night, I changed into my nightie, the long white one with tiny yellow rosebuds, the one that had grown so short, it barely hit my knees when it used to reach my ankles.

It was my mother's night to cook, and so we all wound up with a plate of scrambled eggs and English muffins with a blob of some of Serafina's raspberry preserves she'd sent with us when we left Lost River. It was Sunday, so *The Wonderful World of Disney* was on, and tonight they were showing *The Parent Trap*. Gilly and I were allowed to stay up until 9:30 to watch it, but Angelica and Joaquin were only allowed to stay up until 8:00.

We balanced our dinner plates on our laps as we sat around the small black-and-white TV in the living room.

"Hayley Mills . . ." my mother said. She had opted for dry toast and a scoop of cottage cheese with pineapple, and she pointed her fork at the TV. "She was discovered when she was only twelve by a director who was looking for a boy to play the lead in one of his films."

The movie was about twins, but only one girl was playing both roles. I had been trying to figure out how on earth they managed to make her appear as both Sharon and Susan at the same time. Gilly explained that it was something called a *split screen*, but it was so convincing, I had to keep reminding myself that it was the same actress. That was what I felt like sometimes, like two different girls: one who was tough, a mischievous tomboy, and the other who was soft and scared and girly.

The knock came at the door downstairs just as one twin, Susan (but pretending to be Sharon), arrived in California at the twins' father's ranch house.

"I'll get it!" Joaquin yelled, and took off running toward the stairs, sliding across the floor in his feety pajamas.

"*Allo*, little man!" Henri's voice boomed, and then we heard him coming up, the *clomp clomp* of his boots on the stairs.

I looked up from my plate at Henri, who had a yellow clasped envelope under his arm.

My mother scrambled up from her spot on the couch, balancing her half-empty plate on the edge of the coffee table, and went to him.

"Oh! Are these the photos already?" All her anger from earlier seemed to have slipped away. I thought of it like those Alka-Seltzer pills on TV. *Plop, plop, fizz, fizz*—so much bubbly turmoil, and then just the faint electric buzz and hum.

"Yes," he said. "I knew you were in a hurry, so I went straight to my darkroom."

They sat at the kitchen table, where he slid the photographs out of the envelope. He laid them out like a fortune-teller laying down tarot cards, and my mother studied each one, biting her nails. She was trying hard to grow them out. She'd even gone as far as painting them with a coat of the bitter-tasting tincture she'd used to get me to stop sucking my thumb. It had been in our medicine cabinet for years. I knew it tasted terrible, but she kept nibbling away as she studied the headshots.

She shook her head. *No, no. Too happy. Too serious. My hair looks terrible in this one.* I started getting a creepy-crawly feeling in my stomach as I felt her frustration escalating.

"My face looks so *fat*," she moaned, beginning to tug at her cheeks, pinching the soft flesh there.

"Okay, okay. But here. This is my favorite," Henri said. "I think you will like this, no?"

He laid down the final photo. I peeked over my mother's shoulder at the glossy black-and-white print.

In the photo, she was wearing Guillermo's shirt and loose tie. Her face was beautiful, the sunlight catching a spark in her eye. The beret sat perfectly on her soft hair, and she looked intently at the camera, but a small smile crept across her lips. That was the mother I loved, the one who tickled my feet to wake me up in the morning. The one who would play endless games of Chinese checkers with me. The one who would rub gooey aloe vera into my sunburned shoulders.

My mother's face softened as she picked up the photo. She could see that he'd captured her, too. The *real* her. I thought, *Maybe there were two of her, too.*

She nodded, rendered speechless for a moment. "This one," she said. "This one is it."

Liliana had come over by then and was admiring the photo.

"It's perfect," Liliana said, squeezing my mother's knobby shoulder. "You look like Ali MacGraw."

"How much do I owe you?" My mother reached for her purse, which hung on the back of one of the chairs. I knew for a fact that she had exactly three dollars in her little purple coin purse. The rest of her savings was in the bank. "I'll need several copies. I know the paper and chemicals are expensive."

Henri shook his head. "No, no. It is my pleasure to photograph you. Someday, when you are a big Broadway star, you will give me tickets to see you perform."

She smiled again and reached for Henri's hand. "Thank you, Henri. Truly."

I was so grateful to Henri. Somehow, her irritation had completely dissolved. The fizzing water was flat and placid again.

"Oh!" Henri said, lifting a second manila envelope I hadn't noticed before. "I almost forgot!" He slipped another couple of black-and-white 8x10s out of the envelope onto the table.

In the first photo, I was sitting on the little stool, sneakered feet resting on the rungs. My legs looked long, too long—almost cartoonish, I thought. The angry bug bite on my knee was a dark spot. You could read the caption on my favorite shirt. My hands were on my hips as I seemed to challenge the camera, Henri, or whomever was looking at the photo. My mouth was set and determined, but my eyes filled with mischief. One of my yarn hair ties had come undone and traveled down the front of my T-shirt.

"Une petite coquin," Henri said.

"Coquette?" my mother huffed. *Fizz.*

"No, no. Co*quin.* A little rascal."

"You shouldn't have wasted your film," my mother said. "Please let me reimburse you."

Then I saw another photo lying underneath this one. As my mother fiddled with her purse again, and Henri protested, I slid it out and studied it. Here was the other me. The *real* me. It made me think of the photo of the girl with the freckles and the daisy swim cap that was hanging in his apartment. I was smiling, yes, but you could also see that I was uneasy. Shy and anxious. As if I knew already that all of this would make my mother angry. I looked *open*—that was the word—like a wound that's lost the protective scab. Raw and vulnerable.

Illumination, 1976

*I*t is a Saturday, September, and it has been raining for three days. Guillermo and Liliana took the kids to the Museum of Natural History to go see the new Hall of Gems. I didn't want to go, but after hours of watching TV and reading, I am bored and wishing I had gone with them. My mother was supposed to be home from her audition by now. She promised Liliana she wouldn't take the subway this time, but getting a taxi is going to be hard in the rain, and she has to come all the way from West 46th Street.

Suddenly, there's a knock at the door. Guillermo told me to lock myself in, not to answer the door for anybody. He promised they would be home before dinner. So, I tiptoe down the steps and listen.

"Allo?" a muffled voice says. It's only Henri. I release the breath I have been holding and run to the door to unlock it.

"Ryan!" He's standing in our doorway, eyes sparkling with excitement. He's wearing one of those caps that snaps to the brim and rubber galoshes. His wool blazer is wet.

"Nobody's here," I blurt out. "Just me."

"But you are exactly the person I came to see."

"Me?"

"Oui! I was out walking and got an idea, but I need your assistance." Everything he says sounds fancy.

"Okay." I shrug. "I was bored anyway."

"Well, then, get your shoes," he says. "I have an umbrella."

"*Where are we going?*"

He lifts his camera, which is wrapped in a plastic bread bag. "*Would you like to make a photo?*"

I remember this is the way he explained it when my mother and I went to his studio. He told us that he is not taking a photo, but that we are making one. Together. "C'est une collaboration."

"I have to leave my mom a note," I say. I scribble on the Holly Hobbie notepad Liliana keeps by the phone. `I'm with Henri. Be home soon!`

Outside, the security guy, Raymond, is huddled in the doorway, trying to light a cigarette. The flick, flick of his Zippo like the pattering of the rain. He nods to Henri and smiles at me. His teeth are long and yellow. He gives me the creeps.

The sky is so heavy, the air so thick, it feels like I am breathing water.

We start walking down West Street, and when I look back over my shoulder, Raymond has gotten his cigarette lit and is taking a big, long suck on it. I see Jackie-O, as well, down at the end of the street, standing underneath an awning, battling with an umbrella.

The sky rumbles angrily, but the rain has stopped.

We walk quickly down West Street. The sidewalks are mostly empty, but warm lights glow inside the bars, where I can hear music and see, through smudgy windows, men sitting at tables and shooting pool. Outside of one bar, a man with a droopy mustache like Henri's leans against the brick wall. The sign overhead says RAMROD. And the black-and-white-striped awning beyond says THE UNDERGROUND.

"Henry!" the man drawls, and steps away from the wall to shake Henri's hand.

"Allo, Gus," Henri says with a smile.

"Who's your friend?" The man looks at me. His mustache twitches.

"This is Ryan. Ma petite muse. Going down to the pier to make some pictures."

The piers. We're not allowed to play out there. Too dangerous, Liliana said, but didn't elaborate. But I am with Henri. Safe.

"Stop by and shoot some pool later?" Gus says. "I'll buy you a beer."

"Peut être," Henri says, and we keep walking. "Hold my hand."

After crossing West Street, we walk down the pier. I step into a puddle, and the water soaks through my socks. When the thunder rumbles, I feel it in my bones. Lightning streaks across the sky, illuminating us briefly, like a flashbulb going off. The river shimmers for a moment in its blue light.

The pier is dilapidated and smells like a bonfire. Graffiti slashes the crumbling concrete. Twisted metal and slivered wood. It looks like wreckage, but is also strangely beautiful. Like a sculpture or the dinosaurs at the museum, the looming and terrifying architecture of bone.

"It is beautiful, no?" he asks.

I nod. He sees it, too.

We keep walking down the pier until he says, "Stop here." He puts his hands on my shoulders and turns me to face him, my back to the river. To the storm. He carefully lifts each of my braids and brings them forward, so they run down the front of my T-shirt. He backs up then, slipping his camera out of the bread bag.

There's something happening behind me. I hear people talking, or laughing, or something. Men, I think. I feel a little scared. Thunder rolls through me again.

"Now close your eyes and just stand as still as you can," he says.

The rain begins again, suddenly and hard, soaking my T-shirt and jeans. I shiver as the water drips down my bare arms.

"Lift your chin?" he says, and I raise it toward the sky.

The rain batters my face, soaks my hair. I am brave, I think. I am safe. But when the lightning flashes again, my eyes fly open. I am scared. And the shutter clicks.

I let out a little cry as the thunder cracks, and I run to Henri, who wraps an arm around me. He removes his coat and slips it over my shoulders.

"Beautiful! Merci," he says. "Now let us go home and have some hot tea."

He begins to steer me away from the river. I hear laughter, look back over my shoulder, and see two men slipping into the shadows.

New York City
August 2019

"It was just one guy out there," Liliana explains. "I assume he was paparazzi. He had a camera." The photographer had been loitering in the Bank Street courtyard for hours, Liliana said. She'd been on the lookout before we got there, just in case there were any more.

New York City is a contradiction. Here, you can be discovered, become a star. But it is also supposed to be a place where you can be anonymous. It's where you go to pursue fame, but also where celebrities go to be left alone. After a few sightings, my mother and I had quickly learned proper celebrity etiquette. Whenever we spotted someone famous out on the street or in a restaurant, we learned not to make a fuss. My mother would simply dig her nails into my arm and whisper, "Holy shit, that's Mia Farrow!" Or, "That's Steve Martin! From *Saturday Night Live*?" And once, with a sort of hushed reverence, she pointed at a lovely older woman who was smoking a cigarette in a window of the 21 Club and said, "My god, that's Lauren Bacall."

It used to be that I could come and go from Westbeth without anyone in the world caring. For the first year or so after I started working, nobody knew where I lived. But then, word got out. The photographers were easy to spot back then; their cameras were clunky giveaways, especially the ones who shot from a distance with their long telephoto lenses. After a while, I even started to recognize them. Like the barn cats at Lost River, and then the rooftop kittens at Westbeth, I gave them names: *Grumpy,* for the one with the permanent scowl and ratty fedora. *Dr Pepper,* for the one who was always drinking from a can of Dr Pepper. *Bandanna,* for the one who tried to look like he was just one of the dancers in Mr. Cunningham's studios: dance clothes and a red bandanna on his broad forehead.

Regardless of who was waiting, trying to get the next shot, I was always polite. This was something my mother insisted upon from the very beginning, despite her disdain for the men she called "vultures," the second the doors closed behind us. I would *not* garner a reputation as a brat. Or, god forbid, one of those celebrities who looked down on people who were just trying to make an honest living.

"Good morning," I'd say into the bushes as I left for school.

"Sure is hot . . ." I would nod with sympathy to Dr Pepper, who was overweight and wiping a hankie across his sweaty head.

"Cheese!" I'd grin at Bandanna and give him my biggest, cheesiest grin as he clicked.

We had an arrangement of sorts, these photographers and me. They kept their distance, and I offered them my smiles. By then, I understood that my face was simply a commodity, one that could be traded, purchased, or sold.

The photographers back then were on a lighthearted quest—to get a shot of America's "favorite teenager" going about her daily life. The photos that appeared in those magazines were of me looking like most other kids: backpack slung over my shoulder, sitting at a diner with a milkshake and my homework, or running to catch a taxi.

It wasn't until some guy stalked me all the way from midtown to our front door that my mother freaked out. I was fifteen then, and perfectly capable of handling myself. I'd been navigating the city, negotiating creeps, on my own for over a year. But my mother had been spooked, and had gone so far as to buy a can of pepper spray, which she made me carry everywhere.

She also, somehow, got the word out that we had purchased a

home in Connecticut, and leaked the address to *People*. However, there was no house in Connecticut. Any lookie-loos or aspiring paparazzi would have found themselves staring at a grassy cow field in Danbury if they followed this mis-lead. She even invited a reporter from *Life* to do an exclusive interview, which took place at some stables in Danbury, where I cooed and nuzzled "my" horse, Penny. I was allergic to horses, though, and the photos show me with watery red eyes and a puffy face. Of course, the tabloids ran with that—speculating that I had been crying. That my "country dream" was a "country nightmare." But for a while, anyway, the ruse worked, and the paparazzi disappeared.

The idea that some newspaper or tabloid or gossip site has dispatched a photographer to try to capture a shot of me—middle-aged me—because of the news of the portrait, of Henri, of my mother, makes the fillings in my molars ache.

"Try not to worry about it," Liliana says, but I catch her looking over my shoulder to the courtyard as we go inside. "You're safe here. I'll talk to the security guys, too. Have them keep an eye out."

Westbeth. How long did I live here? 1976 was when we moved in, but when exactly did I leave? When did I flee? It wasn't the abrupt departure that we'd made from Lost River. Instead, it took me years to depart. To pull myself away. To separate myself from my mother. I try to remember the last time I walked through these doors but can't. My memory in the last few years has gone from the tight trap that it used to be to something more pliable, less reliable. Fallible, even. It had to have been 1987? '88? More than thirty years ago, either way.

But the moment we walk into the lobby, my eyes are immediately drawn to the brightly colored tiles of the ceiling—in a variety of shades of red and pink—and I remember. The smell of the clean floors also sends me reeling back in time. For a moment, I want nothing more than to turn around. To grab Sasha's hand and run all the way back to the Jane Street Garage and get into the car headed home.

When we moved into Westbeth, the hallways had been pasted with CARTER/MONDALE signs; FOR FREEDOM WE SHALL ALL LAY DOWN OUR LIVES; BURY APARTHEID. That summer of '76, in South Africa, almost two hundred schoolchildren were killed by the police during the Soweto uprising. The signs have changed, but the sentiment is the same. BLACK LIVES MATTER. I CAN'T BREATHE. HATE HAS NO HOME HERE. Sasha studies the walls; she is no stranger to protests, even as a Vermont kid. She grins at the giant drawing of a naked Trump, sucking his thumb, sagging cartoon diaper.

Liliana throws her arm around Sasha's shoulder. Their heads lean in together as they walk toward the elevators, and my throat feels swollen.

Gilly and I trail behind. There are a few people milling about in the corridors, but no one I recognize. I feel suddenly, oddly, territorial. As if this is my home, and it has been invaded by strangers. I know it's ridiculous. I abandoned Westbeth; it didn't abandon me.

As the elevator ascends, I feel my stomach bottom out. I study the numbered buttons and resist the impulse to press 2 for Henri's floor.

"Second floor!" Gilly used to call out in a deep, silly voice, pretending he was one of the fancy elevator operators in the luxury apartment buildings and hotels that we sometimes passed on the street. We used to pretend they were those guards with the fuzzy hats who guarded the Queen of England, and we'd always try to make them laugh. But now, Gilly just stands quietly as we keep rising. On the ninth floor, we get off, and I take a deep breath.

"It's okay," Gilly insists, as if he can simply manifest my well-being with his sheer will.

A door flies open down the hall, and a woman comes walking briskly toward us. She looks vaguely familiar, but I can't place her. Then I realize it's Mrs. Lake, the opera singer (the witch!) from down the hall. She is old now, of course, but her hair remains the jet-black it was all those years ago, parted in the middle and hanging to her waist, though an inch of pure white at her scalp is a giveaway that the black likely comes from a box. Her face is shrunken and pinched, like the apple-head dolls we used to make at Lost River, wrinkled. Bright blue eye shadow glistens on heavy eyelids, and peach-colored lipstick bleeds into the cracks around her mouth. Her milky eyes are wild as she searches our little crew.

"Liliana," Mrs. Lake says, her hand pressed to her breast.

Liliana nods. "Is everything okay?"

"No," she says, shaking her head. "Two men were just here. Looking for Fiona." Her voice is a trembling vibrato.

Liliana pales, and I feel my fingers start to tingle, my body hum like a live wire. *No, no. Not now,* I think.

"Was it the police again?" Liliana asks. Gilly had told me there were investigators; the neighbors all questioned. They'd searched Henri's home to confirm there was no foul play. They'd spoken to my mother extensively, taken her statement as the coroner took his body away.

"No," Mrs. Lake says, shaking her head. "They said they were *FBI.*"

I t has been at least a decade since I've had an anxiety attack. The last time I felt like this was the night things finally fell apart with Andy, the night he packed up and left. Sasha was just a little girl then, but she knew something was wrong. Somehow, I'd managed to keep it together long enough to call my friend, Effie, who came and picked her up, and I spent three days getting myself together again. Years of therapy, of meditation, have stripped my anxiety away, like so much old paint. I have shed my fears, sloughed them off, leaving me exposed and vulnerable, but free. Now, though, my fingers tingle, and I feel my throat closing again. The banging drum of my heart feels loud enough for others to hear. I force myself to calm down. To breathe.

When I was growing up, my mother never knew what to do with my fear. My anxiety. She'd never known what to do when fear turned my knees to jelly. When my heart was racing so hard, I had to sit down and press my hand against my chest, as if it might beat hard enough to leap from my body. She was particularly irritated when the trigger was something simple: a crowded sidewalk; a heavy storm that battered our windows with rain; a sound I couldn't identify, traveling across those wavelike ceilings in the middle of the night.

It happened once in Times Square, when we were looking for a nail salon recommended by a girlfriend. My mother's nails had finally grown, and she was going to treat herself to a fancy manicure. The moment we stepped around the corner onto the busy street, I started getting that breathless, electric feeling, and I took a deep breath. But the air was ripe with something rotten: fish, bananas, body odor. When I opened my eyes again, I was assaulted by the signs advertising X-rated movies. Blinking neon lights with the silhouettes of ladies with big breasts and round bottoms, impossibly high heels. Like the mudflap ladies we counted on the semis on our road trip from Vermont to New York. Movie theater marquee after marquee: *Sweet Cakes, Young Nympho, Taboo.*

As we hustled down 42nd Street, girls who looked not much older than me leaned into men's cars, their skirts barely covering their panties. So much skin and sweat. Men, loitering in doorways and on benches, whistled and grabbed their crotches as my mother and I walked by. It was dizzying and awful.

We reached the open doorway of a place called Hubert's Museum. I sat down on the sidewalk, my back against the wall, hunched over, trying to curl into a ball. Gilly wasn't here to hold me, and my mother stood over me, insisting I get up.

"Ryan, are you *kidding* me?"

People shoved past me to get to the turnstile into the museum; I could feel their pants brushing against my bare legs. Next door was an arcade called Playland, and I could hear the Skee-Ball games, the hard balls knocking against wood. I pressed my hands against my ears.

I felt her hand reach for mine, and I thought she was going to sit down with me, but instead, she yanked me to my feet, almost pulling my arm out of its socket.

"Get *up*," she hissed in my ear, and tears burned my cheeks. "Let's go. What is *wrong* with you?"

I'd had no choice but to try and stand. But just as I got to my feet, someone bumped into me, and when I looked up, the tallest man I had ever seen was standing there. He had just come out of the museum. He had to be at least nine feet tall. A giant. I had seen giants in my copy of *The Guinness Book of World Records*, but never in real life.

"Excuse me," he said and smiled, tipping his hat, but I was filled with terror. As his giant freckled face gazed down at me, I felt dizzy. Upside down.

My mother gripped my arm, and I stumbled after her down the busy street. Eventually, feeling returned to my limbs, and she didn't have to drag me anymore. But I almost fell as she ran down the steps to the subway, still gripping my arm. She fumed. "You want to get us raped?" she said. "Murdered?"

The subway smells were overwhelming. I pulled away from her, but the vomit was burning my throat and filling my mouth before I could get to the trash can.

At the foot of the subway stairs, two men stood, arms crossed. Both were wearing red berets, and it made me think of my mother's headshot, her jaunty cap. Their T-shirts said GUARDIAN ANGELS with a pair of angel wings.

"You ladies okay?" one asked.

"We're *fine*," she said. "Thank you."

The bigger man nodded his head and then smiled at me.

I kept looking back over my shoulder as we hurried toward the southbound 3 train, which had just screeched to a stop on the tracks, until the Guardian Angel disappeared behind me.

My mother didn't speak to me the whole way home, and I had to chase after her up the stairs of the 14th Street station.

"I'm sorry," I kept saying to her back. "I can't help it."

Back at Westbeth, she simply said, "Go brush your teeth." When Liliana asked if everything was okay, my mother nodded and smiled. "Upset tummy," she said. "Probably something she ate."

"You okay?" Liliana asks now, as we reach the door to their apartment.

"Yeah. I just need some water," I say.

"Of course, honey," she says.

But I can see that instead of being the calming presence she has always been, she is rattled, too. She fumbles as she unlocks the door, apologizes nervously, and then the lock gives. "It's the humidity. It always makes the casing swell. There we go."

Coming home to Westbeth, to this apartment, is like stepping into a time capsule. While Liliana has aged, the apartment itself is almost exactly as I remember it. We enter the small downstairs room, which is nearly identical to my memory of it, though the big bed beneath the window is gone, replaced with a worktable and Liliana's art supplies. Large paintings in various degrees of completion still lean against the walls or hang from their canvases' wooden frames on the tall white walls. The heady smell pulls me backwards through time: bitter linseed, woodsy pine, and the nose-burning kerosene scent of white spirit.

"Is that Ry?" a voice bellows from upstairs. *Joaquin.* I didn't know he would be here.

I follow Liliana up the steep stairwell, Gilly and Sasha close behind, and Joaquin is waiting for me at the top of the stairs, his arms open. He encloses me, and I continue to slip into the past. He is so much like his father. The soft flannel shirt, the tobacco smell of him, his big hands on my back. He could be Guillermo, and I could stay here. I could live inside his hug.

I will my heart to still.

"And Sasha, goddamn, when did you grow up?" he asks, as we finally separate.

She goes to him, and he holds her, too.

"You're taller than me now!" he says, laughing. "Though that's not hard, I suppose." Joaquin, like Guillermo, is a stocky five foot eight.

Gilly puts our suitcase on the other side of the divider, which separates the living space from the bedroom, where I assume the missing bed from downstairs has gone. I see that the loft bed above the closets remains. My nest. Our nest.

Where on earth has my mother gone? I was sure that by the time we got back here, she would have returned. She'd have some excuse for her absence. Some explanation. The text I sent her remains unread.

When Sasha was in the fourth grade, her school did a production of *Seussical,* and she had played Mayzie, the bird too lazy to wait for her egg to hatch, who passes off that task to the unwitting elephant, Horton. I had sat through the play with tears running down my cheeks. Sasha's sweet performance had moved me, of course, but it was the *story* that had really done me in. That mother leaving her job to someone else. Whimsical, selfish bird.

But now, I am worried. The FBI came to question her, and she was, conveniently, not here. I think of the letter in my pocket and shake my head. No. I refuse to let her hijack this moment. I'm not here to see my mother. I'm here to honor the life of my friend. To grieve with my makeshift family. Still, my skin vibrates. Like the aftershocks following an earthquake.

As Liliana reaches into the open cupboard for a glass, I see her sneaking a peek at me.

"How are you doing, honey?" she asks. Liliana was always there to pick up the pieces when my mother was AWOL. We know this dance.

She hands me a glass of water, and I sit down at the kitchen table, trying to remember the tools I've acquired over the years to manage this. But the toolbox latch is rusted shut.

"I'm okay," I say, forcing a smile. "It's just so hot in the city. I always forget."

It's her job now to believe me. Or to pretend to, anyway. Liliana pats my arm.

Gilly comes back into the kitchen and, thankfully, recognizes what this is: The beads of sweat at my hairline are not from the heat but from the inferno raging in my body.

"Hey, Mom," Gilly says, nodding, purposeful. "Why don't you and Joaquin take Sasha downstairs to the gallery?" He smiles at Sasha.

"It's not the Met, but there's a pretty cool show up right now. Mom has a couple of her larger pieces in it."

"Oh, yes!" Sasha says, clapping her hands together. "Please! I'd love to see more of your work."

Sasha has been staring at one of Liliana's paintings every day since she was born. It was a gift for my baby shower, and I hung it above her crib, where she could delight in the bright splotches of color. Over the years, it has been moved around the room, and in a few weeks, it will be loaded into the back of her car to find its new home on a wall in LA.

Gilly sits down opposite from me at the table. I hear the door shut behind Liliana and Sasha downstairs.

"Why is the FBI looking for my mother?" I ask. "You said the police already took her statement. Is this about Henri?"

I search Gilly's face, his kind face I've been looking to for answers for most of my life. But when I don't see any answers there, the buzzing begins. It fills my ear, blocking out all other sounds. I watch my hand reach for the water, feel the lip meet my lip, register the flood on my tongue, but swallowing is hard. I need to focus.

"What if it's about the photo?" I say. "About Zev Brenner."

I think of that cryptic inscription on the back, the way it had sounded like she and Brenner were old friends. Chummy, even. *Love, Fi.* If they knew each other—or were friendly—maybe they needed her to make a statement. To testify? But to what? The photo was of *me*. The article had made the photo something ugly, something salacious. And I am pretty sure this is the reason why Henri is dead now, why he took his own life. My throat burns.

Gilly's mouth twitches, a telltale sign that I have struck some sort of nerve.

"Drink first," he says, and I obey. The water, cool and clean as water from the spring in Lost River. I'd forgotten how good New York City tap water is.

"What is it?" I demand.

"It's probably nothing, but there's been some talk about Margie."

"Margie?" I ask.

Margie was my modeling agent. The woman who *discovered* me. My mother would tell the story a thousand times, my story added to the list of life-altering chance encounters she'd been clinging to for years. Margie got me my first job, which then set off the chain reaction that was my unlikely career. Margie had been there through it all. Had I ever heard her utter the name Zev Brenner?

Gilly rubs his knobby throat with his hand, another tell.

"Margie knew him?" I say. "Zev Brenner?"

"They're saying," he says, "she *worked* for him."

New York City
Halloween, 1976

"I have an audition tomorrow," my mother announced at breakfast, as she often did. She hadn't been cast in anything yet, but she remained optimistic. It had only been a couple of months. I knew money was tight, though. I'd heard her whispering on the phone with Serafina, and two days later, a check came in the mail for her.

"Where is it?" Liliana asked. After that first day, when we all thought she'd been mugged or murdered, Liliana had demanded to know exactly where my mother was going, just in case.

"West Thirty-Eighth Street," she said, reading the ad in *Backstage*. "A couple blocks from Penn Station?"

"Oh, that's in the Garment District. Mind if I come along? I need to pick up some fabric for our Halloween costumes."

"Can I come, too?" I asked. It was Saturday. No school.

My mother shrugged. "I guess. Can you watch her while I'm in my audition?" she asked Liliana.

"Of course. It'll be a girls' day," she said, and smiled at me.

I was going to be Tiger Lily from *Peter Pan* that Halloween. There would be a huge parade in the Village, Gilly explained, that started in the Westbeth courtyard and traveled all the way to Washington Square Park. There would be life-sized puppets made by one of the Westbeth artists. Everyone got dressed up, even the adults.

In Lost River, we always had a Halloween party, because we

didn't have neighbors close enough to trick-or-treat. In the fall, when all the summer stock people were gone, I was the only child left behind. Serafina did her best; she decorated the big house with cobwebs and the pumpkins we carved into jack-o'-lanterns. I'd always help her stuff her boyfriend Joe's old flannel shirts and dungarees with leaves to make the harvest dummy, who guarded the porch.

She'd let me pick out anything I wanted from the costume shop, but the costumes were always too big, and my mother would have to safety-pin the dresses or suits to fit me, lift their hems so the cuffs and skirts didn't drag on the ground. The parties were fun: spooky drinks, steaming with dry ice, and a live band in the barn. But I was one of the only kids, and usually, I'd just wind up falling asleep in the hayloft above the music. Joe or one of the other guys would have to carry me down to our cabin when everyone had gone home.

This year, I was excited to dress up. To be surrounded by children. To gorge on candy and march in the parade.

It was Gilly's idea for us to be characters from *Peter Pan*. Liliana had already made his Peter costume, a green tunic belted at the waist with a little feathered felt cap and shoes. A pair of green tights. Angelica would be Tinkerbell. Gilly had wanted Joaquin to be Captain Hook, but he'd insisted on being The Fonz from *Happy Days* instead. He planned to wear Guillermo's old motorcycle jacket and cuffed jeans, a plastic Fonzie mask from Woolworth's. He'd been practicing his catchphrase, *Ayyyy*, jutting his thumbs in the air and cocking his head. Guillermo had stepped in to be Captain Hook, and Liliana and my mother were going to be mermaids. Liliana had been searching for the perfect fabric to make their shimmery tails.

At Lost River, Liliana oversaw the costume shop, which I thought was one of the most magical places on earth. At Westbeth, she had a sewing machine in her studio, and she had set to work with our various costume requests right away. She somehow procured the softest brown suede I had ever felt, and she made my Tiger Lily dress with fringes at the bottom. I already had a worn pair of moccasins that still fit. I would braid my hair and wear a turquoise-colored headband with a big red-and-white feather affixed to the back. Guillermo was borrowing his Hook costume from one of the theaters he worked with. The mermaid costumes were the only ones left.

Going out with Liliana was exciting. Unlike my mother, she had grown up in the city. She knew every street, every alley. She didn't need a map or a kiosk telling her which way to go.

On Saturday morning, the three of us walked to Bleecker Street to wait for the bus. We sat together on the green plastic seats for the ride up Eighth Avenue. I felt so grown up on the bus, sitting sandwiched between my mother and Liliana, who were both dressed up for a day on the town. My mother was auditioning for a shampoo commercial. The casting call had said they were looking for blondes, but my mother was determined. "At least, I'll stand out," she had said. She'd slept with her hair wrapped around the orange juice cans again and then borrowed Liliana's hot rollers in the morning. I could smell the steamy heat of them now as we sat pressed together on the bus, headed toward midtown.

The bus was filled with people, young and old, men and women, everyone going somewhere. It seemed a miracle to me that the world was so full of people, each of them with their own lives. In Lost River, at any given time, there were no more than fifty people in my world. But here, I almost never saw the same face twice. Not outside of Westbeth, anyway. Even within the building's walls, I was always spying someone I hadn't seen before. The seats were all along the edges of the bus, with its fishbowl-like windows, not like a school bus with its tidy rows. We sat across from an elderly man. He was wearing a long trench coat, and he had a freckled bald head with wisps of hair over the top that reminded me of the baby robins Gilly and I had found in a nest in the barn's rafters. His shoes were glossy, and I wondered if he'd gotten them polished by one of the shoeshine boys with their chairs lined up at the subway stops. I looked up at his face; he was smiling at me, and I began to offer him a smile in return, when I felt my mother yank my arm as she stood up.

"Fucking pig," she spat, and the man's face bloomed red.

Confused, I stumbled after her and Liliana, who had also stood up, toward the other end of the bus, but snuck a peek back at the man. I caught a glimpse of his open coat, his hand down the front of his pants, moving up and down, his glassy gaze still on me.

I sat down again, but she remained standing, hovering over me, blocking my view of the seats we'd just abandoned. Her hand gripped one of the straps overhead, and she held on as the bus hurtled forward, the other passengers oblivious to whatever had just happened.

"Fucking pervert," she said, even louder this time, and a bunch of people looked up from their newspapers and books.

Liliana reached for her arm as if to comfort her, but my mother jerked it away.

"She's *ten years old*," she said loudly. Though I didn't know what this had to do with anything. Why anyone on this bus would care how old I was.

We got off at the next stop, even though it meant we'd have to walk five more blocks to get to the address my mother had jotted down.

We all walked together until we found the line of women— there must have been a hundred of them—which curled around the corner and halfway down the next block of Fifth Avenue. Every one of them had a head full of blond hair. It looked like a beauty pageant, all these glamorous ladies lined up. We walked past them, the assault of their perfume and shampoo almost as strong as the scent of garbage and motor oil I had come to associate with the city.

My mother grimly stood behind a woman with the prettiest blond curls I had ever seen. My mother jutted out her chin and reached into her purse for her cigarettes.

"Should we wait with you?" Liliana asked.

My mother drew on her cigarette and exhaled, shaking her head. "No. I'll just meet you at that little restaurant we passed on Thirty-

Eighth. Terra Nova, I think it was called? Plan to be there at one o'clock; that should give me plenty of time. If I get done early, I'll just do some window-shopping."

My mother had discovered the joy of window-shopping on our first weekend in the city. We must have walked up and down Fifth Avenue for two hours while she looked with longing at the fancy shops' window displays.

"I feel just like Holly Golightly," she'd said as we stood in front of Tiffany's, the diamonds in the window catching the sunlight and sending it back to us like the light from a star.

"Terra Nova, one o'clock," Liliana said.

"Keep an eye on her," my mother said to Liliana; then, to me, "And stay away from the freaking pedophiles."

I hadn't heard that word before, but I knew she was talking about that man on the bus. I felt sort of sick, and tears sprang to my eyes. I felt so stupid for smiling at him, for being kind to a stranger.

Liliana and I spent the next three hours searching for the perfect fabric to make mermaids' tails. We entered shop after shop on 39th Street, wandering through the rows of fabric bolts. It felt like we'd stepped into Candyland, the endless maze of beautiful colors and textures. I ran my fingers along the edges, trailing behind Liliana, who was on a mission. But she couldn't find what she was looking for. She almost settled on a bit of glittery green material, but then changed her mind.

I was getting hungry. Even the excitement of all that possibility started to feel overwhelming. It was 12:45 already, which meant we needed to be back on 38th Street to meet my mother in fifteen minutes.

"It's almost time to meet my mom," I tried, as we reached a floor where every bolt of fabric was some sort of fur. The air smelled musty and stifling.

She did an about-face; we returned to the floor where we had been before, and I tried again.

"She might be there already, if she finished her audition," I said.

"There!" Liliana said, pointing up at a bolt of fabric.

I looked at my watch, the Cinderella one I'd gotten for my last birthday, her long white-gloved arm pointing almost to the twelve. I thought about my mom arriving at Terra Nova, expecting to find us, and us not being there.

A little lady, with a long yellow measuring tape around her neck and a pair of reading glasses slipping down her long nose, climbed up on a step stool to get the bolt of fabric down. I shifted my weight from one foot to the next as she brought the bolt to a long cutting table and slowly and meticulously cut the shimmery fabric with her sharp scissors.

By the time she had folded it, rung Liliana up at the register, and put the fabric in a little plastic bag, it was 1:10. Would my mom leave? That would mean she'd be on the bus by herself. What if that awful man in the trench coat was on the bus again?

"It's perfect!" Liliana said, oblivious to the electricity running through my body, as we made our way back to 38th Street.

I had run through every possible scenario I could imagine by the time we rounded the corner and saw my mother walking toward us from Fifth Avenue, waving.

I ran down the sidewalk, rushing into her, grabbing her around the waist, almost knocking her over. Breath returned to my lungs as I smelled the familiar smell of her and felt her hands on my back.

I didn't let go of her, even as the host at Terra Nova showed us to our table on the little patio out in front of the café. I had the overwhelming urge to curl up in her lap, the way I used to when I was little. But I was too big for that now; I would have looked silly. Like a baby. And so instead, I just pulled my chair next to hers and leaned my head against her shoulder as she told Liliana all about the shampoo commercial.

"Well, of course they looked at me like I was insane," my mother said, laughing as she squeezed a lemon slice into her Tab. "I was the only one in there who didn't look like Farrah friggin' Fawcett. But the casting director let me audition anyway."

"And . . . ?" Liliana said, and we both waited for the exciting news that she had finally been cast in something.

"He said, and I quote, 'You've got some balls, Miss Flannigan. You're not getting this job, but why don't you come back next week. I'm looking for a brunette for a Kool-Aid commercial.'"

"That's terrific!" Liliana said.

Now that we were reunited, the world around me came into focus again. It was a beautiful autumn day. Here in the city, there were trees, but nothing like the rainbow of maples and aspens and birches at Lost River. Still, the sky was bright blue, and the air was crisp. To celebrate, my mother told me I could have a Shirley Temple, and she and Liliana each ordered a glass of wine. We clinked our cheers and then studied the menu.

I saw the woman watching us from across the patio. She was dressed in a champagne-colored jacket and skirt, with a fancy chocolate silk scarf at her throat. Her platinum hair was cut razor-sharp to her chin. She had large, round sunglasses, which she removed. I looked at her, taking a giant sip of my Shirley Temple, letting the sweet grenadine linger on my tongue before swallowing.

The woman smiled at me. I smiled back reflexively, then remembered how I'd smiled at that horrible man on the bus, and looked away.

I had ordered spaghetti and meatballs. My mother said she wasn't hungry, so she'd just asked for a second glass of wine. I didn't notice the woman approach, because I was so intent on spinning the spaghetti on my fork. I was humming the tune of *On top of spaghetti! All covered with cheese* . . .

"Excuse me," the woman said. "I'm so sorry to bother you."

I looked up at her. She was very tall, and her body blocked the sun.

Liliana and my mother looked at her, bewildered.

"I'm a modeling agent," she said. "I used to be with Ford, but I've just started my own agency."

I looked at my mother. *This is it*, I thought. I could practically see her memorizing this moment. Someday, she would recite the story of her discovery. *We were sitting at a little café in the Garment District, eating meatballs . . .* It was finally, finally happening.

"I hate to interrupt your meal," she said.

"No, no," my mother said, and I could hear a sort of pleading threaded through her words. "Please, have a seat," she said, beaming.

The woman sat in the empty chair and crossed her legs. Her fingernails were painted the pale pink of the inside of a shell, and she smelled like the perfume counter at Bloomingdale's—one of my mother's favorite spots in New York.

My mother fiddled with her hair, which still held the big, loose curls she'd made for the audition. But the agent wasn't looking at my mother. Instead, she was gazing intently at *me*.

"How old are you, dear?" she asked, as I slurped one long strand of spaghetti.

I swallowed. "I'm ten," I said.

"You're very tall," she said, studying my legs, which were looped around the back legs of my chair. "How tall is she?" she asked, and I saw the shift in my mother's expression.

I knew exactly how tall I was—at least as of August—because at Lost River, we marked my height on the woodwork of our cabin door every summer.

"I think she's five feet?" my mother said, her voice flat.

"How tall are *you*?" the woman asked, and life returned to my mother's eyes.

"I'm five-nine and a half," she said. I knew this wasn't quite true, that she had just given herself an inch. But she'd told me that most modeling agencies wouldn't even talk to you if you weren't at least five-nine. My mother was smiling now.

"I'm sorry. I should explain. I'm starting a children's division," the woman said. "For young models. I always like to get a sense of their genes. How tall their mothers and fathers are. Weight," she said.

My mother bristled and stared at my meatball.

"She's really not interested in modeling," she said. "But thanks so much."

For some reason, I spoke up.

"I am interested!" I blurted out. The woman smiled at me warmly.

"I'm sure *you've* been approached before," she said to my mother. "Clearly, she's inherited her lovely bone structure from you. Your complexion?"

My mother's mouth twitched, and I could see the compliments melting her iciness.

"I'm an actress," my mother said. "I actually just came from an audition. I've done a little modeling." My mother had modeled exactly once. Last month, a painter friend of Liliana's at Westbeth had posted a notice that he needed live models for a class he was teaching.

"Well, then, it runs in the family," the woman said. "Anyway, I'll let you get back to your lunch. If you're *interested*," she said, and grinned at me, "come by on Monday."

"She has school," my mother said. "Until two-thirty."

"Then how about three-thirty?" the woman said.

My mother took a deep breath. "I'm sorry," she said. "Your name again?"

She reached into a small clutch she was carrying. She pulled out a card and handed it to my mother. "My agency is called Papillon Model Management."

The business card was creamy white with a simple butterfly embossed next to the company name and number.

"I'm Margaret Schine. But please, everybody calls me Margie."

"What do you mean Margie worked for Zev Brenner? Isn't he some kind of Wall Street guy?"

We are in the living room now. I am lying on the couch, and Gilly is sitting in the giant beanbag chair under the window. I've had three full glasses of water, but I still feel parched. Gilly situated me under the ceiling fan and gave me a cool washcloth to lay across my forehead. It's a worn red one I remember from my childhood.

"Have you been following the stories about him at all?" he asks.

I sit up and put the damp washcloth on my knee.

I consider how little I know about this man. This man who had a photo of me hanging in his Paris apartment, a photo apparently gifted to him by my own mother. He is nothing more to me than the two strikingly different images the news keeps showing of his face. The photo of him standing in a high-rise office, his back to a window framing the city skyline, arms crossed and a smug grin. And the one of him taken the night of his arrest, the mug shot photo of him with his thick head of hair in disarray and bloodshot eyes: the bemused, even *amused*, face of someone who believes himself to be untouchable.

There was a raid, an arrest, rumors of pedophilia. Prostitution. Sexual abuse. None of it seems particularly surprising. Disgusting, yes. But not shocking. Men like this, I think, do what they want.

"Just the basics," I admit.

In Lost River, I feel untethered from the world. It is part of the reason I love to be there, as irresponsible as that might be. It is an easy place to bury one's head in the sand. The local newspaper that peeks out of its wire rack at the grocery store rarely features the atrocities of the world on its front page. Those horrors are relegated to the back, while local human-interest stories (spelling bees and quilting bees; a local farmer's prized *honey*bees) take up that above-the-fold real estate. Our Internet is spotty at best, and I am usually able to avoid my phone. To keep myself from complete oblivion, I listen to the public radio station in the mornings and, once a week or so, click onto NPR's website. I know I'm fortunate, being able to simply extricate myself from the world. Sasha is always reminding me to check my privilege, how lucky I am to simply *opt out*. It angers her, I know, to watch me disconnect. She is one who is always engaged. Enraged. This is a gift from her father. He is Fight, and I, like my mother, am Flight.

Sasha doesn't know, of course, the reasons why I hide. She doesn't know the anxious spiraling that can begin with the news of another teen shot in their classroom, another woman held captive, another child separated from her mother. I have spent the last eighteen years ensuring that I live outside the news instead of inside it.

"Talk is that Margie has been *procuring* girls for him," Gilly says. "Models. *Underage* models. Through the Paris division of her agency. That she's been doing this for decades."

"Seriously?" I say, sickened.

"I don't know. It's just talk."

"How does my mom know him, Gilly? And why on earth would she give him my photo? *That* photo?"

Gilly rubs his mouth with his hand and takes a deep breath.

"Have you read her note?" he asks.

I shake my head. "Have you?"

"No," he says. "I only know that Fiona wanted to talk to you about it herself. Before Henri—" he starts. He looks physically pained, his eyes glossy. He shakes his head, covers his mouth with his hand.

"If she wanted to explain, then why did she take off?" I say. "Gilly. I can handle it. Just tell me what is going on."

"I honestly don't know, Ry. Maybe it's in the note."

I hear footsteps running up the stairs, and Sasha pops into the living room like a little fairy sprite, followed by Liliana and Joaquin.

"Oh, Mama! Liliana's paintings are so beautiful. You have to go downstairs and see."

"I will!" I say. She comes to me, sitting down on my lap like she's still a little girl. I have spent the last eighteen years making sure that she never stops doing this.

"What are you guys doing?" she asks, and pulls the wet washcloth out from under her. "Ew. Gross."

"Gilly and I are just trying to figure out where your grandmother has run off to." I am trying to treat her disappearance as if it's just one of her many quirks. Sasha doesn't know her grandmother well enough to question it.

"*So . . .*" Sasha says, in the way I know means she's about to follow up with something I will say no to. "I called Zu-Zu, and she's out of class at five tonight. Is it okay if I meet her at the ballet studio and go get some dinner? I mean, since Fiona isn't back yet?"

She acts as though we're still at home, and she is just going to drive ten miles to Gormlaith to meet her.

"How will you get there?" I ask her.

"The *subway*?" she says.

"You don't know how to use the subway."

She rolls her eyes. "The map app on my phone has public transit directions. It looks like it's basically a straight shot on the 1 train."

Her independence is her father's, as is her fearlessness, even in a strange city.

"I guess it depends on what everybody else is planning for tonight?" I say, hoping someone will stop her, tell her that we need her here. But then again, maybe she *shouldn't* be here when Fiona comes back. It might be best if she's out of range of whatever that might mean.

"*Go*," Liliana says. "Have fun with your friend. We'll just be here putting Henri's photos together for the memorial." She turns to me and says, "She'll be *fine*."

"Actually, if you and your friend are interested, they're doing an outdoor movie over at Pier Forty-six tonight," Joaquin offers.

"At the *piers*?" I say in disbelief.

"I *know*," Liliana says. "Who'd have thought? They are definitely not the piers you grew up with."

"I think it's that Kate Winslet movie," Joaquin says.

"*Eternal Sunshine*?" Sasha asks, and claps her hands together. "Oh, I love Charlie Kaufman. Have you seen *Being John Malkovich*?"

"Dad was *in* it," Gilly says.

"*Get out*," Sasha says.

Liliana laughs. "Gilly, that hardly counts. He was on screen for about three quarters of a second."

"Did he get to meet him?" Sasha asks.

"John Malkovich?"

"No, Charlie Kaufman!" Sasha has never been starstruck over movie stars. But writers? Writers, she moons over. Her dad's a screen-writer, after all. It's no wonder.

"I don't know. He did meet Tarantino once, though," Joaquin says. "Said he was a super prick."

"Oh my god!" she says, clearly delighted by this sort of gossip. "Anyway, I'll ask Zu-Zu. She loves Kate Winslet. Maybe she can meet me here instead. If the pier's close by, it wouldn't make sense for me to go all the way up to Lincoln Center, anyway. She could just come here, and we can grab something to eat nearby."

Relief washes over me with this compromise.

"That sounds like a good plan. Maybe I could go with you guys?" I suggest, thinking suddenly that a movie in the park sounds a lot more desirable than having a confrontation with my mother here. "We could put together a picnic, bring popcorn?"

Sasha nods in the way that she does, in the way that I do, when I am agreeing to something I don't really want. Mustering enthusiasm by vigorously nodding. Here is my legacy. Of course, she doesn't want her mother tagging along. She's eighteen now. Grown.

"Actually," Liliana says, reaching for my arm, "I was really hoping you and Gilly could go through Henri's photos, for the memorial. There are thousands of them, and we only have room enough for a couple dozen or so. You know his work better than anyone. You should be the one to choose."

It's my turn to nod in manufactured agreement. Of course. This is why I'm here, after all. To honor Henri.

Zu-Zu arrives at five o'clock, and Sasha introduces her to everyone. Zu-Zu is outgoing and sweet. I can't help but think Henri would have loved to photograph her. She's biracial, with Devin's brown skin and Effie's startlingly blue eyes. She has that ethereal quality that so many ballet dancers have, as if she were made of vapors or glass. That contradiction has always fascinated me, the way these girls, whose strength is so profound, could appear so delicate. Whenever I see Zu-Zu, I am reminded of how I had once longed to dance. But there are only so many lives we can live, and that one slipped away like so much chiffon and ribbon.

"Should we go get pizza or something?" Sasha asks, stuffing a batik tapestry from Liliana into her backpack to use as a blanket.

"Oh my god, yes. I am starving," Zu-Zu says.

"Text me when you get there," I say to the closing door.

"Do you want me to go down to Henri's apartment with you?" Liliana asks tentatively. "Or would you and Gilly like to go alone?"

I look to Gilly, who is washing the dishes from our dinner.

"I mean, I'm happy to come along," she says. "But like I said, I have no idea where to start. With the pictures."

"We can go," I say to her, nodding. "Stay here. Maybe my

mother's come back. I've been texting her, but I don't think she's getting them. Or reading them, anyway. We'll go check on her while we're down there. She might be home by now."

This is, I think, just as possible as it is impossible. My mother is predictably unpredictable. But even as I imagine her answering her door, hair turbaned in a towel as though this were any other day, Mrs. Lake's words feel like a punch. The *FBI.* Jesus. They probably wanted to talk to her about Margie. Another blow lands in my solar plexus. The FBI could very well want to talk to me, too. I should have asked Mrs. Lake what they said.

"Thank you," Liliana says. "I honestly haven't been able to bring myself to go down there yet. I'm not sure I'm ready. If I'll ever be ready."

I nod again, though why she thinks I would be more equipped emotionally for this is beyond me.

Gilly and I quietly make our way down the empty corridor; there is an eerie stillness, less like the Westbeth I remember and more like a mausoleum. He reminds me that most of our neighbors on the ninth floor had been families with children. Like us. Those children are grown now, and the new families who have moved in don't let their children roam the way we did. We were wild then, but this new generation of children has been domesticated.

In the elevator, Gilly says, "You sure you want to do this? I'm happy to grab the photos and bring them up. We don't have to sort through them down there."

I shake my head. I need to do this.

"Okay," he says, and the elevator doors close. *"Second floor!"* His voice breaks, and I look at him, tears filling both of our eyes.

All Hallows' Eve, 1976

*T*he parade is dizzying. Life-sized puppets swoop over the courtyard on strings and sticks: ghosts and bats and towering skeletons. Hundreds of costumed children and their parents assemble in the courtyard, us included. Our ensemble—we refugees of Neverland (plus Fonzie)—huddles together in the courtyard before making our way en masse to Jane Street, where the parade will begin.

Gilly and I spent almost an hour getting ready as Liliana made last-minute adjustments to our costumes. She and my mother look otherworldly, like real mermaids. They both wear bikini tops made of giant clamshells that Liliana had from a trip to the coast of Maine. Their bellies are bare—Liliana's, soft and round; my mother's, tiny like a child's. Their shimmering, glimmering tails sweep the ground behind them as they walk. They both wear their hair down, with shells and starfish threaded through their curls.

"You look pretty, Mama," I said earlier, as she was fussing with her emerald sparkly eyeshadow in the mirror.

She waved a dismissive hand. "Not as pretty as you. You look like a real Indian princess."

Guillermo's long, black wig has transformed him into Captain Hook. And Mr. Lee, the puppet-maker in charge of the parade, made a papier-mâché crocodile puppet, which Gilly and I operate with two sticks. It slithers across the ground and even makes a tick-tock sound.

Angelica started coming down with a cold on Friday, and by this morning, she was feverish. But she insisted on joining the parade; her Tinkerbell costume is complete with fairy wings strung with lights. I haven't been feeling very well, either, but I haven't mentioned my sore throat or stuffy nose to my mother. I don't want anything to spoil our plans for the night.

A Dixieland jazz band leads the way, followed by the tenants of Westbeth, with a group of men playing drums behind us. When I press my palm against my chest, I can feel the rhythm of them beating there. I feel like I am Tiger Lily. I imagine that I am a real Indian princess, captured by Captain Hook. The sound swells inside me. I feel brave.

However, after the last bit of sunlight has disappeared from the sky, I begin to shiver. I am wearing tights and a turtleneck underneath my costume, but I am trembling all the same as we move, like a swiftly rushing river, through the streets of Greenwich Village.

At a certain point, Tinkerbell gets too tired to walk, and Captain Hook carries her. Henri—who has joined us, dressed in a striped shirt and red cap as Smee—clicks a photo of Tinkerbell burying herself into Captain Hook's neck, sucking her thumb, and cheeks ablaze, one nostril a bubble of snot.

It hurts to swallow, and my teeth are chattering now as we pass a pizza shop, and the bright neon lights hurt my eyes. I press my fist to my cheek and feel it burning. My head pounds in time to the drums behind me. I don't have the energy to make the crocodile slither, and so he drags behind me.

"You okay?" Gilly asks.

"I don't feel good," I say, and my voice sounds like gritty sandpaper. Every word hurts.

"I'll take this," he says, and takes the stick from me, maneuvering the crocodile as best he can. It's a job for two people, though, and so the tick-tock of his clock doesn't work.

When we finally get to Washington Square Park, all I want to do is sit down. To lie on the grass or on one of the benches, but the park is crowded, and the air is filled with loud music. The drums are too loud now, incessant.

My mother and Liliana have found two men who live across the street from Westbeth. They're both dressed like sailors, with white caps and bell-bottom pants, though shirtless with red ties around their knobby throats. They plead with Henri to take their photo.

Finally, feeling like I can't stand up for even another minute, I spy an open spot on the concrete edge of the fountain. Behind me, the beautiful arch-way glows ghostly in the autumn night.

"I need to lie down," I say to anyone who might hear. My mother is busy hamming it up with the sailors, who are kissing each other and mugging for Henri's camera.

Gilly hears, though, and follows me. It's cold at the fountain, the spray spattering my goose bump–riddled skin, but at least I can lie down. I curl up on my side and pull my knees up to stay warm. Gilly puts his hand on my head.

"You're burning up," he says.

Sitting on the ground near us is a guy, maybe a teenager, his back against the concrete. His sleeve is rolled up, and through one eye, I watch as he wraps a sickly yellow rubber tube around his arm.

"Ryan." I hear a voice.

"Is she okay?" Henri asks.

"She's sick."

The man taps at a needle, and I watch with fascination as it disappears into his flesh, his head rolling back.

"Let us get her home," Henri says, and Gilly stands.

But before Henri lifts me up, I hear the shutter click.

I was still a little sick on the Monday after Halloween, but my mother said I had to go to school if I wanted to have my meeting with Margie at Papillon later that day.

When the bell rang after school, I walked outside with my new friend, Cathy, who had pierced ears and was allowed to wear Kissing Potion lip gloss. My mother was waiting for me by the gate.

Normally, my mother dressed in bell-bottoms and peasant blouses. Dangly earrings. But today, I hardly recognized her. She was dressed elegantly, in clothes I hadn't seen before: a white fuzzy turtleneck and camel-colored slacks. Her hair was slicked back into a bun, like a ballerina's. She looked like a stranger.

"Ry!" she said and Cathy, whispered, "That's your mom?"

"Coming!" I hollered, and ran toward my mother, who sighed heavily when I reached her. She studied my face with a frown.

"I told you not to mess up your hair. What did you do?" she asked.

I absently touched the top of my head; during recess, I'd been playing on the merry-go-round. We liked to lie down on our backs when we spun; sometimes, our hair dragged on the ground.

As we walked away from the school, she fished in her purse for a hairbrush and stopped me at the corner to run it through.

"Oh my god, it's filthy!" she said, and there was a sort of panic laced through her words. She tugged at the tangles and then looked around, as if someone might be able to help her. Finally, she located a rubber band in her purse and quickly whisked my hair back into a ponytail.

She sighed again and studied my face, searching for the answer to something—maybe why it was that Margaret Schine had discovered me instead of her.

The offices for Papillon Model Management were on the Upper West Side, somewhere in the 70s and just off the park. It was a cold day, and we were running late. My mother's cheeks were flushed red by the time we found the address on the Papillon business card. My own cheeks felt numb.

My mother made one last cursory and critical check before we went inside. I was wearing my favorite denim jumper, which had an embroidered strawberry on the front. A red turtleneck and red sweater tights. Mary Janes that I had outgrown. I could feel a blister forming on each of my heels and was trying to walk so that the sharp edges of the shoes wouldn't bite in.

"Why are you walking like that?" she whispered as we opened the heavy wooden door.

"I told you they're too small," I said.

"Well, try not to do that," she said. "We'll put a Band-Aid on it later."

Inside, we were greeted by a large reception desk with gold vases of white hydrangeas on either side. A blond-haired woman sat behind the desk, looking at us expectantly.

"We have an appointment with Margie," my mother said, careful to use the nickname the woman had told her to use. "Ryan Flannigan? I'm her mother, Fiona."

"I can tell! You look exactly like each other," the woman said, smiling. She looked like one of the ladies in those Breck commercials. Shiny hair and a wide smile. Her hair looked so soft, I wanted to touch it.

I sneezed and then sniffled to suck my runny nose back in. My mother tensed.

"You can have a seat right over there," the lady said, pointing to a small waiting area, where two other girls and their mothers sat waiting. "She'll call you in just a minute."

We took a seat on a soft, baby blue couch. I took a peek at the other two girls. Both were blond, like the lady behind the counter, with big soft waves in their hair. I started thinking that letting my hair drag in the dirt at school had not been such a good idea. These girls both looked like they just walked out of a beauty salon. One girl had big green eyes and a scatter of freckles. The other had brown eyes, and something about her face reminded me of a deer. Both mothers sat primly at the edges of their respective chairs, pretending to glance through magazines.

On the walls were giant framed photos of girls' faces. At least half a dozen. All of them were wearing makeup: glossy lips and dark lashes. Some were smiling, while others looked over their shoulders at the camera with serious expressions on their faces.

I saw my mother looking at them, and I thought about the picture we had brought with us, one of the photos that Henri had taken of me while she was changing for her headshot: the one with my ribbon unfurled, the bug bite blazing on my knee. With the Halloween celebrations, we hadn't had time for him to take another one. "It'll do," my mother had said. "It's the kids' division, right? And you look like a kid."

"The Flannigan ladies!"

Margie had popped her head out of the door and spotted us. My mother stood up quickly, and I rose to attention, as well, immediately thinking of that goofy soldier, Gomer Pyle from TV, which made me giggle.

Margie came toward us, and with her came a tsunami of the spicy perfume she'd been wearing when we met her at the restaurant. "Opium," my mother had said. "Yves St. Laurent." My mother could identify the designers and name brands of almost anything. I think she must have gone to department stores and memorized them. I stifled another sneeze.

"Come with me," she said. "Would you like a soft drink?" she asked my mother.

"A Tab would be nice," my mother said.

"Hot chocolate?" Margie asked me.

I nodded.

"And you look like a girl who likes a marshmallow," she said.

My mother winced, but I nodded again.

We followed her into her office after she gave the secretary our drink order, and as she motioned for us to sit in the two high-backed chairs across from her desk, I felt like royalty.

"Well," she said. "I am so delighted you came! Sometimes I'll speak to a girl and her mother on the street, and never see them again."

My mother flinched, probably unsure whether this made us better or worse than those other girls and their mothers.

"You have some very strong genes," she said thoughtfully, and her gaze traveled from my mother to me. "What is your background. Ethnically? Italian?"

My mother shook her head. "My father was Irish. My mother was Cree Indian."

Margie clapped her hands together again, as if she were a contestant on *The $25,000 Pyramid*.

"So *that's* where that gorgeous skin and cheekbones come from," she said. "I'm usually really good at this, but this one stumped me. Cigarette?" she asked my mother, as a crinkly pack of Virginia Slims materialized in her hand.

My mother thanked her and accepted one of the long brown cigarettes that Margie tapped from the pack. Margie lit her cigarette and then passed the lighter to my mother. They both inhaled and exhaled silently, the smoke swirling around in the air.

The secretary came in, carrying a little tray with a bottle of Tab, a glass with a seedless lemon wedge and crushed ice, and a steaming cup of cocoa with one oversized marshmallow bobbing in its center.

She poured the Tab for my mother, handed her the cut glass tumbler, and then carefully handed the hot chocolate to me. I was grateful for the napkin, which I dabbed at my runny nose.

I took a sip and immediately burnt my tongue. I always made this mistake. I was always impatient when it came to treats like this. The roof of my mouth must have been scarred with blisters from the bubbling hot cheese of a thousand slices of pizza. Now my taste buds felt like sand.

"Okay," she said, as she stubbed her cigarette out. "Let's see your photos. Then we'll take some weight and height measurements."

I saw my mother's mouth twitch at the mention of weight. The scales we had brought from Lost River were used every single day, sometimes two or three times a day, by my mother. She kept track of her *fluctuations*, as she called them, in a little spiral notebook she stored in her underwear drawer.

"She put on some weight over the summer, but she always does that right before a growth spurt. She goes *out* before she goes *up*." My mother laughed nervously.

I had never heard my mother talk about my weight before, my body. But suddenly, it seemed as though she had been paying very close attention.

"How old are you again, sweetheart?" Margie asked, turning her attention to me.

"She'll be eleven on Valentine's," my mother offered, but Margie kept studying me.

"She's very tall for eleven," Margie said. "Is her father tall?"

My father. This was something my mother and I never spoke about. I knew nothing about him. When I was really little, my mother said she found me in Serafina's vegetable garden, curled up beneath a cabbage. I knew this wasn't true, but I also knew better than to ask my mother about who my father was.

"Six foot three," my mother said softly.

"Oh, that accounts for those legs, then," Margie said. "Stand up, Ryan?"

I set my mug on the little end table next to my chair and stood up. Margie came around from her desk and grabbed both of my hands as she examined me.

"She has a quite mature face," she said, without taking her eyes off me. "Very unusual in a child her age to have such a precocious face."

I didn't know what *precocious* meant, but the way she said it made me feel special.

The paper on my mother's cigarette crackled as it burned.

"She'll need a portfolio, of course," Margie said, turning back to her desk.

My mother shook her head. "I'm sorry, we don't have the—um—resources for that," she said. She stubbed out the cigarette in the ashtray next to Margie's butt and grabbed her purse off the back of her chair, setting it in her lap. "I didn't realize there would be any costs associated . . ."

"Oh, no, no . . ." Margie said, waving her hands dismissively. "There will be no costs. We have a team of photographers in-house. But it will mean we need to schedule a session." She looked down at her calendar desk blotter and grabbed a pencil from a silver holder. "How is next week at the same time?" she asked.

I ran my wounded tongue across the roof of my mouth, feeling each individual inflamed taste bud.

"I don't know," my mother said. "She's still such a little girl, and I have auditions myself. I'd have to check my calendar . . ."

I knew that her datebook was inside that purse. I also knew that she had her schedule memorized up until Christmas.

Margie's tone suddenly changed, from lighthearted and earnest to irritated. "If you're not interested," Margie said, "there are plenty of other pretty girls out there. I guess I am just not sure why you bothered to come at all."

My mother's face reddened. Would she start to cry? Or would she lash out with angry words? I had seen both things happen after her face turned this particular shade of crimson.

She shook her head then and fumbled in her purse. "Oh, look, I do have it here," she said, and pulled out the datebook. She quickly licked the pad of her thumb and flipped to the calendar for the second week of November.

"We're free," she said.

"Wonderful," Margie said, her friendly tone returning as quickly as it had departed. "We have a full wardrobe, so no need to wear anything special. She doesn't need a bra yet, right?" she asked, gazing at my boyish chest, and I felt my own face flush red.

"No," my mother said. My mother rarely wore a bra herself; her breasts, unlike Liliana's, were small.

Margie jotted down a few notes and then called her assistant in.

"Nell will take her to get measured," she said to my mother, "and you and I can chat for a bit."

Nell took me to a stark-looking room that seemed like it might be a storage closet. Metal shelving, with stacks of banker's boxes, and a row of tall metal filing cabinets. She turned on the overhead light and asked me to take off my jumper.

"You can keep your panties and your undershirt on," she said.

I felt like I was at the pediatrician's office. She had me step onto a set of scales first that registered my weight at eighty pounds. She then told me to stand against a yellow wall marked with measurements.

"Five feet, two inches," she announced. "You're only ten?"

I nodded.

She pulled a yellow cloth tape measure out of a drawer and circled it around my body: my chest, hips, and waist. The metal tab at the end of the tape was cold on my bare skin. She even measured my head circumference.

"Sometimes our clients use hats," she explained.

I nodded quietly again.

She located a Polaroid camera on a metal shelf and said, "Just hold still and look at me."

It made me think of those mug shots of criminals. I giggled.

"No smiling," she said seriously.

The camera spit out the undeveloped photo. "Now turn to the side," she said, and she snapped again.

When she was finished, and my image appeared in the two photographs, she told me to put my clothes back on, and she showed me out of the room and back down the hall. I could hear Margie talking and my mother's laughter.

They were smoking again; I could smell it as we approached the open door.

"Oh, you live at *Westbeth*?" Margie said, delighted. "I used to date a sculptor who lived at Westbeth. Perfect human specimen, but dumb as the day is long."

My mother laughed and said, "Was his name *Roger*?"

"Yes!" Margie said, laughing. "My god, hung like a donkey . . . but such a *jackass* . . ."

As we entered the room, Margie sat up straight and again stubbed out her cigarette. My mother was smiling, the creases at her brow softened into a smooth plane.

Margie, a pair of reading glasses perched at the edge of her nose, looked over the photos Nell had brought in. After a while, she looked up and put her hands together, like a prayer, her fingertips touching her chin.

"So, we'll see you both next week? Same time?"

My mother sprang from her seat. "Yes," my mother said. "Next week. Is there anything special I need to do, with her hair? Makeup?"

I thought of those girls in the picture frames in the lobby. Their glossy hair and shiny lips. I wondered who their mothers were.

"Not at all," Margie said. "Just have her come in with a fresh clean face and hair. We have people who will take care of all that."

I thought about the dust from the playground in the ends of my hair. About the smudge of ketchup my mother had rubbed off my cheek with a wet thumb while we hurtled underground in the subway. I thought about what all of this meant. How it was that my mother went to an audition, but it was *me* who was discovered. Sitting, eating spaghetti and meatballs. I had never even thought about being a model or an actress before, but it was the only thing my mother had ever wanted. My chest ached with guilt.

Margie stood up, came around from her desk, and bent down, just a little, so she could look me in the eyes.

"You, my dear," Margie said, studying me, "are an extraordinary little girl. I think this is the beginning of something very, very special. We are so delighted to welcome you both to the Papillon family."

I finally stole a glance at my mother, and to my surprise, it wasn't hurt I saw, but pride. She was beaming. Alight.

Margie thrust her hand into the air between them, and my mother accepted it. I bit the tender tip of my tongue as they shook hands. And then I sneezed.

"Did you want to go see if your mom's back first?" Gilly asks as the elevator doors open to the second floor. He's looking down the hallway, as if my mother might just materialize before our eyes. And who knows; she just might. She has disappeared before, but she always comes back.

"Can we do it after we look at the photos?" I ask, and my voice feels like a fuzzy bumblebee in my throat.

"Of course," he says.

I try not to think about where my mother might have gone. And *why*. The FBI wants to question her. About Margie, I imagine. They had been friends, after all. For decades. I couldn't imagine the FBI would be very happy about her running off right now. And if she has nothing to hide, then why is she hiding?

I remember the note again. Know I should read it. Leave it to my mother to toss a live grenade like this into the room and then flee.

Gilly unlocks the door to Henri's apartment and leads me down the corridor to the living room. Henri's apartment, too, is an untouched tomb, an ossuary of his things, of memories.

Tears spring to my eyes as I spy the STRANGE GIRLS circus poster, the bookshelves still overflowing with books. A mug with a petrified tea bag sitting on the coffee table. I don't need to look at the paper tag to know that it is Earl Grey.

"Where?" I ask, hardly able to finish my sentence. "Where did Fiona find him?"

Gilly motions with his chin to the bathroom, and I feel compelled to follow his gesture. The room is small and square and smells of clean Ivory soap and something stringent. The counter is cluttered: his shaving brush, his razor. A scatter of black bristly hairs on the countertop. A styptic pen. I pick up the razor and run it across the backside of my wrist, the fine hairs there appearing on the blade.

There are pipes in the bathroom that run across the ceiling, carrying water or heat through the innards of this building. Pipes strong enough to hold a man. The blue stool, *my* blue stool, is next to the toilet, where it doesn't belong. He must have stood here before he leapt. Suddenly, the soapy smell is too much. My ears start to fill and buzz. My vision vignettes. I grip the cold counter of the sink and look at my face in the mirror.

It is my mother who stares back at me. It is my mother who has always stared back at me.

Where *is* she? I pull out my phone again and check. She still hasn't read my text.

I return to the living room.

"We came in and cleaned out his fridge a few days ago," Gilly says. "Management has given us a few weeks to empty the rest out. They'll have to renovate before they move someone in. He's been here since Westbeth opened. One of the originals."

I look at the walls, plastered with art, and am amazed that I recall each photo and painting, every line drawing and collage. I trace my fingers across their surfaces. There she is, the girl in the swim cap, defiantly looking back at me.

"What will you do with everything?" I ask, looking around at a lifetime's worth of stuff. My mother is a minimalist; for this, I am grateful. When she is gone, there will be little to sift through, I imagine. Henri has no family. No children or grandchildren. Gilly said that he willed his meager savings to Westbeth and his belongings to us.

"We'll have an estate sale for most of the stuff. A few things will go to auction. Some of his art collection, signed books. Mom knows someone at Sotheby's who is coming to do a valuation, next week, I think." Gilly picks up the mug and peels the tea bag that has stuck inside. The faint scent of Henri's tea wafts to me, and my eyes sting. "But, of course, you are welcome to take anything you like. You have first dibs. No holds barred. If you can't take it back with you this trip, we'll hold onto it for you."

My fingers graze the objects on his shelves. The collection of antique cameras, the vintage toys, the drawers of that card catalog filled with all the curiosities. How would I ever decide what to keep?

"Come on," Gilly calls out, and I follow him down the hall to Henri's studio.

The room looks the same as it always did: exposed brick wall, scuffed floors. But in the center of the room are three or four boxes filled with framed photos, and on his worktable are stacks and stacks of loose prints. Thousands of them. A lifetime's worth of art.

"What will happen to his photos?" I ask.

"You can take any of those you want, as well. I figure we'll pick the ones to show during the memorial tonight, but anything you want, just let me know. There's a collector who's expressed interest in his body of work," Gilly says. "A *completist*."

"A completist?"

"A fan. Totally obsessive. His collection includes photos from back when Henri was a student in Paris. He's been collecting his work since the eighties."

Henri never achieved the fame that some of his contemporaries did. That some of his neighbors at Westbeth did. Diane Arbus became a household name after her suicide here. Henri's mentor Robert Doisneau's iconic prints can be found in every college dorm room. But Henri's humanist photography stemmed from the obsessive need to capture a moment, rather than achieve notoriety. He exhibited his work, of course, selling a few select pieces to pay his rent. To fill his refrigerator. But many of the photos were too personal, he said; they didn't quite *belong* to him. So, whenever he could, he returned these borrowed moments to their rightful owners. Like the little fish Gilly and I caught in the river, the ones too small to keep, he returned them to the waters.

On the streets, whenever he snapped a photo, he made sure to get the phone number and address of his subject. Later, after he had developed the film and made a print he found satisfactory, he would track the person down and give it to them. Once, I was with him in his darkroom when he developed a photograph he had taken on one of his many trips to the piers. It was of two boys, teenagers, embracing. One of the boys cupped the other's head with the palm of his hand. The boy being held had eyelashes like a girl's: thick and black. When Henri enlarged the photo, you could see a single tear clinging to those lashes, catching the light as it hung on. I knew this photo was magical. "We need to find him," I had said. "To give him this."

Henri had frowned and looked at me, cocking his head in a way that I was coming to understand as fondness.

"It is not a photo I think he would like to have," he said.

"But it's beautiful," I argued.

He shook his head. "To you and to me. But to this boy, it is the image of a wound." And so, he had not tracked them down, these boys who snuck away from the world to the piers. Like Gilly would later sneak away himself. Instead, Henri filed it away in a glassine photo sleeve.

He had kept these prints, the ones that captured his subjects' hurt, their shame, in a single drawer in the old architect's desk. The hardware on the drawer supported a little cream-colored card, noting the contents in Henri's delicate handwriting; *Tristesse*, it said.

"Do you remember this one?" I ask Gilly, holding up the print of the boys embracing.

Gilly nods.

"You should have it," I say. "He would want you to have this one."

★ ★ ★

For hours, Gilly and I sit on the floor of Henri's studio, searching through his photos for ones to hang in the gallery for his memorial.

"How do we choose?" I ask, feeling overwhelmed.

"Just pick the ones you love most," he says.

Henri's street photographs are my favorites, though he made many posed portraits of the residents of Westbeth, as well. Not just of the actors and actresses, the dancers needing headshots, or the novelists and poets needing author photos. He captured pictures of *everyone*: the reclusive painters, the shy musicians, the eccentric sculptors whose faces were always specked with clay. We decide these photos should cover one wall in the gallery.

I have always disliked when photographers seem to be judging their subjects. Some photographers' work reveals more about the person behind the camera than in front of it. Part of the magic of Henri's photography is that it is absent of judgment. His photos are somehow collaborative, an agreement between both artist and subject. There is reverence and compassion in his work. He told me once that his photos were a tryst. A secret meeting of viewer and the one being viewed. I know this was true of the photos he took of me. Always.

We gather the portraits of the residents. Some of them dead now. But many of them are still here, still living in this building, even. I pause when I find a photo of my mother. Henri photographed my mother often. After those first headshots, she went to him, and he obliged her desire for whatever it was she was yearning for. Initially, she went under the guise of wanting to have up-to-date headshots: ones that would reflect a new haircut or weight loss. She studied the photos when he returned them to her, searching for something, though I am still not sure what.

But this one is different from those self-conscious portraits. The longing in her eyes in those photos always made me feel uncomfortable. Her need bleeding through the paper.

This one is recent.

She sits on that blue stool, the one he used for these sessions, the one I sat on in his darkroom for hours and hours as I watched him work. The one he climbed to his death. In this photo, she stares at the camera, not with need, but with something that feels like dread. The shadows beneath her eyes are dark. She looks gaunt. Her hair is slicked carefully back into a chignon, but it is white. Shockingly white. *She is an old woman*, I think. When did this happen? But it is Henri I see here, too. Imagine the words he must have said before his shutter clicked. He was old now, too. Both of them with so much to fear.

Gilly takes the photo from me when I hand it to him, and he sets it in the pile.

At eleven o'clock, we have only gotten through about half of the photos; we haven't even touched the ones Henri took of me. I have been avoiding them.

The deeper bottom drawer of the cabinet has always been dedicated to our photos, our history secreted away. This must be where he stashed the copies of the blackout photo. The enlargement of *Blackout, 1977* found in the raid was not the only print. I know, because I was with him when he made it. I was with him as he painstakingly dodged and burned. As my face and body emerged again and again until he got it just right. I need to see it again. I wonder if it will help me understand.

I brace myself. I haven't seen many of these photos in decades. But when I open the drawer, it is empty. Every one of the prints is gone.

New York City
December 1976

The pictures the photographer at Papillon took for my portfolio were meant to show my "range," Margie explained: smiling with pigtails in one (commercial), loose hair and serious in others (editorial). Taking these pictures was nothing like making photos with Henri. I felt like a doll: dressed and posed. Directed to smile or pout, to look surprised or shy.

But for a whole month after we took the photos for my portfolio, there was nothing but a lot of waiting. Every few days, my mother would call Papillon, twirling her finger through the spiraling coil of the phone cord. I'd hear her brightly asking the secretary to speak with Margie, and the pause while she waited to be connected; then, I'd watch as my mother stood up straighter, and said, "Hi, Margie! Just checking to see if you've heard anything from Sears yet?"

Margie kept my mother apprised of all the clients who had expressed interest in my portfolio. She had a lot of local clients looking for a child to model for their Christmas sales ads: boutiques and department stores. Margie had told us she was holding out for national ads, that she wanted my first assignment, my introduction to the world, to be *big*.

"Sears is looking for a girl for the cover of next year's Wishbook," my mother said one November morning after she got off the phone with Margie.

I loved the Sears Wishbook, the catalog that came to us each fall at Lost River. I would lose myself in the colorful pages for hours, imagining what it would be like if I could call the number and order the beautiful clothes and toys in the pages. The covers always featured wide-eyed little girls and boys in pajamas, sitting beneath a Christmas tree or peering up a chimney, searching for Santa Claus.

"The look-see's on Saturday," she said. She had just gotten out of the shower and smelled of that exhilarating combination of Noxzema and the Jean Naté body splash she used. She sat at the kitchen table and worked baby oil into her freshly shaved legs.

"What's a look-see?" I asked.

My mother snapped the lid of the baby oil shut. "Remember? Margie explained. It's when a client has models come in, to *look and see* if they want them for a job."

Liliana didn't get the Sears Catalog at Westbeth, so my mother was on a mission to track one down. She figured if we could study the models, then we could get a feel for what they might be looking for at the look-see. After thumbing through the huge yellow pages, she said the closest Sears and Roebuck was in Brooklyn. Before this, we had had no reason to go to Brooklyn. We could get almost anything at Shopsin's General Store on Bedford. With Serafina's money, we had done my school clothes shopping at Mays in Union Square. Everything we needed was in Manhattan, within a few blocks or via a quick subway ride. Brooklyn was nearly an hour ride on the Q train. It felt like we were prepping to go to the moon.

The weather had been mild for the early days of December, especially compared to this time of year in Vermont, but that morning, it had dropped at least twenty degrees. My mother and I dressed in long underwear under our clothes and then wrapped ourselves in scarves and heavy parkas. Mine was red with toggles, and too small for me. I thought it was funny that it was originally from the Sears Catalog, though my mother had purchased it at a church rummage sale in Quimby.

At the 14th Street station, we walked down the steps, past two men in suits and ties, who nodded and smiled at me. Because it was a Saturday, and because we were leaving the city, the train wasn't full, and we were able to get seats. After we'd gotten settled in, I pulled a book out of my backpack. Gilly had taken me to the library, where I got my own library card, and it had felt like magic. I'd had a library card at home, too, but the Quimby Library was small, and I had read almost every book for kids my age by the time we left. The Jefferson Market Library looked like a castle, an enormous Victorian Gothic building with a clock tower, like Big Ben in *Peter Pan*. Gilly told me it had once been a courthouse, but the stained-glass windows reminded me of a church. There was an entire room dedicated to children's books.

I was a bookworm, reading at least two or three books a week. When I was feeling anxious or out of sorts, words calmed me. Slipping into the worlds between the pages was like slipping into a hot bath; I instantly calmed. I was lucky not to get motion sickness on the train, so I was able to read during the ride. This time, I was lost in Narnia—as if the pages of the book had been the door to the wardrobe, I slipped inside until the train came to our stop. And as we walked from the subway station to the looming Sears building, it had started to snow, and I felt like I was still inside the story: The two worlds blurred.

We walked hand in hand inside the building and located the customer service area, where catalogs were situated for people to peruse before making their orders. I thought of the pattern catalogs in the fabric shop in Quimby: so much possibility in those glossy pages.

My mother left me leafing through their fall catalog, which featured a couple in matching sweaters with their bicycles leaned against the fence, a sea of fallen leaves around them. It made me miss Vermont. When was the last time I'd ridden a bike? Gilly and I had practically lived on our bikes at Lost River. We rode thousands of miles on our bikes. We'd had to leave them behind when we came to the city. My hope was that we would be spending the summer at Lost River again next year.

My mother returned, grinning, two catalogs in her arms. She couldn't wait to tear into the brown paper they were wrapped in, and so, as we exited the building back into the frigid air, she unwrapped them with ungloved fingers and cast the crumpled paper into a trash can.

We went into a drugstore across the street and sat at the counter. I ordered a hot cocoa but said no to the marshmallow. She asked the waitress for lemon water, set the catalogs down on the counter, and studied the covers. On the front of the first one was a typical Christmas scene: a tree decked in twinkling lights. Two children, a boy and a girl, with identical blond bowl cuts, wearing pajamas with Winnie-the-Pooh on them. The little girl clung to a stuffed Tigger, and the boy held a bright yellow Pooh, wearing his trademark red T-shirt. They looked about Angelica's age, maybe six.

My mother took a deep breath and pulled out the second catalog. It was the 1975 Wishbook, which I remembered from last Christmas. The cover of this catalog also featured a twinkling Christmas tree and two very young children, but with the addition of a mother, who wore a fur-collared coat that matched her daughter's.

She shook her head. "These are *little* kids," she said. "You're as tall as that woman," she continued, studying the lady in her glamorous coat.

I drank my cocoa quietly as my mother simmered in her disappointment.

"Maybe they're doing something different this year?" I tried.

"Maybe," she said. "Or maybe Margie's blowing smoke up my ass."

That expression was one of my mother's favorites, but I hated it. I thought of Margie and her Virginia Slims, smoke curling upward.

My mother was right, of course, about the catalog. We went to the look-see, and within minutes, the man who was in charge shook his head and flicked his wrist.

"How old is she? Fifteen?"

"She's *ten*," my mother barked. As if my actual age would change anything.

I heard her on the phone with Margie that night, demanding to know why we'd wasted our time when it said right in my file that I was five foot two. She was on the verge of shouting, when suddenly, her voice softened.

"What?" she asked.

And then her expression changed. It had been filled with a sort of fury only moments before, but now she looked manic. She grabbed my arm, and I could feel her fingers digging in.

"Ouch," I mouthed, and yanked my arm away.

"Really? When?" she asked, pulling the kitchen drawers open, searching for a pen. She found one and scribbled the info Margie was relaying down on a scratch pad.

I looked over her shoulder, which she shrugged, as if to shake me off.

But I made out two words in her careful cursive: *Baby Love.*

I knew exactly what that was. I'd gotten a bottle of the perfume for Christmas. It had a shiny pink cap and smelled like baby powder and flowers.

She hung up the phone, shaking her head in disbelief.

"They saw your portfolio. The people at Baby Love. They have a new campaign."

"Another look-see?" I asked, trying on the word.

"No," she said. "They *want* you."

New York City
August 2019

"Where are my photos?" I ask Gilly, panicked, as I stare into the empty drawer. "All of my photos are gone."

"What?" he says, looking up from a black-and-white picture of a pair of weathered hands holding a lit cigarette.

I try and fail to remember exactly when I last opened that drawer. The photos are gone, but most of the images are burned into my memory. They've been published in books and exhibited in galleries. Over the years, Henri had gifted copies to my mother, to Serafina, to Gilly. To me. But not the one from the blackout.

I can't remember the last time I saw the photo. I wonder if it is even as I remember it. The way we see ourselves changes over time. The way we remember ourselves, as well. If I can't find the photo, I can't confirm my memories. And if there is no confirmation of my truth, then how can I refute what they are saying?

Zev Brenner is a pedophile. A pig. And the fact that my mother would offer him this particular photo, this one where my fear and longing are laid bare, shatters me. I gave her this image because I wanted her to see what her absence did to me, how lost I was without her, and she offered it up to a monster. Turned my vulnerability into a cheap thrill for a wolf who devoured little girls. *Les loups ne se mangent pas entre eux—wolves do not eat each other,* she had said. But what did this mean?

I feel a sort of chasm opening in me.

"You didn't find any of them in here?" Thousands of prints are scattered about us like a game of 52-card pickup. It could take us a week to go through them.

"No," I say. "They're not here."

"He probably just moved them, for safekeeping. Maybe after the article came out?"

"Maybe?"

Or did he get rid of them? I try to imagine him tearing the images to pieces, perhaps flushing them in the toilet or stuffing them into the trash bin. I think about the slivers of my face, my body, finding their way to the incinerator, the boiler room, the dark bowels of this building. I imagine him returning to the apartment, bringing the stool to the bathroom . . . *No*. Gilly's right. He probably just hid them somewhere to keep them from getting into the wrong hands. But what now? I wonder if the police searched the apartment after they found him. Had *they* taken them?

"Your mom will know," he says. "We'll find them. I promise."

Still, I feel a gaping hole in my chest. A terrifying crevasse.

I check my phone. Nothing from my mother. Nothing from Sasha, either. I click on Life360, the tracker app I installed when she got her license ("Big Brother," she calls it). She'd argued that when she turned eighteen, I should uninstall it. That it was creepy to have your mom able to see where you were at any moment of the day or night when you were an adult. And then she'd decided to drive across the country by herself, and I made my case that she could either have a creepy mom or one who kept her sanity. "If I can just look at the app, I won't be texting you every five seconds to make sure you're okay," I said. "You choose."

"When I get to LA, though, Mom, will you please, please get rid of it?"

"We'll talk then," I said.

I did promise her that I would only use it if I hadn't heard from her, and so instead of clicking on the app, I text her first. **Hey Sash . . .**

finishing up at Henri's. Movie still playing? When she doesn't immediately respond, I click on the app, just to make sure she's okay. It's eleven o'clock, after all, and she and Zu-Zu are in a park. In the dark. The little icon with her sweet face is, as expected, at the pier where the movie is playing. Though it also shows she has less than 7% juice in her phone, which creates another wave of anxiety.

I take a deep breath and start to gather the photos I have set aside for myself, slipping them into a cardboard portfolio we located in Henri's closet.

"She okay?" Gilly asks, nudging his chin toward my phone.

And, as if on command, the phone dings. **Just finished, coming back. We'll come to Westbeth and get an Uber for Zu-Zu from there.**

Cool, I return. Sasha knows only a fraction of my worry. My acting skills have come in handy as a nervous mother.

"We can finish in the morning," Gilly says. "We have more than enough to put up for the memorial, but I wanted to make sure you got any of the others you wanted before you went home. Don't worry about the missing ones. I'll find them and get them to you."

Gilly locks up Henri's apartment, and I look down the quiet hallway toward my mother's, the apartment we moved to when she finally got off the waitlist, nearly two years after our arrival. It's one of the smallest studios available at Westbeth. Just a few hundred square feet. It was small for one person, but for the two of us, it had been claustrophobic and, eventually, unbearable. For four years, we lived there together, until things between us began to crack. I got my own apartment at just sixteen years old.

With me gone, my mother had needed to argue her case to the building's management to stay. At that point, she wasn't a working actor anymore, had really *never* been. Not in the city, anyway. Westbeth was a place for artists, and she had left her work as an artist behind her so that she could be my manager not long after our arrival. I offered to buy her an apartment; there was plenty of money by then. But she dug her heels in. This was her *home*, she said; she'd made a life inside these walls. This was her community. Besides, she argued, she was writing a book. An autobiography. She set up a writing desk in the living area and outfitted it with a typewriter and reams of clean white paper. She took writing classes at The New School and found a publisher willing to publish it. The print run was small, and it sold modestly before being remaindered. The few reviews it received were harsh, though; her selling our story seemed to confirm everyone's suspicions that she had been little more than a peddler, hawking her own daughter. The allure of the book was not her story, but *mine*, and even then, it was just morbid curiosity. But the publication had been enough to qualify her to stay at Westbeth, and when it became clear that she wasn't going to write another book, she took up painting. She took lessons from Liliana and replaced her writing desk with an easel. She sold some of her work, mostly to collectors who were intrigued because she was my mother.

My fame, by then, had become a wild and terrifying thing. It surrounded us, like a hurricane. It was the creature that she had fed and fed until it had grown into something she could no longer control. She sold her paintings, the sad knockoffs of those 1960s paintings of children with enormous eyes. Her art made me sad in an inexplicable, almost angry way.

They said I left the city because of my mother, to break free. But that is not true. I left the city when I began to pity her. When love turned to shame.

"Should we go see if she's back?" Gilly says.

I nod. Better to get this over with now rather than tomorrow, the day that belongs to Henri.

Gilly knocks on her door, because for some reason, my body is frozen in place.

There is nothing, and so he knocks harder.

I imagine her, rising from the designer couch I bought for her, stubbing out her cigarette in the pottery ashtray I made for her in the fifth grade. I strain my ears to hear the sound of CNN on her TV; the white noise of bad news. But the quiet is depthless.

"She's not in there," I say.

Gilly shakes his head. "Not yet."

"I'm exhausted," I say, forcing a yawn. "I could sleep until next Tuesday."

"Me too. Let me get you settled in upstairs. I told Howard I wouldn't be home tonight. I'll crash on the couch. You and Sasha can have the loft."

We head back to the elevator, which lurches as we rise. I squeeze my eyes shut and see the image of my mother. Rail-thin and afraid, staring at Henri. What was she afraid of, I wonder. Why has she fled this time?

"You okay, Ry?" he asks. "She'll be back soon."

How do I tell him that a little part of me hopes she is, finally, gone forever?

New York City
December 1976

The day of the photo shoot for Baby Love, my mother was not in the bed when I woke up. This didn't alarm me; instead, I nuzzled into the hollow her body had made in the feather bed that served as our mattress. But it wasn't warm the way it was most mornings. It was as if she had been gone a long time. Or hadn't been there at all.

In Lost River, she often put me to bed at night and then went back to the barn for rehearsals or to hang out with the other cast members. Actors kept odd hours, she explained. But she wasn't in a play now. And even then, she always came home before I woke up.

I rolled over and looked down at the beds below, where the other kids slept. Angelica had her own little cot tucked into the corner. She called it her cubby bed. Guillermo had stretched a clothesline on the diagonal, from one wall to the next, and Liliana had draped an old sheet printed with orange and yellow flowers over it. Angelica crawled in each night as if she were an adventurer climbing into her tent. Gilly slept curled up in a tight little ball, but Joaquin lay on his back with his arms thrown over his head. Both boys were shirtless, wearing only their white briefs. It got hot in the apartment, even now that it had grown cold outside, the radiators steaming. It was almost Christmas, and we'd had two separate dustings of snow already; soon, it would be winter. Our first in the city.

Guillermo had left the first week of November, the day after

Jimmy Carter won the election. We'd had a going-away party, and he'd roasted peanuts in Jimmy Carter's honor. He would be in Los Angeles shooting his film for the next six months. This was why we were here, after all: so that Liliana wouldn't be alone. With Guillermo gone, Liliana no longer got up early in the morning. Especially on the weekends, when she and my mother stayed up late drinking wine and talking. I'd lie in the loft bed, trying to make out what they were saying, but the sound of their voices, their trying-to-be-quiet voices, usually lulled me to sleep. I would only wake up when I felt the bed shake as my mother climbed up the ladder and crawled under the covers with me. I'd roll over, thread myself around her, and hold on tight.

Gilly, Joaquin, Angelica, and I had the apartment to ourselves on Saturday mornings as our mothers slept. We'd pour ourselves giant bowls of cereal—sugared cereal, now that Guillermo was gone (Cocoa Puffs and Count Chocula). We'd pile the couch cushions on the living room floor and watch *Dr. Shrinker* and *Electra Woman and Dyna Girl*. Sometimes, we'd hang out in our pajamas, watching TV all the way until *American Bandstand* came on at twelve-thirty. Liliana would make hot pastrami sandwiches, and she and my mother would join us to see whatever new band was on. The host was Dick Clark, the same guy who hosted *The $25,000 Pyramid*. Liliana thought he was cute. My mom favored the rock stars. Elton John was her favorite.

"He's gay, you know," Liliana had said. "As a two-dollar bill."

Gilly and I had both looked up at the TV screen, where Elton John, in his big round glasses and plaid jacket, was singing "Don't Go Breaking My Heart" with Kiki Dee.

"No, he's *not*," my mother had said, laughing. "Well, maybe bisexual. At least that gives me a fifty-fifty chance."

I knew what *gay* was, because many of the people who came to Lost River were gay. The set designer, Fernando. Kip, the actor who played Puck in every production of *A Midsummer Night's Dream*. And here, in the West Village, there were a lot of gay people. Mostly men. I had seen them at the piers and on the streets, holding hands or ducking into doorways to steal kisses. The first time I saw two men holding hands, it had startled me, like hearing thunder during a snowstorm. Or finding a four-leaf clover. Unexpected. But nobody thought much of it here at Westbeth, and so I didn't, either. Liliana had explained that some people hated the gays, though. That they had to be careful; sometimes, they got beaten up in the streets. That was upsetting.

"Do you think Henri is gay?" I had asked Gilly once, and his face had gone sort of blank.

"Why?"

I shrugged. "He's not married. He doesn't ever go on dates."

My mother had gone out on at least three dates with men she'd met since we got to the city.

"I don't know," Gilly had said, sounding annoyed. "And I don't care."

"Me either," I had said, and felt a weird, heavy feeling. Gilly never got annoyed with me.

This morning, I shimmied down the ladder to the kitchen, where I took a glass from the cupboard and poured myself some orange juice. I got a big bowl out of the cupboard and reached for the box of Freakies. Because they were my favorite, Gilly and the others usually left them for me. But the plastic bag inside the box had only colored crumbs. I slumped down at the kitchen table and drank the glass of orange juice, but it was the kind with chunks of pulp, and I hated that.

I figured my mother might be taking an early morning dance class with Mr. Cunningham upstairs. She said she wanted to keep in shape, even though she hadn't had any auditions since we signed my contract with Papillon. I had asked if I might be able to take ballet lessons now that I, too, needed to watch my figure, but she had just laughed. "You're a stick," she had said. "Look at the way you eat. I would die for your metabolism." Yes, she was probably just in a class.

But when I looked at the Felix the Cat clock, with his ticking tail, that hung in the kitchen, it said it was only eight a.m. Dance classes didn't start until nine. After nine, our apartment hummed with the sound of feet moving across the floor above us. But now, all was quiet.

Maybe we were out of coffee, I thought. We were always running out of things without Guillermo here. He did all the grocery shopping, and since he'd left, the cupboards were either brimming with food, or there was almost nothing. The only thing my mother could not survive without was coffee. But when I popped the lid on the canister where Liliana kept the coffee grounds, I was greeted with the heady scent of freshly ground beans.

Maybe she'd gone for an early morning walk. Liliana had pleaded with her not to take these early morning treks, but she said sometimes she felt claustrophobic in the building, and that she needed fresh air. She missed being able to go outside in nature like she did at Lost River.

I ran to the door, where we kicked off our shoes, and counted the pairs. My mother's shoes were all there: suede boots, winter boots, Keds. She kept her high heels in our little closet space. The only thing missing were her Dr. Scholl's wooden sandals. But it was December. Too cold for sandals.

I started to feel dizzy and knew enough to sit down, put my head between my knees. This is where Gilly found me.

"Where's my mom?" I asked.

He put his skinny arm across my back and said, "She's probably just visiting somebody in the building."

We'd only been at Westbeth for a few months, but she had made friends. Something was always going on in the building: movie screenings and parties; rooftop performances and art installations. Westbeth was like a playground for us kids, but it was for the grown-ups, too.

I nodded even as snot filled my nose and started to run; I licked my lip and tasted salt.

"I have to go get my pictures taken this afternoon. What if she isn't back in time?" I asked.

The Baby Love photo shoot was all that Mom had been talking about ever since Margie called. We'd planned this day down to the minute. At nine a.m., I'd take a shower and wash my hair. They had said not to worry about styling it, so my mother's plan was to let it air dry, maybe use a little conditioner to keep the static electricity down. Now that winter had come, the air was practically buzzing. We kids chased each other around the apartment giving shocks; the Oriental rug in the living room, combined with wool socks, made sparks fly from our fingertips. She said we should start walking to the subway by one. The appointment was at two, which would give us plenty of time, even if there were delays.

"I'll make us breakfast," he said. "It's early. She'll be back soon."

With Guillermo gone, Gilly did the things his dad usually did. He was good at making banana pancakes. He knew how to stop the toilet from running. He also was the unofficial caretaker of us younger kids on the weekends when Liliana and my mother liked to sleep in.

He went to the fruit bowl, where all that remained from Liliana's last trip to Sloan's were three brown bananas. Their skins slipped off, and he put the mushy fruit in a turquoise mixing bowl, the smell of rotten bananas sickening.

"You want to go see the kittens today?" he asked. "After you get back?"

The kittens were hardly kittens anymore. Three months old. Most of them had been adopted by people in the building, but there were a couple left. My favorite was the runt of the litter, a scruffy brown kitty that I called Fraidy Cat after one of my favorite cartoon characters, the timid kitty who had used up eight of his nine lives. He was still small enough to curl up in my hands. I brought him sardines from the little red tins I found in the back of Henri's cupboards. Henri helped me unroll the lids with the silver key that came at-tached.

"After I get back," I said.

I had no idea how long a photo shoot would take. It was uptown, not far from Margie's offices. Margie had offered to meet us there, and my mother had agreed that that would probably be a good idea. We wanted to be as professional as possible.

But now, my mother was gone.

"Chocolate chips?" Gilly asked.

I shook my head. I was watching my figure, after all.

I took a shower at nine, then sat down with the other kids in front of the TV as I ran the detangler and my wide-toothed comb through my hair. I was so nervous about my mother, I could hardly focus on the story line. At ten o'clock, the anxiety I'd somehow kept at bay started to creep into my shoulders. That's where it always went first. Fear was like a river, I thought, dammed up somewhere inside me. But it took hardly anything at all for that dam to give way, and then it rushed through my body. To my shoulders, down my spine, into my legs and hands, leaving my head light and breathless, bobbing like a buoy.

"Let's get my mom up," Gilly said. He could always sense when the dam was breaking.

He disappeared down the stairs to Liliana's room. A minute later, she came upstairs, yawning and stretching.

"Hi, baby girl," she said to me, and enclosed me in a big hug. She always smelled like white spirit; the smell seeped into all her clothes, her hair, even her skin.

"Do you know where my mom is?" I asked, and suddenly, I felt like that character in the book my mom used to read to me when I was little, *Are You My Mother?* The one about the little bird whose mother leaves him alone in his nest to get food, and when she does, he sets out looking for her, asking a kitten, a hen, a cow, even a car and a power shovel if they are his mother. When he finally gets back to his nest, she has returned. I was waiting for that part of the story to happen. But it was ten-thirty a.m. now, and she was still gone.

"What did they say you need to do to get ready?" she asked. "I'll help you, and by the time we're finished, I'm sure she'll be back. And if she isn't, I can take you to the photo shoot. Okay, hun?"

I nodded.

Liliana helped me finish combing the tangles out of my hair. She also helped me pick out something to wear that was dressier than the T-shirts and jeans I always wore to school. The denim jumper was clean, but the white blouse with the Peter Pan collar was wrinkly, and so she set up the ironing board in the kitchen and sprayed it with starch and ironed the wrinkles out.

I got dressed and looked at my reflection in the mirror. I tried to imagine my face in a magazine and couldn't.

When I came out of the bathroom, Liliana and Gilly were talking about Christmas. Joaquin and Angelica wanted to stay in New York, but Liliana wanted to take Guillermo's van to Lost River for the holiday. When we still lived there, I always looked forward to Christmas, because Gilly's family often spent the holiday with us. I had never spent a Christmas anywhere but at Lost River.

"Do you even know how to drive the van?" Gilly asked his mom.

"I thought *you* could drive," she said.

"Very funny, Mom."

"Is she back yet?" I asked, though I knew the answer.

"Not yet, sweetie."

It was noon now.

"Do you have the address where you're supposed to be?" she asked.

"It might be in Mom's calendar," I said. She kept her calendar in her purse, and I figured if she were out somewhere, she'd probably have her pocketbook. But when I looked to the hook above the shoe mat by the door, it was hanging there. How did I not notice that before? I didn't know whether to be alarmed or relieved. Why wouldn't she bring her purse? What if something happened to her? How would the police know how to find us?

Liliana grabbed the purse and started digging through, searching.

"Voilà!" she said, and pulled out the calendar. She thumbed through to today's date and ran her finger down the page.

"Baby Love," she read, and smiled at me. "One fifty-five West Seventy-Second Street, two o'clock p.m."

Okay. It would be okay.

When *American Bandstand* came on, everyone gathered in the living room to watch. It was a repeat, with Elton John and Kiki Dee again.

"Okey doke," Liliana said at around 12:45. "Why don't we head out a little early? Just to be safe?"

I put on my coat and wrapped my scarf around my neck. It crackled with static, giving my cheeks tiny little shocks. Liliana bundled up, too.

"Good luck!" Angelica said.

"We'll go see Fraidy when you get home," Gilly said.

The halls were full of Westbeth kids, roller skating and running at full tilt. For a minute, I wanted nothing more than to just go back to the apartment and get my skates. We could skate on the rooftop to see the kittens.

But I thought about how excited my mother had been about my first job, and so I just stared ahead at the elevator doors as we descended.

We stopped on the fifth floor, the fourth, and then on the third, where, as the doors opened, I was startled to see my mother standing.

She was wearing the clothes she'd had on the day before: a soft, patched pair of bell-bottoms and a pink turtleneck. Her hair was messy, and makeup had smudged under her eyes. She was wearing the missing Dr. Scholl's. She looked surprised to see us.

Liliana held the door open, and she stood there awkwardly for a moment before she stepped on.

My mother reached over and hit the number nine button. "I need to get my jacket and boots upstairs," my mother said.

Liliana bit her lip.

"Do we have time?" I asked.

"It's not even one o'clock," my mother snapped. "I told you we'd leave at one."

I knew better than to argue, and so we ascended again, back up to the ninth floor, where my mother quickly changed, twisted her hair up into a bun, and pulled on her coat and her boots.

"I've got this," she said firmly to Liliana. "Thanks, though."

She grabbed my hand, and we headed out into the city to my first job.

When we came home, my mother was buzzing. Liliana wanted to hear all about it, and my mother was happy to oblige. She unzipped her tall, soft boots, peeled off her pantyhose, unhooked her bra, and dragged it out through the sleeve of her sweater, all while narrating our adventure. Whatever frustration she'd felt earlier at Liliana for stepping in to make sure I got to the shoot on time had slipped away—as diaphanous and slippery as her nylon stockings.

I went straight to the bathroom to wash the makeup from my face. I dunked my head under the running faucet in the tub, and then ran a comb through my hair to get rid of those rigid curls. My hair was sticky with hair spray, so I ended up washing it, as well, and then rinsing and rinsing, turning the water hotter and hotter until it burned my scalp and the bathroom filled with steam.

My mother had insisted we stop at a bodega on our way home, where she found a dusty bottle of sparkling wine on a shelf near the back. Now, I could hear her pop it in the kitchen, and the *glug, glug* as she poured it into two of Liliana's jelly jars. The clink of their glasses.

I rubbed the steam away from the mirror and stared at my reflection. I recognized myself again. Somewhat. The rouge they had used on my cheeks, combined with the bitter cold outside, made me look flushed. Almost feverish. I rubbed at my cheeks with a washcloth, but it only made it worse.

"I'm going to go see the kittens," I said to my mother and Liliana. "With Henri."

"Okey doke," she said cheerfully, and beckoned me over.

Her arm circled my waist. "We were just celebrating your first job!" she said brightly. "I told Liliana about how much they loved you. The photographer said to me that you were a real natural. Like you'd been doing it for years."

We had returned home in silence, so this bit of news took me by surprise.

"Oh," I said. I didn't know whether this should make me feel flattered or something else. My mother was beaming and pouring herself another glass of wine. I watched the bubbles rise.

"Did you have a good time?" Liliana asked, her voice the same as when she asked us if we were feeling okay if one of us sniffled or sneezed.

I shrugged. "It was okay."

A shadow seemed to cross my mother's face, and her arm dropped from my waist. "A national ad campaign, and it was *okay*." There was meanness in that word. Mocking. It made my cheeks burn even hotter.

"Where's Gilly and everybody?" I asked.

"They're out playing," Liliana said.

The weekends were filled with opportunities to play, with every kid home from school. Liliana's only rule was that we stay inside the building. People left the doors open on the weekends, and we wandered in and out of the other kids' apartments, getting snacks or stopping to play with their toys or listen to their music. Every now and then, some of the boys would sneak down into the basement. I hadn't been down there; Liliana said it was easy to get lost.

"If Gilly comes back, can you tell him I went to go see the kittens?" I said.

"Sure thing," Liliana said.

Henri had said we were welcome to go into his apartment as long as the door was unlocked, but I still knocked a couple of times before pushing it open. I usually came with Gilly, but I was familiar enough with his apartment now to know he was probably in the studio when I found the living room empty.

I walked through the room, stopping as always to look at the photos on the wall. I felt like Henri's studio was like that Sears Wishbook. Every time I opened the catalog, I saw something I hadn't seen before, and every time I came to Henri's, I discovered something different, too.

He wasn't in the studio either, which meant he was in his darkroom.

I went to the door and knocked gently.

"One minute!" he said, and so I sat down on the little blue stool to wait, looking out the window at the darkening sky. The days were so short now, the sun setting before five o'clock.

When he emerged, he smiled and clapped his hands.

"*Allo!* How was your first job as *une model*?"

I shrugged again. Everyone was so excited about this, but I had been underwhelmed. It had felt strange to be fussed over. To be moved about and posed like a mannequin. I had felt like the doll in that book I loved, *The Lonely Doll*, the one with the pink gingham book jacket—the main character of the story a doll who lives in the city. In the black-and-white photographs of Edith, a doll who befriends two stuffed bears, she is somehow both animate and inanimate.

"Can we go see Fraidy?" I asked.

"Of course, of course. He is getting so big!" he said. "Go get some sardines."

I located the little tin of sardines in his cupboard, and together, we made our way to the rooftop.

Little Fish, 1976

*I*t is freezing on the roof, the sky above us black-and-blue, and I start to worry about the mama cat. How will she stay warm this winter? I don't understand why somebody can't just take her in.

Henri and I wrap our coats around ourselves and go to the little corner alcove, where she made her nest. But when we get there, both the mama cat and Fraidy Cat are gone.

"Where are they?" I ask.

Henri's mouth twitches. "Well, I don't know. Maybe they got inside somehow. It is very cold; perhaps someone allowed them in."

What I don't say is that Fraidy is *my* cat. At least in my mind. The cats at Lost River had been mine, too. They were free to roam all over the property, coming and going as they pleased, but they still belonged to me. It was our cabin door they came to each night, waiting for us to let them in.

"Ryan," Henri says. "I am certain they are safe and warm. It is okay. I will come back later and check. I will also ask the neighbors. Do not worry. Animals know how to survive outside."

I nod. I trust Henri.

"Here," he says, and puts his hand out for me to give him the tin of sardines. "Try this."

He pulls the silver key from the bottom of the tin and inserts it in the tab of the lid. Slowly, he rolls the lid back, and the fishy smell reaches my nose, which twitches at the pungent scent.

"If they are out here, this will make them come," he says, and smiles.

Together, we sit, waiting for the smell of sardines to lure the cats to us. Henri takes out his camera and clicks a few photos. My wet hair is starting to freeze, and I can feel my teeth chattering, as well. Underneath my parka, I am just wearing the tank top I changed into when we got home. When a gust of wind blows across the rooftop, I shiver and hug myself harder.

"I really wish I could keep him," I say. "But Guillermo doesn't like cats."

"Isn't Guillermo in Los Angeles?"

"Only until spring."

"And then?" he asks.

I haven't thought about what will happen to my mother and me then. I know we are on the waitlist for our own apartment. But I am not sure how long that will take. Liliana said not to worry about it, but while the apartment is big, it would be crowded with another adult.

I shrug. "I don't know."

I stare at the open tin of sardines, at their silver scales. The cold wind carries the scent off the river, and it feels like we are on the docks.

"Sardines stink," I say, stating the obvious. "I wouldn't eat them if it was the last thing left to eat on earth."

"Really?" Henri says.

"Not if all the food was gone."

"I dare you to try," Henri says.

"What?"

"You are a very cautious little girl."

I don't like how that word makes me feel.

"What do you mean?"

"I mean, you are not an adventurer. You are someone who likes things to stay the same."

"That's not true!"

But it is true. I had a book called Mister Dog when I was little. It was one of those Little Golden Books with the gold foil edges. It was about a dog named Crispin's Crispian, a dog who belonged to himself. He liked things in their place. He liked routine. The story called him a "conservative." I remember thinking that I was just like that droopy dog. I liked things in their places, too. I told my mother that I was a conservative. She laughed at me, and her laughter felt like a hundred beestings.

"I am not," I say. "I am very brave. Gilly said I'm brave. I even swung all the way across the river."

"Is that so?" Henri says.

"I did." But even as I recall that afternoon, I remember how afraid I was. The way I felt as he beckoned me to swing across the river to him. The awful feeling of being unable to let go of the rope, and the sharp reprimand as the bank hit my back. The breathlessness.

"Watch," I say, and pick up the little can.

With my thumb and pointer finger, I reach into the tin and pinch the tail of one of the sardines. It is slippery and slimy, and I feel like I might gag.

Henri raises his camera to his eye.

I want him to capture this. Proof that I am not afraid. Not of some stupid little fish.

I bring the sardine to my mouth and close my eyes as it meets my tongue. It tastes gritty and fishy and wet, but before I can swallow, I feel something at my bare ankles that startles me.

Fraidy Cat peers up at me, his tail curling around my leg.

Henri is waiting with his camera. Fraidy Cat seems to be waiting, as well, so I swallow the little fish whole, feel it slithering down my throat. A smile spreads across my face. Click.

I bend over and pick up Fraidy. His body is warm, and his little motor is humming. "Where is your mama?" I ask, holding him to my cold cheeks, and as Henri focuses the camera, I whisper into his silky little ear, "It's okay, Fraidy! Don't be scared."

New York City
August 2019

Gilly makes tea. Joaquin has gone home to Queens to his family, and Liliana is asleep downstairs. We wait for Sasha and Zu-Zu to come home, the tracker app revealing their slow journey from the pier back to Westbeth. I try not to think of all the things that can go wrong, all the bad things that can happen to two young girls in the span of a few city blocks.

I remember reading a news story once about a little boy in Brooklyn, a member of the Hasidic community. He'd pleaded with his parents to allow him to walk home from his school's day camp. Reluctantly, they agreed, and then the unthinkable happened. He was kidnapped and murdered, his body dismembered and discovered a couple of days later.

This is the kind of story that lives in my mind. The kind that haunts me.

"Do you remember when I did the Baby Love shoot?" I ask Gilly.

He dips his tea bag in his steaming cup.

"Sure," he says. "I remember girls at school talking about it. They couldn't believe I knew you."

I shake my head. "It was a horrifying photo," I say. "I didn't realize it then, but it was awful. How could she have let me do that?"

"Well, I guess it was a different time back then," he says.

He's right, of course, but the photo has always made me uneasy. It has been the subject of much scrutiny before, criticism dismissed by my mother. "Did anyone hurt you?" she had demanded once when I confronted her. A few years ago, a graduate student, writing a thesis on the history of the sexualizing of young girls in American advertising, found my phone number and called to ask me to speak on the ads I made. Those images. I hadn't known what to say.

In the photo, my hair has been curled into tight coils, which they sprayed with so much hair spray, I started to wheeze. I am wearing fake eyelashes, pink rouge on my cheeks, and lip gloss so thick and shiny you can almost see your reflection in my pout. I am holding a pale pink stuffed bunny. But you can't tell if I am a child made up to look like an adult, or an adult made to look like a child. When I found the ad years later, it felt like someone had punched me in my throat. Sasha was ten at the time. The same age that I was in the photo.

Even worse was the slogan: *Even good girls can be a little naughty sometimes.*

What I remember from that Baby Love photo shoot was that my mother had been angry after we left Liliana. She had yanked my arm so hard that my shoulder ached: all the way to the subway, on the train, and as we took the narrow stairwell to the studios, where we arrived with one minute to spare.

I remember when they had me change into the soft pink nightie, the wardrobe lady had said, "Oh, you're just a little girl" when I pulled my jumper over my head. "Your face is so grown-up! How old are you, sweetheart?"

"Almost eleven," I said.

"Oh, goodness. You're practically a baby."

I remember feeling insulted. I wasn't a baby. I was in the fifth grade already. Going to middle school the next year.

But when I found the ad years later, which my mother had razored out of *Seventeen* magazine and kept in a scrapbook for me, I wondered what that kind woman had been thinking as she dressed me in a baby-doll nightie and passed me to the makeup artists who painted my face. I wonder what all those women thought when they posed me on the canopy bed and slipped the strap of the nightie off my shoulder. I wondered what all those people thought: the makeup artists and hair stylists, the wardrobe people and secretaries and handlers. All the ones who silently transformed me from a child into a woman. The photo looks seductive. My expression coy. A babyish pout on a face that might have belonged to a woman twice my age.

"Without that campaign, you wouldn't have had an acting career. You know that, right?" my mother argued.

She was right, of course; that photo changed everything. It appeared in dozens of magazines, from *Mademoiselle* to *Seventeen*. It was the ad that Valentino Moretti saw, the legend being that he was at the dentist, about to get a root canal, when he was thumbing through a magazine and found the girl he'd been looking for for over a year, the one to play a precocious child nymphet in his most recent project, a film about a carnival worker and his daughter.

But I was not trying to be coy. I was not trying to *seduce* anyone. I was, instead, thinking of the ache in that shoulder, and my mother's angry hands. The way she'd been furious with me, silent the whole subway ride, as if I were the one who had disappeared that morning. As if I were the one who could not be relied upon.

In interviews later, people would ask about that first photo. The first inklings of how far she'd be willing to go. "Yes," she would say to the interviewer. "She has always known how to use her beauty to get what she wants. Since she was a baby, really. Just a little pout, and people's hearts melt. It doesn't work on me, of course," she would say, laughing.

Her words were like the golden thread that Rapunzel spun, turning something ordinary into something glittering. Something dangerous.

The phone chimes with a notification from the tracking app that Sasha is home, and soon, I hear her and Zu-Zu's soft giggles downstairs, muffled so as not to wake Liliana. And I breathe.

New York City
Christmas, 1976

We were supposed to go to Vermont for Christmas. Liliana would drive; we'd leave on Christmas Eve and then return to the city before New Year's. Serafina had called and said she would make the buttery sugar cookies I loved, the ones with the hard candies melted in the center like stained glass. She said that there was a lot of snow on the ground already, and another storm would bring enough to go sliding. (This is what we called sledding in Vermont.) I thought of the dented aluminum saucer I had, and how much I loved sliding at night: the crunch of fresh snow as we traipsed up the hill to the barn, the hush of it, and snowflakes like moving constellations above us.

Liliana had already picked up the van from the garage in New Jersey. Guillermo had told her where to go to get it tuned up. Now it was in a spot on the pier, a makeshift lot where Westbeth residents with cars paid to park them.

Gilly and I had stayed up late for two nights in a row, talking about all the things we wanted to do when we were back at Lost River.

"Do you think Santa will find us there?" Angelica asked.

I was starting to have my suspicions about Santa, but giving them voice made me feel sort of hollow and sad, and so I nodded and assured her that he would.

"Just make sure to bring your stocking to hang," I said. Angelica had curled up in my lap and hugged me.

Christmas was on a Saturday this year, so we'd gotten out of school a whole week before. We had put up a fake Christmas tree in the apartment, decorated with god's eyes we made from sticks and yarn. Liliana and my mother had threaded cranberries and popcorn to make garlands, and Angelica made an angel out of a paper-towel roll and tissues in her first-grade class.

Gilly had been excited to show me all his favorite New York holiday traditions. We'd watched the skaters at Rockefeller Plaza, of course, and then stayed to see the enormous tree illuminated. But he also brought me to see the origami tree at the Natural History Museum, decorated with hundreds of paper insects and intricately folded animals. When we got home that day, Liliana found a stack of origami paper she used for her art classes, and we spent hours learning how to turn the delicate pieces of paper into cranes and frogs and dragons. But best of all were the tickets Guillermo got from a friend, who was a light designer for the New York City Ballet, to see *The Nutcracker* at Lincoln Center. I had been completely and utterly mesmerized. It took every ounce of my strength not to plead with my mother to please let me take ballet lessons. After watching the performance, there was nothing else I wanted more. If I made enough money doing modeling, I thought, maybe I could pay for lessons myself.

On the Tuesday before Christmas, my mother and I went Christmas shopping. We had gotten my check for the Baby Love ad and put most of it in the bank, but my mother said there was enough left over to treat ourselves and our friends. We found a *Happy Days* board game for Joaquin, a Cher doll for Angelica, and for Gilly, I bought a T-shirt with shimmery silver stripes across the front spelling out NEW YORK and the Peter Frampton album he wanted. When we'd checked everyone off our list, we walked up and down Fifth Avenue, window-shopping. She loved to look into the display cases at Tiffany's, just like Audrey Hepburn.

"Someday, I'm going to buy a tennis bracelet, just like that," she said, pointing to a glittering diamond bracelet circling a velvet wrist.

I couldn't picture my mother wearing diamonds. She only had one necklace in her jewelry box, one that had belonged to her grandmother that I wasn't allowed to play with. A gold filigree clasp and a hundred shimmering pearls. Most of the time, she opted for big silver hoops for her ears, or dangly silver and turquoise. She bought her jewelry on the street from the men who called out to her, *Hey, mami!*

"I'll buy one for you," I said. "Someday when I'm rich."

This had broken the spell, and she'd looked at me. For a moment, I worried I'd said the wrong thing, but then she slipped off her glove and stuck her pinky out. "Pinky swear?"

I did the same and linked my pinky with hers. "I swear."

When we got home, my mom sent me to hide the gifts in our closet.

"Margie called three times while you were gone!" Liliana said.

"Oh, really?" my mom asked, with that excited edge to her voice. "I wonder if she has another job for Ry. Did she say?"

Liliana shook her head. "No, she just said to call her as soon as you got home."

"Where the hell were you?" I could hear Margie's gravelly voice booming through the receiver as my mother balanced the phone between her ear and her shoulder and pulled off her coat and boots. It was warm in the apartment; I stripped out of my winter coat and sweater, my hair crackling with static.

"We were window-shopping," my mother said, and smiled at me. She took the phone, stretching the curly cord as she walked down the steps and perched near the bottom.

I tried to eavesdrop, but Margie was doing all the talking. I wondered if this meant I might get another job. The Baby Love one had been okay. Kind of boring. But it was fun going to the bank and opening an account. I had my very own passbook, which showed how much was in there. I thought about that diamond bracelet. Maybe I could buy my mom something like that for Christmas if I got another job. Maybe I could pay for ballet class.

After a long time, my mother ran up the stairs and slammed the phone down. She looked at me, excited.

"We aren't going to Vermont for Christmas," she said.

"Why?" I asked, crestfallen.

"*Because*," she said, "you have an audition."

I knew from my mom's experience that auditions often led to absolutely nothing. You could spend all day waiting in line, only to be dismissed because you were too short or too tall, too fat or too skinny. I didn't want to go on an *audition*. I wanted to go to Lost River: to go sliding with Gilly and Joaquin and Angelica, to eat Christmas cookies and drink cocoa and wake up on Christmas morning to open my stocking. I wanted clean white snow and quiet. I wanted to go *home*. If only for a little while.

"Can I do it later?" I asked.

My mother's smile faded. "Are you kidding me?" she asked. " 'Can I do it later?' "

I hated when she mocked me. The voice she used always sounded like a baby. I wasn't a baby. She briskly started clearing dirty dishes from the table, avoiding my gaze.

"I'm sorry, Mama. What's it for?"

She turned around, hands on her hips, and snapped, "It's for a *movie*. With Robert De Niro. The director saw the Baby Love ad, and they *want* you. It's a friggin' feature film. It could be your big break. But I suppose we can go to Lost River instead. Forget about it. They'll be able to find somebody else. Maybe Jodie Foster."

I swallowed, and it felt the way it did when I was sick and my glands were swollen.

"I'm sorry, Mama. I want to do it. I do."

But I could tell I had already ruined it for her and spoiled her excitement.

★   ★   ★

The director was in the city from his home in Italy just for the holiday, leaving the following Monday morning. He had asked to meet me on Sunday, which meant there was no way we could be in Lost River for Christmas.

Liliana offered to stay in New York with us, but my mother wouldn't hear of it. "Serafina is so excited to have you. Ryan and I will have a nice Christmas here."

I had been curled up in the loft bed, feeling sorry for myself, avoiding my mother for hours after she got off the phone with Margie. My socks were damp from our long walk, and I didn't even care if the sheets got wet.

Of course, the idea of being in a movie was exciting. I also knew Robert De Niro was a famous actor, but I couldn't quite picture his face. He was in that movie *Taxi Driver* with the girl Mom was talking about, Jodie Foster. She was in the Disney movies and *Freaky Friday,* which had just come out. The director was very famous, my mother explained. But I hadn't heard of any of the movies that he directed.

There was a rumor that Robert De Niro's father lived at West-beth, that he was a painter, but Liliana said she didn't know him. This idea thrilled my mother, though.

I refused to come down for dinner. Said I didn't feel good. And even though my stomach was rumbling with hunger, I stayed in the loft, reading old *Ramona* books, until I finally fell asleep.

In the morning, it was Gilly who woke me up. "Psst," he said.
"What?" I grumbled.

My mother wasn't in bed. I could hear the John Denver Christmas album that Liliana had been playing for weeks now. I smelled something delicious coming from the kitchen. Bacon and cinnamon.

"We have a surprise!" Gilly said.

In the living room, everyone was sitting around the Christmas tree in their pajamas. I rubbed my eyes and looked to my mother for an explanation. That was when I spotted Henri, sitting on the couch next to Liliana.

"What's going on?" I asked.

"It's Christmas!" Gilly said. "Sort of!"

There were, indeed, gifts under the tree, and Henri was holding my stocking, which appeared to be stuffed.

"Santa came?" I asked, and then felt silly. Santa wasn't real. I knew it with a sudden and heartbreaking certainty.

"He brought one of your gifts a little early," Liliana said.

I padded into the living room and sat down on the floor cross-legged. My nightie was so short now, and my wet socks were still sort of icky and damp. I peeled them off.

Liliana came in from the kitchen with a tray full of food: apple muffins and bacon and cups of cocoa and coffee.

"I think she should probably open her stocking first," Liliana said. "Henri?"

Henri stood up and brought me the stocking. It was heavy. And warm. I was confused and looked at him for some sort of explanation.

I set it in my lap and felt the tiny motoring hum.

My chest heaved. I pulled back the edge of the stocking, and there, inside, was Fraidy Cat. He looked up at me and squeaked out a little meow.

"Mine?" I asked, unable to form a full sentence.

"*Oui,*" Henri said.

"But what about Guillermo?" I asked Liliana.

"Sometimes it's easier to ask for forgiveness than for permission." She shrugged.

I looked to my mother, expecting her to say *no*, but she clapped her hands together and smiled. "Since you're being so understanding about having to stay in the city for Christmas," she said. In an instant, I knew that she was sending me a message. There was to be no more moping or complaining about not being able to go to Lost River. And I wouldn't. I pulled Fraidy out of the stocking and snuggled him against my chest, where he purred and purred. *Mine*, I thought.

We exchanged gifts, as if it were Christmas morning. Liliana gave me a book called *A Very Young Dancer*, about a real girl about my age who was in the New York City Ballet's *Nutcracker*. Angelica gave me a beautiful rhinestone barrette. Joaquin wanted to play *Happy Days* right away and set up the game board at the kitchen table. I held Fraidy Cat on my lap. I wouldn't have cared if this was the only gift I got.

Gilly gave me a Magic 8-Ball.

"Ask it a question," he said.

I held the ball in my hand; the idea that it could predict my future felt amazing. Scary and wonderful all at once.

"Will I get the part in the movie?" I asked, knowing this would make my mother happy. I shook the ball and waited for the answer to materialize in the little blue triangle.

My mother peered at the 8-Ball hopefully, as if it were, really, a glimpse into the future. IT IS DECIDEDLY SO, it read.

"One last one," my mother said dramatically, locating a box underneath the tree.

She handed it to me, and I carefully unwrapped the ribbon and paper. Inside was a wooden doll, wearing a hand-painted red dress with tiny blue flowers.

"I don't have a present for you yet, Mama," I said.

"You don't need to give me anything. Look," she said, pulling the doll apart at the middle, revealing another identical doll, though smaller, inside. "It's like you and me!" She laughed. "The same, but smaller."

The smaller doll also had a seam in the middle.

"Go ahead," she said.

I pulled this one apart gently, revealing another smaller but identical doll inside that one. "And someday you'll have a daughter, and she'll have a daughter, too."

I kept opening the dolls until the very last one, which was as small as my pinky finger but still exactly the same.

New York City
August 2019

Sasha and I sleep curled around each other in the loft bed, and I dream that I am with my mother again, limbs and hair entangled. Mermaids, she used to say, braiding our hair together as we fell asleep, and I would dream that she and I were swimming, the swish-swish of our tails and the hush of the ocean in our ears. I remember looking at the concrete waves above us and dreaming of the sea.

Sasha smells like weed, the scent making me tense. It's legal in Vermont now, but not for her, and not here. Until now, anything she has done, she has done at home. I remind myself that soon, she will be outside of the protective bubble I have made at Lost River.

When the girls came home from the movie, she and Zu-Zu devoured a bag of tortilla chips and half a jar of salsa that Liliana got for them. I have always adored Zu-Zu. She has my friend Effie's tenacity, and Devin's passion and gentle humor. She is the kind of child people call an *old soul*, wise and mature, cautious and meticulous, while Sasha is more of a hatchling: impulsive and vivacious. Trusting and adventurous. Sasha devoured handfuls of chips, licking the salt off her hand and shrugging off the plop of salsa that landed on her shirt, while Zu-Zu delicately nibbled the corn chips and spilled nothing. Sasha guzzled a whole can of seltzer and let out a loud belch, grinning widely.

"Classy," I'd mused.

"The classiest," she'd countered, and then thrown her arms around me.

Now, her arms are draped over me again. I have to delicately extricate myself from the tangled knot in order to get out of bed.

I hear stirrings below in the kitchen and assume it's Gilly. He's gotten a sub at school for the rest of the week, but he's an early riser. However, when I climb down from the loft, I see that it's Liliana, puttering around the kitchen.

"Good morning, sunshine," Liliana says when I hug her. She smells soapy and clean, and her hair is damp from a shower. When I hold her hands, I see her skin is delicate, the veins close to the surface, mapping out the two years since I last saw her. When did she get so old? Like my mother, her hair is white now. Her skin transparent. She looks breakable.

"Can I make the coffee?" I ask.

"Already made," she says, and goes to the counter. She pulls a mug from the cupboard and pours a full cup for me. No cream or sugar.

"I've never understood how you and your mother can drink it like this," she says. I've been drinking black coffee since I was thirteen.

I sit down at the kitchen table, and she joins me.

"Where's Gilly?" I ask.

"Out for a run," she says. "I told him I wanted some time alone with you. To talk."

"Oh," I say, surprised.

She lifts her chin toward the loft, eyebrow raised.

"She'll be dead to the world for at least another hour or two," I say, and smile.

Liliana sips on her coffee and sets it down, and then looks directly into my eyes in that disarming way she has.

I force a smile and wait.

"Your mom called me this morning."

"She did?" I ask. I think of the jangling phone, loud enough to

jar us all out of bed. But then I remember that no one has used the
landline here in a decade or more. She would have called Liliana's
cell phone, and Liliana would have been discreet.

Once again, I feel a pang of something. That snarly sense of in-
justice. Henri is dead. My heart is broken, and my mother has disappeared yet again.

"Well, where is she?" I ask.

Liliana shakes her head.

"I don't know. She wouldn't tell me. She said it's to protect us."

"What is she, some sort of spy?" I joke, but my laughter falls flat.

"She said she hopes you understand that she had nothing at all to
do with this. That Margie, that Papillon . . ."

"What are you talking about?"

The coffee is bitter and strong. My eyes water. She reaches across
the table and pushes the *Times* toward me. "I was going to wait until
after the memorial, but I knew people would probably text you
about it."

I reach for the paper. "What section?"

Her long finger taps at the front page.

The headline reads "Modeling Agent Arrested in Brenner Sex
Trafficking Scheme." Margie's headshot, at least a decade old, sits
below the headline, next to a pixelated photo of her being escorted
from the Papillon offices, men in suits on either side of her. I linger
on her face, her razor-sharp bob and razor-sharp jaw and razor-sharp
gaze.

Jesus. This is serious. This isn't speculation, gossip. This is a fed-
eral case. I think of the FBI, who had been here looking for my
mother. Could *they* be the ones who took the photos from Henri's?
Was that even legal? If so, what would they be thinking as they
looked at those pictures of me? I feel nauseous.

My eye is drawn to a graphic below the text that takes up a good
portion of the page, a chart that looks almost like a family tree.
Perched at the top is a circle with Brenner's face. Three branches
stem out below. Two of the names I have never heard before, but the

third is Margie's. And like descendants, branching below her are the names and photos of her alleged accomplices: suspects and those who have been indicted in a major sting operation. Scouts. Other models. The names and faces are those of all the people who had, once, been like a family to me.

My eyes burn as I read the names of girls I once knew. Charlotte Revere. Betsy Nelson. Brigitte Bonaventure. These girls, all five or six years older than me, had been my mentors. I shake my head. I can't understand what any of this means. I've only begun to ponder what Margie's involvement with a man like Brenner could have been, but these girls? The ones who helped me curl and feather my hair, who taught me how to use tea bags to take away dark circles under my eyes, the ones who gave me tips on how to fight jet lag after international flights. The girls who coddled me and treated me like a baby sister. They were *complicit*?

Then I see what Liliana wanted me to see.

Fiona Flannigan.

My mother's face, grinning from inside a circle, perched on her very own branch below Margie's.

New York City
December 1976

I remember the way he studied me. I was growing accustomed by then to people gazing at me in this way. Assessing, evaluating. But it was as if they were looking at me without truly seeing me. This was the way that Margie had looked at me that day in the café. The way the cameraman had looked at me during that photo shoot for my portfolio, for the Baby Love ad. I didn't know what to do when this was happening, and so I slipped away. I imagined myself floating up, up, up into the sky. I thought of the rooftop with Henri, nothing but clouds all around me. I was there but not there. I simply left my body, even as the makeup artists brushed rouge onto my cheeks and gloss onto my lips. Even as they tugged at the tangles in my hair or fussed with the clothes that hung on me like a mannequin.

We met at the Russian Tea Room on the Sunday after Christmas.

My mother and I had gone shopping that week, using some of my Baby Love money. She'd purchased me a white wool coat and a furry red muff and matching crimson earmuffs. A new pair of white, patent leather Mary Janes. They made me feel like a baby, the little hearts punched out of the leather, but the coat was beautiful.

This time, my mother was there when I woke up. Alone in the apartment, we both got up early to get ready. She set my hair with hot rollers and used a little lipstick to rouge my cheeks. We left with an hour to spare and took a taxi rather than risking the trains running late.

Margie had arranged to have the script for the film, *Midway Girl*, sent over by a courier. My mother read it first; then together, we read the scenes I would need to memorize. She said if I got the part, then she would have me read the whole thing. "It's pretty heavy," she explained. "Let's see what he says first."

Margie said the director was interested in me for the role of Sadie, a girl growing up with her single dad, a carnival worker who operated the Wonder Wheel at Coney Island. Sadie was sassy and smart. Brave. She was nothing like me.

"That's why they call it *acting*," my mother said.

And after the first few times of reading through the scenes, I started to feel like I *could* act like Sadie. It was fun, pretending to be someone else. At Lost River, Joe had built a stage in the forest for us kids to put on our own shows. We pillaged Liliana's costumes for clothes to wear. We made up stories, sometimes on the spot, and acted them out under the eaves of leaves. This was the same thing, my mother explained. Just making believe.

Mr. Moretti, the film's director, was staying at the Ritz-Carlton, just across the street from the Russian Tea Room. We arrived with twenty minutes to spare, so we wandered around the bottom of the park for a bit. She was happy, nervously excited, her cheeks pink.

"Just be yourself," she said. "Act natural."

"Acting" natural seemed to be a silly idea, but I nodded.

When there were only five minutes left, my mother took me by the hand, and we made our way back to 57th Street and located the red awning for the Russian Tea Room, right next door to Carnegie Hall.

My mother had gone from being chatty to a still sort of quiet as we entered through the revolving doors and gave our coats to the coat-check lady. Her voice was hushed as she told the hostess our names. The lady led us to the table, where Mr. Moretti was waiting.

I had never been anywhere like this before. I was gawking as we walked into what looked, to me, like a palace. Rich green walls with framed oil paintings, lush red upholstered seats. Chandeliers with a million red glass ornaments. And so much gold.

Even as we shook the man's hand, it took all my energy to keep my jaw from dropping and my eyes from wandering. The people at the booths and tables looked so elegant and at ease. As if it were no big deal for them to be having lunch underneath a sky full of crystals.

"It is such a pleasure to meet you both," Mr. Moretti said as we took our seats. He looked at me but spoke to my mother. "Margie told me that she was quite beautiful, and I have seen your portfolio, of course, but I truly had no idea she would be so very *breathtaking* in person."

I thought about that word, remembering that horrifying sensation of hitting my back on the riverbank. My breath stolen.

"Truly, truly stunning," he said, shaking his head as he kept looking at me. The man had thick eyebrows, like two fuzzy caterpillars above a pair of beady eyes. "How old is she?"

"She's ten," my mother said. We were both accustomed to people directing their questions about me to her.

"Oh," he said, frowning. "But Sadie's thirteen."

"I'll be eleven on Valentine's Day," I chimed in, and it was Sadie's voice that came out.

"She does look older than her age," he said. "Remarkable."

He continued to study my face, as if looking for evidence of our deception. People were often surprised to hear my age. I thought of my little girl shoes, my toes pinched inside.

"You don't have any experience in film, I understand," he said, suddenly speaking to me.

I came back from where I had been floating (somewhere near those glittering glass bulbs and lights).

"Film?" I asked, and I thought of Henri's drawers full of film. I thought of the way he taught me to roll the film into the developing canister in complete darkness.

"*Movies*," he said, and laughed heartily. "I guess that's a no?"

My mother laughed uncomfortably.

"I'm an actress, too," she said. "She's been around theater people her whole life. She was born at the Lost River Playhouse, summer stock?"

"Well, then, not only beauty but talent must be in her blood," he said, and my mother blushed.

A waiter in a red silky uniform approached the table, and Mr. Moretti said, "We'd like two vodkas, the Ballet Russe for the lady and a Bloody Mary for me. A tea for this one, please. With cherry preserves. Are you ladies hungry?"

I was starving. We hadn't eaten breakfast, and it was past noon now.

"No, thank you," my mother lied. "We had a late breakfast."

"I'm hungry," I said, again channeling Sadie.

"Me, too," he said, and grinned at me. "*Famished*." He then ordered several items from the beautiful menu: caviar blinis, kabobs, a fruit platter, and a duck meat platter, all of which arrived in short order. There was enough food to feed a family.

I tried not to gorge myself, but everything was so beautiful and delicious. As I savored every bite, I looked at the beautiful paintings, all framed in ornate gold frames. Several of them were of ballet dancers.

"Do you take ballet classes?" Mr. Moretti asked when he caught me studying the paintings.

I glanced furtively at my mother and shook my head.

"Oh, you *must* put her in ballet class. It will give her discipline and grace. Invaluable," he said. "Did you know that football players often take ballet class?"

My mother shook her head.

He leaned across the table and whispered conspiratorially, "Do you see that man in the back corner?"

My mother and I both turned our heads to look toward the back of the restaurant, where a man was sitting at a table, reading the newspaper.

"That is Rudolf Nureyev," he said. "The Russian ballet dancer?"

We nodded. We had heard of Nureyev. Everyone had heard of Nureyev. He was famous, but he looked so alone. I wondered what it was like when everyone recognized you.

Mr. Moretti asked a lot of questions—about our lives in Vermont, at Westbeth. He told us how it was that he happened upon the Baby Love ad when he was at the dentist's office.

"I stole the magazine," he said with a laugh. "Stuffed it in my briefcase. It took a half a dozen calls to finally track you down."

He told us about the film, as well. That the role would be very demanding and possibly a bit *controversial*. I wasn't sure what that meant. Maybe that's what my mother meant by *heavy*?

"I'm looking for a girl who can be part urchin, part *ingénue*." I didn't know what that word meant, either, but it sounded French. I would ask Henri later.

He ordered another round of drinks, and I watched my mother soften. Alcohol had this effect on her. She became pliable when she was drinking, as if the liquor planed away her sharp edges. She was always more affectionate when she was drinking, wanting to hug and to touch.

"She has an agent?" he asked my mother.

"Margie is her agent," my mother said. "For modeling."

"No, no, she needs an agent for acting," he said, slicing into a tender piece of duck. "A manager."

My mother looked flustered, though I couldn't tell if the flush in her cheeks was from the vodka or from embarrassment. "I'm her manager," she said.

"Aha," he said, clasping his hands at his chest as he leaned back in the booth.

I snuck a peek at Nureyev in the corner. He was paying his tab now. I watched as he rose from the table and walked toward us. I looked up at him, and he smiled at me as he passed.

"Can I take ballet?" I asked my mother, as if I hadn't asked before, again and again.

"Of course," my mother said, as if we had never battled about this.

"Listen," Mr. Moretti said, raising his hand to the waiter for the check. "The producers are going to want her to do a screen test, of course. As soon as possible. Something we can show Bobby. But do you have someone? Who can review a contract?"

"A contract?" she said.

"Yes," he said. "Of course, like I said, Bobby gets the final say. But I *want* her."

I had been floating again as he studied my face. I was somewhere else—my slippered feet dancing across a floor, ballet music, and chiffon swirling about my hips.

"For the movie?" my mother asked.

"Yes, darling. For the movie."

"Do they have champagne here?" my mother asked, her eyes sparkling like the crystals of the chandeliers.

He grinned. When the check arrived, he shook his head and gave it back to the waiter. "A bottle of champagne, please—the Private Couvee."

We took a taxi home that night after spending hours more at the Russian Tea Room. They drank the entire bottle of champagne, save for a tiny glass they allowed me to sip. Now it sat sour in my stomach as the taxi hurled through the city and then deposited us in front of Westbeth.

"Hi, Jackie!" my mother said to Jackie-O, who was talking to someone on the corner.

Jackie tilted her head in concern as my mother tripped on the curb.

"Oopsie," she said as she righted herself.

My mother was swaying and mumbling as we entered the building. In the elevator, she leaned against the back wall and slid down until she was sitting on the floor. I could see the white cotton crotch of her pantyhose. I knew what was coming next, and there was nothing I could do to stop it.

I handed her my new muff, that beautiful red puff, because I didn't have anything else to give her. When she threw up into it, I knew it was ruined, the smell almost unbearable as we rose to the ninth floor.

New York City
August 2019

Sasha comes down from the loft, rubbing the sleep from her eyes, mumbles her good mornings to Liliana and me, and disappears into the bathroom.

What will I tell her? I look to Liliana for guidance, but she appears just as lost as I feel.

"What do we do?" I ask Liliana. "About my mother?"

"She needs a lawyer," she says. "A good one. I'm certain this is just a mix-up. Because of her friendship with Margie. Their history."

What she doesn't mention is *my* history. The blackout photo. The insinuations and accusations that have been circling my mother like bees around a hive for years.

"It says she's a person of interest. Do you think they have evidence? I mean, other than the photo?"

Liliana rubs her temples.

"Were those FBI guys here to *arrest* her?" I whisper. "Do you think they had a warrant?"

Liliana puts her hands up. "She didn't tell me anything. She just said to tell you that she was not involved in any of this. That she hardly knew him. Brenner."

"*Hardly* knew him? What the hell does that even mean? She gave him a photo of me, and now, she's some kind of *suspect*. She's a fugitive, Lil."

The toilet flushes, and Sasha comes out of the bathroom, stretching. Her hair stands on end, and she looks like a little girl.

"Coffee?" she asks.

"I think we need to go back to Vermont, hun," I say.

"*What?*" she asks as she reaches for the coffee pot. "But the memorial is tonight. Gilly's taking me to MoMA today. We promised Zu-Zu's mom we'd bring her home. What's going on?"

I shake my head and hand her the paper. I am so tired of secrets, of lies. My mother was never honest with me; I will not lie to my daughter. Not anymore. Even if the news is difficult. Even if it hurts.

Sasha's eyes widen as she scans the article, absorbing what it means for her grandmother, who has been more of a myth than an actual presence in her life. This deception is mine. I have painted this portrait, spun this dream of the grandmother I thought that Sasha deserved. I am done.

Sasha looks at the front page and then at me, waiting for an explanation I can't give her.

"I want to leave before the media figures out I'm here," I say. "It's going to be a total circus once they find out I'm at Westbeth. Henri deserves a private memorial. You said there was a paparazzo lurking around out there yesterday. I guarantee there will be a half dozen more soon. They're like cockroaches. You see one, it means there's a zillion more of them hiding out."

Liliana shakes her head. "Listen, I'll talk to security. We'll make sure nobody gets in who doesn't belong here. Gilly's going to talk to his brother-in-law; he's a lawyer. He'll get somebody to help your mom. To clear this all up."

I nod. But what I don't say is that maybe there is nothing to clear up. Maybe everything they are saying is true. I need to leave, to go home. My heart aches at the idea of missing the memorial, but my mother has left me with no other option.

"You can still go to MoMA," I say to Sasha. "We'll leave this afternoon when you get back." I am trying to appease her, the way I did when she was small. *No, you can't have cake; here, eat this banana.*

Offering her a crumb to distract her from the cookie. "I'll let Effie know we had to leave the city early. Maybe Zu-Zu can take the train. Or Devin can drive down and pick her up. They'll understand."

Sasha scratches her head. "What about Fiona? What's going to happen to her now?"

"I don't know." I reach for her hand, those tiny hands so much smaller than my own. "This has nothing to do with us, though. This is *not* our problem."

Sasha's eyes plead. "But she's your *mom.*"

New York City
February 1977

My birthday, as always, was on Valentine's Day. This year, it was a Monday, which meant I would be at school for most of the day. Liliana had made some cupcakes for me to bring to share with my class, but they would probably be lost in the shuffle of all the other Valentine's treats.

Earlier in the week, our teacher had us decorate shoeboxes with pink and red construction-paper hearts; she used a box cutter to carefully make a slot in the lid of each one. During lunch, we were to distribute the valentines we'd brought with us to our classmates. I'd always shared my birthday with this tradition, and most of the time, people just doubled up, added a birthday message to the paper valentine.

My mother, however, always made sure to make a big fuss about my birthday. At Lost River, Serafina and she would go out of their way to decorate our cabin with red balloons while I was at school. Serafina once made a menu, as if we were in a fancy restaurant; I got to choose what to "order," and my mother pretended to be the waitress.

Ever since we met with Mr. Moretti at the Russian Tea Room, my mother had been so happy. After that episode in the elevator, she'd stopped drinking. Not even wine with Liliana after dinner, like usual. Of course, she had done this before. But it didn't mean that I enjoyed the break any less, didn't hope that maybe this time, she just wouldn't start again.

I had taken a day off at school to do the screen test, and she had, in short order, found an agent to handle the film contract. Her name was Susan Freed, someone Margie knew. Someone who handled a lot of Margie's older girls who'd crossed over from modeling into acting. She'd even met with a financial planner, who would help her manage the payments I would be bringing in now. I half-listened as she explained how it would all work. It felt grown-up to me, outside of my realm of understanding, like the stock market and politics. She seemed to thrill at the idea of being my manager. She loved all the details she needed to attend to. Seeing her happy made me happy, too. She said she'd "turned over a new leaf." I loved this expression; it made me think of the shiny green undersides of the ferns and other foliage along the river. Untouched by sun or rain, silky in my fingers.

We wouldn't start filming until May. The film would be shot entirely on Coney Island. They'd even offered to put us up at a hotel there, and my mother accepted, since Guillermo would be coming home around then, and she wanted to make sure to give him and Liliana space. "The kids can come stay with us at the hotel for a couple of nights if you want," she said. "Give you guys some privacy?" I thought it would be so fun to be in a hotel on Coney Island with Gilly.

But that was months from now. We still had to get through the winter, which was cold and strange in the city. Not at all like Vermont. It was dirty and windy, and people seemed to get even more angry and impatient. When I'd gone to pick out the valentines for my class at the Bigelow Pharmacy, a woman had yelled at me to *just hurry up already*. I'd finally selected a box of Super Friends valentines, since I thought they'd be good for both boys and girls. Gilly picked the same ones, since we went to different schools, and we'd sat at the kitchen table with Joaquin and Angelica, filling them out. Our schools both required that we give them to every one of our classmates.

There were a few kids I would rather have left out; I saved the ones with the villains for them, so they might take the hint.

In the morning, I woke up to my mother tickling my feet.

"Good morning, birthday girl!" she said as I climbed down the ladder and into the kitchen.

The other kids were already at the table, even Joaquin, who almost never woke up in time for the walk to school. In the middle of the table was a giant chocolate cake with red candy roses all over the top and my name spelled out in red frosting.

"Cake for breakfast?" I asked. It seemed like the most decadent thing in the world.

"Why not?" she said, shrugging. "It's got eggs and flour and milk—practically all the food groups."

Liliana lit the candles, and everyone sang. She sliced the cake and served up a piece to everyone except my mother, who nibbled on the corners of some dry toast.

When there was nothing but crumbs and globs of icing left on our plates, my mother handed me a package. It was wrapped in valentine gift wrap, covered with rainbow-colored hearts. I carefully slid my finger under the tape, trying to preserve the pretty paper.

Inside was a box made of pink vinyl with a white canvas strap.

"Turn it over!" my mother said excitedly.

On the front of the box was an illustration of four ballerinas, and it said BALLET BOX.

"Well, open it! Here." She took the box, unsnapping a little flap at the bottom. I reached in and pulled out a pair of soft leather ballet slippers, a crisscross of elastic sewn inside. I quickly opened the main compartment. Inside was a black stretchy leotard and a pair of pale pink tights. Overwhelmed by what this meant, I looked to her for confirmation.

"Now, it's just once a week. The teacher said you may have to be with the younger children to start with, since this is your first class, but—"

I threw my arms around her neck and hugged her.

"But you said I'm too clumsy . . ." I started, and Liliana looked a little alarmed. "That grace is not my forte."

"What are you talking about?" my mother said, standing up and swiping the plates away.

"When Mr. Cunningham said that I should take ballet, you said . . ."

"I said that classes were too expensive," she said, but her smile had gone from big and warm to the kind that wasn't really a smile at all.

The sickly-sweet chocolate cake suddenly made me feel sad.

"But *now*," she said. "There is going to be plenty of money for extras. And Mr. Moretti said that it would be a good idea. Remember?"

I nodded. I remembered. I remembered *everything*.

New York City
August 2019

All morning, Liliana and I hang Henri's photos on the clean white walls of the gallery. It is too late to properly frame them, so we suspend picture wire from one corner to the next, making a sort of clothesline, hanging the photos with binder clips. I feel as though I am slipping back in time as the room fills with the images he created. With the world as he saw it. It is my childhood, here on display. It is nearly impossible not to slip into the ethers of my recollections, only to feel the sharp stab of sorrow, remembering: *Henri is gone.*

The memorial is at six o'clock. We plan to get the photos hung by noon. Gilly and Sasha are going to MoMA, but promised they'll be back by four, so she and I can head home. I have gathered the things from Henri's that I want to keep. His robe. His camera. The only thing missing are the pictures we made. Gilly has searched everywhere, but they, like my mother, have just disappeared.

The news of the FBI's interest in my mother lingers at the edge of every thought. It is a yard sale puzzle missing pieces; I can sense the edges, contained here in the city, but the picture is incomplete.

Here is what I know. My mother, at some point, gifted Brenner, a pedophile billionaire, with a photo of me. As a child. A photo that, out of context, could seem like exploitation. Like pornography. Like evidence. And this, I am fairly certain, is why Henri took his own life. This misinterpretation. This maligning of his art. The implication that he would ever harm me, too much to bear. Also Margie, somehow, was tangled up in Brenner's network. Margie, her employees, her models, my mother.

My mother.

The sun is bright outside, blazing through the windows of the gallery. I wipe the sweat from my forehead into my hair, which I have tied back with a blue bandanna. Liliana is standing on a step stool, stretching the next line of picture wire.

The wall of portraits stare back at me. My mother's is dead center. I look at her expectantly, as if she can answer all the questions racing through my head.

What had she known about this? And what did she have to do with Brenner? Was it possible she was complicit? That she was a cog in this horrifying machine?

Suddenly, the heat is oppressive; I feel vertiginous, swoony. I want fresh air. Water. I need to get out. I make my way out of the gallery, through the doors into the courtyard, and sit down on the nearest bench, putting my head between my knees, trying to remember how to swallow, how to breathe.

The click of the shutter almost doesn't register, what with the pounding of my pulse in my ears, but then I hear it again. I glance up to see a few people milling about. Did I imagine it? How on earth would someone have gotten into the interior courtyard? They would have to pass security. *Security* that Liliana had promised was airtight.

Click. I hear it again and stand up, knees still feeling like jelly. But I can't see anyone. No cameraman lurking in the shadows or perched like a sniper on one of the balconies above.

"Go away," I say softly.

Click.

"Go away!" I say more loudly this time and feel my heart like a ticking clock. I remember the note from my mother. I'm wearing the same jeans as yesterday, and it's still in the back pocket.

I open it up, expecting some convoluted explanation. But instead, it's just a single sentence. My mother and I have a canyon between us. But somehow, she always seems to know exactly what it is that I am thinking. Years and miles apart.

I have them. In Audrey's pocket.

My photos? She *has* them. They're not gone! But Audrey's pocket? Who is Audrey? And why so cryptic?

Then I think of the cedar chest at the foot of her bed. She picked it up at a flea market after we moved into our own apartment in Westbeth. The person selling it said it had once belonged to Audrey Hepburn, when she traveled with Mel Ferrer on the Queen Mary to Europe for their second honeymoon. I doubted it, but my mother believed what she wanted to believe.

I return to the gallery and find Liliana struggling to reach the far corner. "Do you have a key to my mom's place?"

She stops what she's doing and studies me silently, and I know this means that she does.

"I'm not sure that's a good idea," she says.

"Why do you always do this?" I ask, summoning a question that has been plaguing me for decades. "Protect her?"

She looks stunned, as if I have accused her of something instead of asking a perfectly legitimate question.

"What do you mean?"

"I mean, she's on the cover of the *New York Times*. A suspect in a freaking trafficking scheme. The FBI are looking for her, and everyone's just like, *Oh, she just needed to clear her head. She'll be back.* She's not coming back. If she was innocent, she'd come back."

The words feel like marbles in my mouth, hard and round. When I swallow, I feel them lodged there. The ones I haven't said.

"She traded that photo with Brenner for something," I continue. "It was a *quid pro quo*. She gave him my photo in exchange for something, but I have no idea what. Do *you* know?"

Liliana shakes her head. "No. I swear." With this, she crosses her heart, as if she's a little girl instead of an elderly woman. *Cross my heart, hope to die. Stick a needle in my eye.*

"What did she say exactly when she called? You have to tell me."

If my mother had the photos, and went to the trouble of leaving me a note, why hadn't she just called me, too? And why wasn't she reading her texts?

Liliana rubs her temples.

"I swear to you. She hasn't told me anything. I learned about the photo being at Brenner's apartment when you did. When I asked her, she told me that he and Margie were *colleagues*. That was how she put it. She said that he had been a fan of Henri's work, and when he found out that Margie knew one of Henri's neighbors, he asked about purchasing a piece."

I shake my head again. This story makes sense, except for two things. First, why *this* photo? A photo of the worst night of my life. A photo I had given to my *mother*. One she knew I wanted only her to ever see. Second, the inscription. *Wolves do not eat each other.* Who was the wolf here? Were they both wolves? And if so, what did that make me?

But Liliana is telling the truth. She has never been a good liar. She flusters too easily, a red rash climbing up her neck if she even tries. Once, when Angelica was in high school and got caught dropping acid on the High Line tracks with a bunch of other Westbeth kids, Liliana had tried to fabricate some sort of story to tell Guillermo, and by the end of her nonsensical explanation, her face looked as if she had poison ivy.

She's repeating what my mother told her. She is not the liar; my mother is.

"Please. I just need to look for something."

She sighs and reaches into her pocket. She pulls out her set of keys, presses it into my palm, and says, "Your mother is not perfect. But she would never, ever be a part of something like this."

I take the key ring from her.

"I'll meet you back down here in a half hour," I say. "Sasha and I are leaving at four."

I will say my goodbyes to Henri, and then I will take my daughter home.

★ ★ ★

Alone, I take the elevator down to the second floor. *Second Floor!* I think.

But instead of turning left to go to Henri's, I head to my mother's apartment. I fit the key into the lock and brace myself for whatever it is I will find inside.

At least she had the foresight to remove the photos from Henri's, though I know she wasn't thinking of me. She would never have considered how much I needed to see for myself what it is that everyone else thinks they see.

The door creaks open, and I step into the shadowy foyer. I am assaulted by the scent of the essential oils she wears: jasmine and orange blossom. She makes the perfume herself, calls it "Night Garden." I half expect her to emerge from the shadows.

In the living room, the sun is streaming through the windows, and the air is still and thick. My head is swimmy as I walk to the kitchen.

Ravaged. It is the first word that comes to mind. It looks as if someone has picked up the room like a snow globe and shaken it. Hard. It's a disaster. Like Sasha's room when she was a toddler and incapable of picking up after herself. My mother is a lot of things, but messy is not one of them. For a moment, I wonder if her apartment has also been raided. Upended by someone looking for something. But this is not the work of a burglar; rather, someone who left in a hurry. Someone who fled.

I move to the kitchen. There is a pot of water, two poached eggs swimming inside. Two stiff pieces of toast perched in the toaster. The coffee pot was clearly left on until the automatic timer shut it off. The bottom of the glass carafe is black. I feel sick.

I study the room, searching for something, though I hardly know what anymore.

The bedroom, too, is in complete disarray. Every drawer open. The closet raided for her favorite clothes and shoes. I drop to my knees and scan under her bed to confirm that her suitcase, normally stashed beneath, is gone.

I am so stunned by the way she's left her apartment, I almost forget about the reason I'm here. The *photos*.

Audrey's honeymoon trunk remains at the foot of her bed, shut tightly. I move to it and release the clasps on either side, lifting the lid.

My mother had been delighted that this was Audrey Hepburn's, but also by the secret compartment in the bottom, which the man who sold it to her had shown her. A place for love letters or other contraband.

I take a deep breath and slide the door to the hidden recess open.

But there are no photos here. Instead, there is another envelope, again with my name in my mother's loopy handwriting. I feel rage stirring inside me. What does she think this is? Some sort of treasure hunt? She was in too much of a hurry to turn her coffee pot off, but she was able to write me not one but *two* notes?

I grab the envelope and leave the trunk open, return to the kitchen.

Fuming, I sit down at the table and tear open the envelope, slicing my finger in the process. I plunge my finger into my mouth, taste the copper penny flavor of my blood. I use my free hand to shake the piece of paper open.

I need to talk to you. In person, Ry. Face to face. I promise to give you the photos if you come. If you just give me a chance to explain.

This is followed by an address. In Brooklyn.

I am seething. My mother is using my images again as a bargaining tool, but this time, with me.

I look at my watch. It's noon. If I leave now, I can still be back by four o'clock to meet Sasha and Gilly here before the memorial. I will listen to whatever version of events my mother has crafted, get my photos, and then leave.

Coney Island
May 1977

The Terminal Hotel was at the corner of Stillwell and Mermaid Avenue, right across the street from the train station. When my mother and I got off the train, she checked the slip of paper where she'd written down the address and looked at the building in disbelief. She looked up and down the street, as if the giant sign had been misplaced.

"I guess this is it," she said. "Let's get checked in. We have a meeting with Mr. Moretti and the rest of the cast at five."

After our encounter with Mr. Moretti at the Russian Tea Room, I suppose my mother had been expecting more glamorous accommodations. But it was all the same to me: an adventure. For one thing, there was a Chinese restaurant on the first floor of the hotel. Secondly, we could see the ocean from our third-story window.

"Well, this is convenient," my mother said as she spied the liquor store next door, as well. "I'm gonna need a few drinks if *this* is where we're living for the summer."

My heart felt heavy. After the Russian Tea Room, my mother had stopped drinking. Of course, I knew that this new and lovely truth could change in a moment, in a sip, but at Westbeth, she'd gotten into a sort of routine as we prepared for the two months at Coney Island shooting *Midway Girl*. A routine that did not include drinking, or disappearing.

The plan was that we would spend twelve weeks filming, staying at the hotel during the week, and then going to Westbeth on the weekends and days off. Gilly's family would be in Lost River starting in June. In July, when the movie wrapped, we would take the train to Vermont and meet them all there. My mother had been offered the role of "Woman at the Ball" in *My Fair Lady*, a non-speaking role that I knew would mean a lot of standing around in a pretty ball gown, pretending to have conversations with the other background cast. (My mother told me that they usually mouthed the names of vegetables to look like they were actually talking. *Peas and carrots. Rutabaga, lettuce, green beans.*) Normally, she would have jumped at any opportunity to be on the stage, but when Mr. Moretti called to officially offer me the part of Sadie, she told Serafina we'd be tied up this summer, and she'd have to take a seat in the audience rather than on the stage.

When my mother talked about the movie, her eyes lit up. She tried the words on like Eliza Doolittle trying on gowns for the races: *For the first week, call time is at five-thirty each morning; the DP says the light at sunrise is magic. It will be like cinema verité. Raw. Valentino says to just think of the script as a map. There will be a lot of improv. And they plan to use the crowds on the boardwalk as extras, just like they did in Brooklyn for* Dog Day Afternoon. *We'll wrap at the end of July, and then it'll go into post-production. They're hoping to release next summer.*

As we checked into the hotel and carried our own bags up to our room, I watched her taking it in, likely trying to figure out how she'd spin this when friends asked: *Valentino is of the Stanislavski school; he believes that his actors need to fully inhabit their characters' lives. You wouldn't believe the* dive *he set us up in. Said that all that grit and grime was to help her get into character. To* become *Sadie. He says, "Art is suffering," and boy, did we suffer.*

It was, my mother explained, a real fleabag hotel. A single room occupancy, or SRO, for long-term residents, with a shared bathroom on each floor.

"If you need to go, we go *together*," she said. "*Terminal* is right."

After we got our room, we did just that, passing a woman who reminded me of Jackie-O coming out of a room, buttoning her blouse. My mother wouldn't even let me sit on the toilet seat. "This had better be worth it," she said. "God, we're both going to wind up with crabs."

That evening we met Mr. Moretti, David (the director of photography), and the main cast at a fancy Italian restaurant called Gargiulo's, which was just around the corner from the hotel. We met in a special room that Mr. Moretti had reserved exclusively for the cast and crew. It was *Fancy with a capital F*, as my mother liked to say.

My mother's shoulders, which had been as tense and rigid as a clothes hanger since we got to Coney Island, softened. She'd been right. The hotel was just to help the cast immerse themselves in the seedy world depicted in the script.

My mother had coached me on how to greet Mr. De Niro as if I were a commoner preparing to meet the Queen. I had never seen any of Robert De Niro's movies, but my mother had. After Mr. Moretti gave me the role of Sadie, she'd traveled to theaters all over the city to catch *The Godfather Part II, Taxi Driver, Mean Streets*. I wasn't allowed to see any of them, but he had a musical called *New York, New York* coming out in June with Liza Minnelli, and my mother had promised we'd go see that together.

Mr. Moretti told us to order anything we liked off the menu. I wanted the spaghetti and meatballs, thought it might even be good luck, but I was wearing a pale blue dress, the only fancy dress I had that still fit me, and my mother was worried about spills, and so when the waiter came around, she ordered the pasta primavera for me, and a soda water with lime for herself, for which I was grateful.

There were probably a dozen people at the table, and many of them seemed to know each other: mostly men and one older lady who looked very familiar. My mother pinched me and whispered that she had been in that miniseries about the Roosevelts that she and Serafina had watched last winter, but that I probably recognized her from *The Waltons*. After we'd been at the restaurant for about forty minutes, making small talk with the other cast and crew, my mother reached over and touched Mr. Moretti's arm.

"So, when is Mr. De Niro coming?" she whispered. "For dessert?"

Mr. Moretti smiled warmly and patted her hand. "So, I guess we should get down to business here?" he said, loud enough for the table to hear.

And I *knew*. I knew it in the way I knew he wouldn't look her in the eye, and in the way David, the DP, kept studying his plate.

Robert De Niro wasn't coming.

"He's been waiting on a script for ages. Some movie about a bunch of guys just back from Vietnam. He and Walken. Cazale and his girlfriend, some stage actress named Streep. They start filming in Thailand in June. Then Pittsburgh. So it's a no-go for *Midway Girl*."

A collective sort of hush fell over the large table.

"I know," he said, nodding. "It's disappointing. Of course. We all love Bobby, and he would have been perfect. But the show must go on, as they say, and we've found a replacement." He looked across the table then, at a guy who had been quietly dunking his bread in olive oil and red wine vinegar for the last forty-five minutes. He had dark, shaggy hair and a square jaw. A sort of crooked nose. "This is Tony," he said. "He's stepping in, and we're lucky to have him. Pulled him away from Broadway, the Mamet show, *American Buffalo*, that just opened."

"I was just an understudy," Tony said, shyly. I liked him right away.

I watched my mother's hand lift off Mr. Moretti's wrist, like it was something hot, and then she flagged down a waiter.

"I'll have a vodka martini, please," she said.

Luckily, the hotel was close. My mother's words were slippery and her gait unsteady as we walked back to the hotel arm in arm with some guy named Nick, who I thought was part of the crew. Something called the *key grip*, I overheard him tell my mother. He was muscular and had tattoos running up both arms.

I walked for a while with Helen, the lady from *The Waltons*. She told me she was only in a couple of scenes; she played Sadie and her dad's neighbor. She wouldn't be back to Coney Island until June. She was catching a train back to the city that night.

"Five-thirty a.m. sharp call time," Mr. Moretti reminded us, before he took off for whatever hotel he was staying in and the rest of us rounded the corner to The Terminal.

As my mother walked ahead, arm linked with Nick's, the guy who replaced De Niro approached me, hands in his pockets.

"It's nice to meet you," Tony said, removing one of his hands to shake mine.

"You, too," I said. "Is this your first movie?"

He smiled and nodded. "It is."

"Me, too," I said.

At the hotel, we all went our separate ways. My mother and I took the elevator up to the third floor. I changed into my pajamas and crawled into the twin bed that was covered with a worn chenille spread. The pillow was flat, and so I tried to fluff it into shape, though it didn't matter. The train ride, and a night spent making small talk and smiling and trying to remember which fork was which, had been exhausting. I could have slept on a concrete floor.

My mother was antsy, though. She paced the room, no longer charmed by any of it.

"This is bullshit," she said. "I gave up a role in *My Fair Lady* for this?" Her words had teeth. "Never mind all the auditions we turned down for you."

"I'm sorry, Mama," I said, feeling my body starting to curl in on itself. I was a pill bug again. A roly-poly.

"Method acting my ass," she said. "De Niro was the only reason why this film was able to get financing. What do you bet now that De Niro is gone, the money will disappear, too."

She was talking to me, but not really talking to me.

"I need to go get some air," she said, my seven least favorite words in the world. The last time *she needed to go get some air*, she had been gone for a whole day.

But I didn't argue. Arguing did nothing but make her more determined.

She stood on the other side of the door and listened for me to lock the deadbolt before she left. I leapt back into the bed and stared at the lights from the train station across the street. I could hear the waves crashing against the sand from here, and I tried to pretend it was the sound of the river in our cabin at Lost River, or the sounds of the freight ships on the Hudson at Westbeth. I tried to pretend I was anywhere but here.

At some point, I fell asleep, and woke at the sound of my mother on the other side of the door as she fiddled with the key. "Shit," she said, and laughed. "You have to be fucking Houdini to get into these rooms." She was with someone. I heard his low voice and then silence before the door finally gave and she came stumbling into the room. The air was filled with milky light. I feigned sleep but peeked at the clock on the nightstand, which read 2:45 a.m.

I heard her undress and crawl into the bed. She clicked on the TV, but there was nothing but the crackle of white noise. I waited until I heard the hum of her sleep and then crawled out of bed and clicked it off, the dark room filling with silence. The smells of cigarettes and liquor were as heavy as a blanket. I covered my head with the chenille bedspread and fell into a fitful, desperate sort of sleep.

Two hours later, I stood at her bedside, shaking her shoulder. She rolled over and looked at me through rheumy eyes. I braced myself, waiting for her to lash out for not waking her up earlier.

"We have to be at the boardwalk in forty-five minutes," I said.

She sprang out of bed then, stretched her arms over her head, and yawned.

"Just enough time for a cup of joe." She smiled and pinched the tip of my nose. "Are you ready for your first day, my little starlet?"

New York City
August 2019

I return the keys to Liliana and tell her I am going to find my mother. Her expression is alarmed and, perhaps, concerned, but she nods.

"She told you where she is?" she asks. "I mean, where she's been staying?"

"She left an address. In Brooklyn. Why? She didn't tell you?"

I assumed that Liliana knew exactly where my mother was and that she was just withholding that information from me on my mother's request. It troubles me that she seems to be surprised by this.

"No," she says. "She probably knew I wouldn't be able to keep it from you. Or that I might try to convince her to come back."

I nod. It's true. Liliana would never encourage her to run away from her troubles.

"She needs to turn herself in, Ry," Liliana says. "To the authorities."

Hearing these words suddenly makes all of this more real than even reading that article in the *New York Times* did. My mother is wanted by the FBI. This is as serious as it gets, and she's playing hide-and-seek.

An old feeling returns. It's the same awful feeling I had once back at Lost River when I was six or seven and my mother had a toothache. She complained about it for a week, every time she ate something, pressing her palm to her cheek and grimacing. Serafina gave her all her home remedies: clove oil, a wet peppermint tea bag, even a bourbon-soaked cotton ball. But nothing worked. Then one morning, I awoke in the middle of the night to the sound of her moaning. The cabin was cold and damp, but her body was on fire. I remember reaching over and pressing the underside of my wrist against her forehead, the way a mother would to a child. When she refused to get out of bed, I pulled on my winter boots and coat over my pajamas and went outside, where I filled a plastic baggie with snow. I told her to press it to her cheek and that I would be right back. Then I trudged through the snow up to the big house to get help.

It took Serafina and me both to get her out of bed and into Serafina's truck. In the truck, she leaned against me, in agony, as I stroked her hair. I muttered, "It's going to be okay, Mama. You'll be okay." And I knew, even as I comforted her, that this was upside down. That she was acting like the child, and I was acting like the parent. It had made me feel lonely and weird. If she wasn't the mom, then who would take care of me?

"I just want my photos back," I say. "Fiona will do whatever it is that Fiona wants to do."

The heat is oppressive, the sun blinding, as I walk from Westbeth to the 14th Street subway stop. I am grateful for the shade as I descend into the station. Someone is playing the steel drums, and the percussion—along with the roar and clack of the trains—makes my head pound. I need to sit down.

The A train is arriving just as I get to the platform, and I can see through the smudgy glass windows that it is packed with people. Inside, I grab the nearest pole and hang on as we lurch forward. I keep my eyes peeled for an open spot to sit down, but at the next stop, when a couple of people get off, the seats are quickly taken by a pregnant lady and an elderly gentleman.

Luckily, the train begins to empty as we leave the city. Nearly half the remaining riders scurry out at the last Lower East Side stop, and then we are under water. I try not to consider the impossibility of this, all the ways that it defies nature. That it *depends* on it: physics and geometry making it possible for this train to roar through a tunnel beneath the East River.

I find an empty seat near the doors. I sit back and close my eyes, try to imagine that I'm simply riding in a car, with the windows rolled down, a cool breeze in my hair. I try to dream a song on the radio. I try to conjure serenity.

Click.

My eyes shoot open. A group of teenagers congregate at the other end of the car, goofing around, taking photos with their phones. The tension in my neck eases.

I close my eyes again. I remember taking Sasha on the Nemo ride at Disneyland long ago, the way she had marveled through the port-hole windows at the cartoon fish. To avoid hyperventilating with claustrophobia, I had focused on her bright eyes and open smile. It's amazing how your child's joy can distract.

The train screeches to a stop at the Bergen Street station in Prospect Heights, and I study my map app. This is where I need to get off. I excuse myself as I step over a lady's bags that are obstructing the path to the doors, and she nods at me, her head bobbing, her eyes milky with cataracts. Her face, like my mother's in Henri's photo, is drawn.

I emerge onto the intersection of Bergen and Flatbush, and a wave of heat overwhelms me again. I check my phone, orient myself, and begin the two-minute walk to the address in the note.

The streets are residential beyond Flatbush, row house after row house. I pass a school, vacant for the summer, the basketball court oc-cupied by a group of young guys. The sound of the ball dribbling on the asphalt beats in time with my heart.

I get the very distinct sense that someone is behind me. I look over my shoulder, but there's nobody there. Still, the hairs on the back of my neck bristle.

A young couple, with an expensive-looking baby stroller laden with string grocery bags, is coming toward me. After they pass, I take a quick glance behind me again. I'm just being paranoid. No one has followed me to Brooklyn. I'm alone. Nobody on these streets recognizes me or would even care if they knew who I was.

I look at the map again. The address is the next block up. The streets are quiet, empty. I slow as I approach the address and confirm it is the same one on my mother's note. The X that marks the spot on this inane treasure hunt.

There is a waist-high wrought iron gate in front of the brownstone house. I have to reach over to release the latch.

Click. I whip around again, but there is no one there. I must be losing my mind.

I remember the feeling that day a paparazzo followed me home to Westbeth when I was fifteen. I'd had the sense of someone dipping into the shadows, the padding of their feet as they walked behind me. I remember holding my breath, scanning the dark alleys and shop entrances, looking for an escape route or somewhere I might duck to let them pass. As I began to sense the pursuer getting closer, I had started to run, grateful to be wearing sneakers. I had felt like Dustin Hoffman in that chase scene in *Marathon Man*. The sound of the man's footsteps behind me had been the most terrifying sound I'd ever heard. The sound of a hunter.

I close the gate behind me and walk up the steep flight of steps to the massive oak doors. There is a glowing button to the right of the entranceway. Tentatively, I press it, and somewhere in the bowels of the house, I hear the electronic trill of the bell ring out.

The sun behind me reflects in the beveled glass window, obscuring whatever is inside. After several moments, when no one responds, I realize I should probably text my mother. Fugitives don't answer the door.

Here, I type, suddenly realizing maybe the reason she hasn't read any of my texts is that she's concerned that the FBI is monitoring them. That would also explain the handwritten note. Still, this one word could mean anything. "Here" could be anywhere. It could mean anything.

The bubble denoting her typing her response pops up, but then just as quickly disappears. I sigh.

Finally, through the beveled glass, I see the shadow of someone, and a man opens the door. He peers out past me, as if I'm not standing there, and then ushers me inside.

Coney Island
June 1977

Being on set was magical. It only took about a week of working for me to realize that I was good at this. While modeling had been sort of fun, it had all felt a bit silly. The momentary thrill of seeing my photo in a magazine was overshadowed by the fact that my face was being used to sell something (perfume or blue jeans or pudding), which seemed sort of embarrassing. But making a movie? I finally understood why they called it *playing a role*; it really was like *playing*. It was the closest I had felt to the afternoons at Lost River, when we put on our own shows in the woods.

Acting was about telling a story. Like my mother had said, it was *make-believe*. Making people believe that what they were watching was true. And to do this, you had to lose yourself in the character. I thought about the movies and shows I loved, the magic of whatever story was on the screen. Acting felt *important*.

I didn't know it at the time, but Mr. Moretti was a brilliant director, and the way he approached directing was unconventional. There was no memorizing scripts. No running lines. No getting coached between takes. Instead, he had *conversations* with us, the actors. He'd take us on walks down the boardwalk or along the beach and discuss what the next scene was about. What our characters' emotions would be. He'd tell us the story, ask us questions, giving us just a little prompt and a nudge. He would give us the beginning and the end of the scene; how we got there was up to us. Or rather, up to Sadie and her dad, or whomever else she was interacting with.

Tony, who played my dad, was soft-spoken and kind. He had been in several Broadway shows, but this was his first film, and he was just as nervous as I was. He was patient with me, and treated me like the kid I was rather than the way some of the other crew barked orders and cussed around me, as if I were just another adult on the set.

When we had downtime, we played Scrabble or Chinese checkers.

The days were long, but they didn't feel that way. And my mother, while present, felt on the edges. After the first week, she stopped accompanying me and spent her days lying in the sun, working on her tan. For the first time, I felt like I was a part of something that belonged to *me*.

Each day when we finished, the cast and crew would go back to the hotel to rest, and then we'd all convene for dinner. We didn't go back to Gargiulo's—way too fancy—but rather to Meng's, the Chinese restaurant on the first floor of the hotel. I quickly discovered an appreciation for Chinese food, my favorite being the big bowls of greasy lo mein. My mother, always on a diet, ate only the wonton soup, sipping delicate spoonfuls of broth but leaving the fat dumplings in the bowl. She drank mai tais, slipping the wedge of pineapple from the rim of her glass to give to me, the faint hint of rum lingering on my tongue.

I had a teacher on set, and I was able to get some of my schoolwork done during the day. But after dinner, I still had to go upstairs to our room and finish my homework, while my mother stayed downstairs with Nick and the other production crew: the gaffers and camera and boom guys. The makeup artists also loved my mother, and sometimes they all went out dancing together.

In the city, I had hated it when my mother disappeared, but Coney Island felt small; there were only so many places she could go, and the fact that she was with the rest of the crew, like a small family, eased my mind.

I had my own key to the hotel room, and with my mother gone, after my homework was done, I could also watch the shows *I* liked: *Happy Days*, *Laverne & Shirley*, and *Little House on the Prairie*. I was supposed to go to sleep by nine. Call times were often just after the sun rose, but on Wednesdays, I'd stay up late enough to watch *Charlie's Angels*.

My mother always came back, though sometimes it wasn't until the air was tinged with light; still, I felt oddly safe in our hotel. Every room on our floor was occupied by the cast and crew. If I needed someone, all I had to do was go knock on somebody's door. Tony was right down the hall; if he knew my mom was out, he'd swing by and check, just a knock-knock, and then he'd poke his head in to say "Good night." On the nights when I *was* scared, when the sounds of the crashing waves or distant thunder rattled me out of my dreams, I would pretend I was Sadie. Sadie wasn't afraid of anything. She was tough and brave. She didn't even have a mother at all.

During the first few weeks on set, we went to the city on the weekends to visit. Guillermo had come home, and he told us stories about his months in Los Angeles. My mother listened to his stories dreamily. Los Angeles was where the real movie stars lived.

Gilly's family was supposed to go to Lost River for the summer, but then Guillermo got a last-minute offer to play Sancho Panza in *Man of La Mancha* on Broadway. The show opened in September, and so in June, Liliana had gone on to Vermont without him, taking Joaquin and Angelica with her, but leaving Gilly behind after he made his case that he was old enough to take care of himself while Guillermo was at work. Gilly was thirteen now. He'd started babysitting some of the kids at Westbeth, and he thought he could probably make some money if he worked through the summer. With Guillermo gone most days, he could even use the apartment as a sort of daycare facility. Henri was there if he needed anything on the nights when Guillermo was at the theater late.

But after the first couple of weeks, my mother started dragging her feet about going into the city. She and Nick were spending a lot of time together when he wasn't working, and she said I couldn't go alone, especially with no one to watch me at Gilly's house. I missed Gilly so much; it felt like he was on another planet rather than just an hour subway ride away.

Weekends were the loneliest.

One Friday night, my mother had gone out with the crew again and dead-bolted me in the hotel room, where I watched *Donny & Marie,* but it was a rerun. I was planning to stay up late to watch *The Sonny & Cher Show,* since we weren't shooting the next day. We had a little mini-refrigerator in the room, and I found a half a Coke that had gone flat and some leftover lo mein. I sat cross-legged on the bed, eating.

The phone on the nightstand between the two beds jangled, and I nearly dropped my meal. My mother occasionally called to check in, but for the most part, it just sat there, silent.

"Hello?" I said.

"*Allo?* Ryan?"

"Henri!" I said, excited. I hadn't spoken to him since our last visit to Westbeth, nearly a month ago.

"I was calling to see if you are free for a visit this weekend," he said.

"I can't go to the city," I said, feeling angry again at my mother, who had crossed her heart that we would spend our weekends at Westbeth.

"No, no," he said, and laughed. "I will come to you. And I will bring Gilly."

I was so excited, I wanted to squeal, but it was late, and my mother had said that when I was alone in the room, I should try to be as quiet as I could so no one would know I was in there. I even had the TV turned down so that it was barely audible, especially during the musical numbers.

"We will be there tomorrow morning. Maybe we can make some pictures."

My mother was asleep in her bed when I woke up the next morning; I hadn't even heard her come in.

"Mama," I whispered into her hair.

She grumbled and mumbled. "It's Saturday, Ry. Let me sleep."

"Henri and Gilly are coming today! Their train gets here in ten minutes. Can I go meet them?"

She hadn't washed her face, and her mascara was smudged under her eyes. "Okay," she said. "But be back here before dinnertime."

I nodded. "Can I have some money?" I asked.

She sighed deeply and raised one floppy arm toward her purse hanging on the back of the door.

I wasn't a SAG member yet, but the arrangement was that I was paid for every week that we shot. My mother sent the checks to Susan, my film agent, who put them into our account. My mother didn't tell me how much they were, only that they were "barely enough." She explained that I was *paying my dues* with this film, and depending on how it did at the box office, it could lead to bigger and better things. She was a lot less optimistic since Robert De Niro was replaced with Tony, however.

My mother usually kept about a hundred dollars of cash in her purse, but I noticed whenever we went to Meng's, somebody else always picked up the check. Usually Nick.

I pulled one crisp ten-dollar bill from the wad she had, and then, seeing that she'd rolled back over and her lips were parted in sleep, I took one more.

I met Henri and Gilly at the train station and hugged them both long and hard. Gilly had gotten taller in just the single month since I'd seen him last. His voice sounded funny, creaky like the wooden floorboards in the barn at Lost River.

Henri was wearing his usual suspenders and blue jeans. He had his camera, and a small box wrapped in pink paper.

"For me?" I asked as he handed it to me.

"*Oui,*" he said.

Inside was a tiny framed photo of Fraidy Cat. "Your kitty misses you," he said. My heart plunked like an untuned key on a piano. I missed my life at Westbeth. I thought about Fraidy Cat's nine lives, and it seemed so strange how many lives I had already had, and how far away they seemed. The years at Lost River were like those white spots you see behind your eyes after looking at the sun. Even Westbeth felt as far away as the moon.

There were so many things I wanted to show them, so many places for us to visit. I wanted them to meet the others, too: Tony and Mr. Moretti; Sarah, who did my clothes; and Barb, who did my hair and makeup. The cast and crew sort of scattered on the weekends, though, some people returning to the city, others going off and doing things with friends and family.

"How is your mama?" Henri asked as we wandered along the boardwalk.

I shrugged. I didn't really know how my mother was. She was drinking again, most nights, but she also seemed happy. I was pretty sure that she and Nick were in love. Nick was nice, too, but kind of boring. He never really laughed, or even smiled, for that matter. But my mother practically glowed when she was around him.

"Come see!" I said, grabbing Gilly's hand and running toward where a small crowd had gathered to watch the tightrope walker, who spent all day suspended two stories up, walking across a wire. Back and forth, back and forth. I was mystified. How did he pee? When did he sleep?

"Did I tell you about the man who climbed the South Tower?" Gilly said.

I shook my head.

"It was so crazy!" Gilly said. "My mom heard on the news that there was some man climbing up the World Trade Center. Ben and I tried to use my binoculars to see him, but it was too far away, so we got a taxi and went down there and watched him."

"Who's Ben?" I asked.

"Oh, just a new kid at Westbeth. Anyway, the police got in a window-washing basket to try to get him to come down, but he just kept climbing. It took him three and a half hours, but he made it.

They call him 'The Human Fly.' He was on Johnny Carson and everything. I can't believe you didn't hear about it."

Suddenly, the guy on the tightrope didn't seem so special anymore.

"Should we go on some rides?" Gilly asked.

We spent almost the whole day running from one part of Astroland Park to the next, riding the Wonder Wheel and waving at Henri, who stood below, snapping photos of us. The tightrope walker might not have impressed Gilly, but the Cyclone did.

"Do you want to go?" he asked.

I didn't. Not at all. Roller coasters scared me. But I could tell that Gilly wanted to. Really, really wanted to. Normally, Gilly didn't mind when I chickened out, but now he seemed irritated.

"Fine," he said.

"Maybe Henri will go with you?" I said, looking at Henri, who shook his head.

"Oh, *non, merci*." He laughed and took a photo of us studying the recently refurbished wooden roller coaster, listening to the screams of terror and delight, falling down from above like rain.

"Whatever," Gilly said. "We should probably start heading back soon, anyway."

"Are you mad at me?" I asked Gilly as we waited for Henri to take a photo of a woman who was selling cotton candy. It was mesmerizing, watching her spin sugar and air into the pink clouds that she handed to her customers.

"Why would I be *mad* at you?" he asked.

"Because I didn't want to go on the roller coaster?" I said.

He shrugged.

I felt tears pricking my eyes. "We could go to the aquarium. I haven't done that yet. Or we could go up in the Wonder Wheel again." I didn't tell him that it had taken me weeks to get up the courage to do that.

"It's okay," he said. "It's no big deal. It's not like Coney Island is going anywhere, right?" Suddenly, the Gilly I knew, my friend who never pushed me to do things that scared me, was back.

But the idea that something had shifted niggled at me.

At the aquarium, Gilly perked up. He loved animals and fish. He'd pleaded with Liliana for a fish tank, but she'd said that they were too hard to clean, never mind that Fraidy Cat might try to eat the fish. Henri wandered around taking photos, and Gilly and I stood looking down at the dolphins. One of them was showing off, diving and then emerging, blowing water into the air. When we got sprayed, Gilly clapped his hands together and squealed. I was so happy he was happy again.

"*Faggot*," I heard someone hiss, followed by laughter.

There were two teenage boys, nudging each other and laughing as they pointed at Gilly.

Gilly kept staring into the water, but I could see the tips of his ears were bright red.

I didn't really know what the guys were talking about, but it didn't matter. They had just ruined everything.

"They're stupid," I said to Gilly. "And it's not even true."

But he wouldn't speak to me, and when we finally spotted Henri, taking photos of a fat manatee, he tugged on his arm and whispered to him.

I stood feeling stupid and left out.

Henri came to me then and said, "This has been such a lovely day. You are the perfect hostess."

"Are you leaving?" I asked, feeling my throat swell. I had hoped they would stay and meet everyone at Meng's for dinner. Tony. Mr. Moretti. Henri could talk to David about photography.

"*Je suis désolé*," he said. "Gilly is feeling under the weather."

Gilly wasn't sick, but there was something wrong, and for the first time, I didn't know what it was.

I returned to the hotel room after their train departed. Now I didn't want to see anyone. I just wanted to curl up in my bed and watch *Hee Haw* and *Wonder Woman*. Maybe the Saturday Night Movie would be good.

But when I let myself into our room, my mother was there, dressed in the same outfit she'd worn that first night, when we all went to Gargiulo's. Maybe Nick was taking her out somewhere fancy tonight.

"Oh, good," she said. "You're back early."

"Gilly didn't feel good, so Henri took him back to the city." I was on the verge of crying.

Instead of noticing, she just went to the closet and started rummaging through the few things we had hung up, finding my blue dress.

"You need to take a shower," she said.

I knew I was dirty. I could feel the salty water in my hair. The cuffs of my jeans were damp and heavy with water and sand, as well. We had spent at least a half hour on the beach, taking photos with Henri.

"Why?" I asked. I definitely did not want to go out on a date with my mom and Nick. The one time they'd invited me along, they'd gotten drunk, and I'd drank Shirley Temples until my throat burned and my stomach ached.

"Valentino left a note downstairs for all of us to meet for dinner tonight. At Carolina's."

Carolina's was another Italian restaurant on Mermaid Avenue. Not as fancy as Gargiulo's, but inside were framed photos of all the stars who had eaten there. Including Robert De Niro.

We all sat at a long table, the usual crew plus Helen, the lady from *The Waltons*. She'd arrived a couple weeks ago, and it had been like having a grandmother on set. Between takes, she'd taught me how to crochet, saying she'd help me make a poncho for my mom. I sat between her and Tony, who was freshly showered and smelled like Irish Spring soap. He smiled at me.

Everyone ordered drinks, and when they all arrived, Mr. Moretti stood up, and the chatter around us petered out.

"I'm sure there has been some talk," he said, scowling. "Some *chiacchiera?*"

I looked at Tony, but he just looked down at his drink.

"As you know, our producers came on board with the understanding that Bobby would be playing the lead. They assured me that nothing would change with the change in casting, but I am sad to say *si stanno ritirando.* They've got cold feet and are pulling out."

There was a collective gasp. Clearly, there hadn't been any chatter about this at all.

"What does this mean?" someone asked. "For the movie?"

Mr. Moretti shrugged. "Honestly, I'm not sure. Our budget is basically cut in half now. I've got some leads, but for now," he said, and his mouth twitched, "we'll be putting things on hold. Luckily, we're more than halfway through the production schedule. So that's good. But until there's another backer, we're going to need to close up shop. Good news is, we've got enough footage to put together a nice promo to help entice some investors."

"Are we going to keep getting paid?" asked the man who played the scary carny. I was scheduled to shoot a big scene with him this week, the one leading up to the one they hired a body double for.

"Sadly, we have to suspend your paychecks, too. But I anticipate we'll be up and running again shortly. For now, let's consider this a badly needed vacation. You can all go home for the Fourth of July. And hopefully, we'll be back on track later this month. Checkout from the hotel is tomorrow. *Capisce?*"

I looked across the table at my mother, who was signaling for the waitress to bring her another martini.

"For tonight, please, let's enjoy a good meal."

"The Last fucking Supper," one of the grips next to me mumbled.

My mother would not look at me; she was intent, it seemed, on drinking as much free booze as she could, while she still could.

"I'm sure it will be okay," Helen said to me.

"We'll probably be back by August," Tony said.

It was over already? I'd left Henri, Gilly, and Fraidy Cat behind. I'd given up a summer at Lost River. All those days spent working so hard were for nothing. Mr. Moretti was making promises he couldn't keep. I knew, because he sounded just like my mother when she spun her assurances like so much cotton candy.

We weren't coming back. *Midway Girl* was dead in the water.

My mother was uncharacteristically sober as we left the restaurant that night, though when we walked past the autographed photo of Robert De Niro, she stopped and spat at the glass. Mortified, I hurried ahead, out onto the street.

Brooklyn, NY
August 2019

"Ryan," the man at the door says, his bright blue eyes crinkling at the corners. He looks my mother's age, with a full head of white hair, swept back. He's wearing a faded T-shirt and jeans, bare feet, as if he is a college kid instead of a senior citizen.

"Hi," I say. "Who are you?"

"It's *me*," he says, and extends his hand. "Nick."

"Nick?" I say. Oh my god. I haven't seen Nick in nearly forty years.

"Long time, no see," he says.

"Is this your house?"

"Sure is," he says. "I'm usually in Paris in the summer, but when your mom called, I canceled my flight."

Paris? Is it possible he's tied up with Zev Brenner, too?

From what I've read, Brenner has been living in Paris since the mid-nineties. He's a dual citizen of the US and France, so extraditing him would be a tricky thing. Luckily, he's an equal opportunity creep—a creep whose deviance doesn't care about international borders. And so, while France is certain to protect its own—even its felonious own—all bets were off when that criminal became a menace to France's own society. According to the accusations, many of his crimes were carried out in an apartment in a five-story walk-up in the 8th arrondissement. An apartment where he kept his "girls"—

girls who had been sent to Paris by Papillon to model, only to find themselves little more than concubines. Many of them were just past puberty, from broken homes, "discovered" by Margie or by any number of other recruiters or scouts who made them promises that were never kept. Girls who believed their own beauty could save them.

The only difference between those girls and me was my mother. It was *her* yearning, not mine, that drove us into the offices at Papillon. It was my mother, and whatever agreement she seemed to have had with Brenner, that had kept me safe.

"Where is my mother?" I ask. I really just need to get this over with. "She has some things that belong to me."

He motions for me to follow him up a set of steep wooden stairs, the Oriental runner threadbare. When we reach the landing, I follow him through a door and around the corner to another set of stairs. The building appears to have four stories, plus a basement apartment. We keep climbing until we reach the top floor. There is a very short door here, and he moves an overstuffed armchair out of the way and pushes the door open.

My eyes take a moment to adjust to the dim light inside. It is, indeed, an attic. Sloping ceilings and exposed beams. There is one cavernous room, and all the blinds are drawn shut.

"You're here," she says.

Here.

The orange blossom and jasmine scent of her is the same as it was when I was a little girl. When she envelops me in her arms, I feel myself reeling, slipping back into another time. Her bony back, her rib cage. The desperate, sorry clinging. I have lost my footing in this world. I am Alice, tumbling down the rabbit hole, falling backward.

New York City
July 1977

We packed up our things at The Terminal Hotel and went home. But she wasn't finished with the film. When she wanted something, it overwhelmed her. Her need was like a balloon, stretched to its limits. Her eyes were wild with it; her body a bundle of raw energy. She was certain that something could still be done to save the movie. To save my career.

"Look at Jodie Foster," she said, offering up a list of young actresses as evidence of something, though of what, I wasn't sure. "All she had before *Taxi Driver* were some Disney films. Kid stuff, but after that film, she wound up nominated for an Academy Award. At thirteen years old. Sue Lyon? She was fourteen when Kubrick cast her in *Lolita*. She won a Golden Globe for that role. She's worked with John Huston, John Ford since then." There was an urgency in her voice, as if we were running out of time.

Immediately after returning to the city, we began to have meeting after meeting with Susan. With Margie. She was scheming, seething.

I, however, was just grateful to be home. I missed being a part of the film, of course. I missed the beach and our dinners at Meng's. I missed Tony and Helen and all the crew. But after just a few days back at Westbeth, the time away felt like a dream.

It was strange to be at the apartment with Liliana and the other kids gone. Guillermo was at rehearsals for *Man of La Mancha* all the time, and Gilly was busy babysitting or hanging out with his new friend, Ben. Still, I was so happy to be back with Fraidy Cat and Henri.

On the Fourth of July, everyone at Westbeth planned to watch the Macy's fireworks display from the rooftop. They were going to be setting off the colorful explosions from a barge on the Hudson River. I had pleaded with Gilly to take the night off from babysitting so he could celebrate, and he had reluctantly agreed.

Things had been strange with Gilly ever since his visit to Coney Island. He wasn't mean the way he had been that day. But he still felt far away, somehow. Busy with his job, yes, but it also felt like he wasn't really listening when I talked. As if he always had somewhere else he'd rather be. It was the same feeling I got from my mother sometimes, and it hurt.

My hope was that the Fourth of July celebration would return us all to normal again. Guillermo had the day off; he'd promised me he'd help me make the red, white, and blue Jell-O parfaits I'd seen in a magazine. My mother had invited Nick to join us, as well. He lived in Brooklyn, and since the film was on hold, he was out of work for the time being.

She had a meeting with Margie that afternoon but said I didn't need to come with her; they were just going to go over some potential jobs for me to do in the city while we were waiting for the funding to come through for the film. Margie said she'd been speaking with a cosmetics company that was looking for a young girl to be the face of their next major campaign. Someone young, innocent. Margie thought I would be perfect. I knew this was important. Without the weekly paychecks, my mother's wallet was empty now.

Guillermo had been very firm with my mother when we got back to the city about her not being out after dark. Since we'd arrived in New York almost a year ago, someone calling himself the Son of Sam had shot thirteen people. Some in the Bronx, some in Brooklyn; but one girl, a student, was shot in the face after her class at Barnard on the Upper West Side. While we'd been in Coney Island, there had been three more murders.

The grown-ups did their best to shield us from this. But the kids at Westbeth overheard everything, and we shared grown-up secrets like stolen candy.

"He likes dark-haired girls," Misty, a thirteen-year-old from the third floor, said. "My aunt got followed home for fifteen blocks last weekend, and she's pretty sure it was him. She finally lost him when she went into Bleecker Bob's and pretended to look at records."

I thought of my mother, with her waist-length brown hair.

"I heard he usually goes after couples," little Frankie said. He was ten. "Like ones making out in their cars and stuff."

I thought of my mother and Nick. I wondered if they ever parked to kiss. The thought made me feel nauseous.

Gilly was watching a set of twins on the second floor, down the hall from Henri. Guillermo and I had made four perfect parfaits, which we would have after dinner before going up to the rooftop for the fireworks.

"It's good to have you back, Ry," Guillermo said. "Gilly really missed you while you were away."

"I don't think he missed me very much," I said.

Guillermo set down the bucket of Cool Whip he'd been scooping from and frowned.

"What makes you say that?" he asked. "Has he said something to trouble you?"

I shook my head. I couldn't explain how it felt, almost as if he were keeping a secret from me, one I should be smart enough to know on my own.

"*Oye mira y calla*," Guillermo said. "Still waters run deep."

"What does that mean?" I asked. It made me think of the river. The way it seemed lazy until you were submerged, swept up in the rushing current.

"It means that Gilly has a lot of things going on inside of him right now. He's thirteen. He may look peaceful on the outside, but there's turmoil inside. Be patient with him, sweet girl. He is your friend."

Independence Day, 1977

*A*s the sun begins to set, filling the apartment with golden light, Gilly comes home and goes straight to the shower. I've been trying to read a library book, but I can't concentrate. Everything in the story makes me think about Gilly and his deep waters. About my mother and her brown hair and a madman out there with a gun. Even when I think about Lost River, I feel uneasy. Is our cabin just sitting there empty? Or has Serafina given it to another actor or actress?

Guillermo is making his specialty: pollo guisado, a one-pot chicken stew that makes the apartment smell delicious. I am eating the Spanish olives, blowing the pimentos through the holes.

When Gilly comes out of the shower, he has a towel wrapped around his waist, his hair dripping on the parquet floor as he moves behind the divider that separates his room from the living space. For some reason, that hollow place in his chest, the architecture I am as familiar with as my own body's, seems deeper. More cavernous. For a moment, I wonder if someone has reached in and stolen his heart.

He emerges minutes later, dressed, the towel now around his neck. How did I not notice how much he's grown? He is almost as tall as his dad now.

"I made parfaits," I say hopefully.

"Cool," he says. "Hey Dad, so Ben is going to come hang out tonight, too, okay?"

"Sure," Guillermo says.

Ben moved in to Westbeth this summer when I was gone. He and his mom came here from San Francisco. He lives on Henri's floor.

We eat our meal in silence; it's spicy and makes my eyes water.

"When is my mom coming home?" I ask, as the room goes from gold to shadowy.

"I'm sure she'll be home soon," Guillermo says. "The trains are probably full because of the holiday."

But as the sun sets, and we all start to gather our things to go to the rooftop, my mother is still not back. Normally, I would distract myself by talking with Gilly. But Gilly and Ben have set up their lawn chairs together, and when I try to join them, Gilly simply scooches his chair closer to Ben's to make room for me, without interrupting his conversation.

Ben is friendly enough. He's a year older than Gilly and has the thin black beginnings of a mustache. His baseball shirt says, I'M A PEPPER. He speaks so softly, I can barely hear him. Finally, I just stop asking him to speak up.

It is still so hot. It was almost 90 degrees this afternoon. The air feels prickly.

It seems like the fireworks are taking forever to begin, the sky indigo still. The sun is gone, but the air remains bright.

Henri has joined us. He has his camera and is taking photos of a group of kids, who are running around with sparklers. I keep watching the sparks, worried that one might land and catch the rooftop on fire. We would all perish up here, like the people in The Towering Inferno. How would we get out? Would we have to leap to our deaths?

Finally, the first fireworks explode over the river. Henri puts his hand on my shoulder, and I know this means he wants to make a photo. And because he is the only person in the world who seems to care that I am here, I stand up and face him. My hands are in fists at my sides, and my chin juts out. I will not cry.

He frames me through his viewfinder, waiting for the next explosion, I suppose. Then, I see my mother walk through the door and onto the rooftop. She is with Nick, who holds her hand and kisses her neck. Son of Sam has not gotten her. She is alive.

"Mama," I say, but my fists are still clenched tight.

Click.

New York City
August 2019

When my mother releases me, she grasps my hands and steps back to assess me. It's funny how I never noticed that this was always her greeting: embrace and then evaluate. She is looking at me with wonder, but it is not the sort of pleased marveling of my youth, but rather a sort of bewildered curiosity. I have also gotten old. I have not been immune to time's toll, to its cruelty. Beauty is just as vulnerable to time's passage, maybe even more so.

She is wearing a silk kimono, reds and purples and emerald green. Her hair is pure white and in a loose braid over her shoulder. She wears a delicate gold necklace with a tiny pearl nestled in the deep glistening dip of her throat, as if inside an oyster shell.

It is stifling up here.

"Would you like something to drink? Beer? Tea?" Nick asks, as if I'm just a neighbor who's come for a friendly visit.

"Some water would be great," I say, and he leaves us.

"Come in, sweetie," she says, and pulls me by the hand across the room to a living area. I see a film poster of *Midway Girl* hanging among others on the wall.

"Nick?" I say.

"Thank god for dear old friends," she says. "People who *know* me. Know that I am not capable of any of those things they are accusing me of."

"Mom," I say, but she's still talking.

"He's been so good to me, Ryan, through all of this." She's speaking as though she is the victim. Like someone who has been violated. She's waiting for my pity, for my compassion and understanding. To confirm that she has been wronged, and to acknowledge how lucky she is to have a man who protects her.

When she sits down on the sofa and beckons me to join her, I shake my head. "I'm just here to get my photos."

"I need you to listen to me," she says. "To give me a chance to explain. It's not what they're saying, Ryan. But I don't care what anyone thinks except for you. They can haul me off for all I care, as long as *you* know the truth."

"*Truth?*" My laughter comes out like the bark of an angry dog.

I sit down on a chair across from the sofa when it becomes clear she's not going to relinquish the photos until I hear her spin her tale.

The steps creak, and Nick comes in with a tray laden with a blue willow china teapot and teacups. A honey pot and several slices of lemon, a little china bowl of sugar cubes. A glass of ice water. He sets it down on the coffee table before us.

"I'll be downstairs," he says. He touches her bony shoulder, then disappears again.

"I was sick, you know," she says, apropos of nothing. "Last year. Breast cancer."

"What?" I say.

"I didn't want to worry you," she says. "Luckily, we caught it early. It was in the ducts, *non-invasive*, they call it. They said it was probably because I didn't breastfeed you." At this, her face looks pained. "I tried, you know. But you didn't latch on. You just couldn't seem to get the hang of it."

I tense at the implication here, that it was somehow *my* fault.

"Chemo?" I ask, looking at her long white hair.

"Mastectomy," she says, and slips the shoulder off her kimono, revealing the scarred remains, a challenge to doubt her again. "Radiation."

I wince and look away.

"You're okay now?" I ask.

"Yes," she says. "In remission."

"Liliana and Gilly didn't say anything to me," I say.

"I asked them not to. Like I said, I didn't want you and Sasha to worry."

At the mention of Sasha, I remember why I am here, and how very much I want to leave.

"Mom," I start, and she reaches for the teapot. She pours a cup and tries to hand it to me. I shake my head.

"I don't understand any of this Brenner stuff. Clearly, there's something to this story, or you wouldn't have the FBI showing up at Westbeth looking for you. Otherwise, you wouldn't be hiding in Nick's attic."

"Did you know," she says, as if I haven't just asked her to explain how it is that she's affiliated with a man who has committed crimes against children. Against little girls. "They say that all conspiracy theories are twenty percent true. That's how they work. If they are twenty percent true, then that is enough to satisfy most people, and they will be willing to believe the eighty percent that is a lie."

"So you're saying this is some sort of *conspiracy theory*? About you?"

She sets her tea down and stretches her neck to each side, like a boxer about to go into the ring.

"What I am trying to say is that people need a story to hold on to. When bad things happen, they need a narrative, so they keep digging until they find that *little kernel*." She pinches her thumb and finger together and then makes a fist. "And they hang on tight."

"I really don't have time for your riddles, Mom," I say, exasperated. I think of Alice again, her cryptic conversation with the caterpillar, when all she wanted was to just go home.

I look at my watch. I have an hour to get back to meet Gilly and Sasha.

She sighs dramatically and sinks into the sofa, and I recall a night that I caught her in the theater after a production of *Streetcar,* all those years ago. She'd been on the stage after the show, when everyone else had gone. She was lying on the chaise, smoking a cigarette in an ornate silver holder. She'd looked so glamorous. Like a real Hollywood actress. She'd taken a long drag on her cigarette and said, in Blanche Dubois's shrill drawl, "*I know I fib a good deal. After all, a woman's charm is fifty percent illusion . . .*" She'd seen me then, lurking in the third row of seats, a captive audience. But instead of scrambling to her feet, embarrassed, she kept right on. "*But when a thing is important, I tell the truth.*"

"Fine," I say. "What's the kernel, Mom? You knew him. You gave him my photo. A photo that I gave to *you*. A photo of me when I was hurt and scared. Because you left me alone."

She winces, though it would be imperceptible to anyone but me. I have hit that single raw nerve.

"I protected you, Mom. And you never, ever protected me."

"You have no idea," she says, her voice louder. Seething. "You have no clue what I did for you."

Every conversation in our half-century history as mother and daughter has always come back to this. To her *sacrifices*. To everything she gave up for me. First, when she got pregnant with me, and later, when I lived the dream that was rightfully hers.

"*Tell me*," I say. "How did you know him?" I am gritting my teeth, furious with a rage I have been saving my whole life to unloose. "Why don't you go ahead and tell me the *truth*?"

New York City
July 13, 1977

"There's an investor," my mother said excitedly at breakfast that morning.

Guillermo had left for the theater, and Gilly was babysitting.

I had attempted to make pancakes for us, but the edges were burnt, and the insides were uncooked. My mother had eaten only half of an anemic-looking grapefruit.

"What's an investor?" I asked, distracted.

"For *Midway Girl*," she said. "I think Margie might have found someone to get it back up and running."

"Does that mean we get to finish it?"

"We'll see. He's an associate of Margie's. Very, very rich. He has apartments in New York and Paris. A private jet."

"So that's good. Are we going back to Coney Island?"

"With any luck, yes. And maybe this time, they can afford to put us up at a real hotel."

I knew that not only was the film broke, but that we were out of money, too. I'd heard her on the phone with Serafina, asking for a loan to hold us over, promising she'd pay her back as soon as production was back on track. I'd seen her go down to the mailbox three times a day until the check finally came.

Since we'd gotten home, Margie had secured a couple of modeling jobs for me. Susan had also gotten me a few auditions. I was scheduled for a photo shoot that Friday and a screen test for another movie the following week. But *Midway Girl* was all that my mother had on her mind. She was convinced that it was going to be a huge hit. She was sure that Tony was the next De Niro, not just a stand-in. She had convinced herself that if it could just get made, we'd eventually find ourselves on the red carpet at the Academy Awards. It wasn't impossible. Mr. Moretti had gotten three Best Director nominations before. I didn't care about any of that, though. I just wanted to finish what we started, and I wanted her to be happy.

It was a Wednesday, and it was going to be another hot day, too hot to do much of anything at all. My mother had picked up a box of Fla-Vor-Ice, and I ate all the orange ones, but it was so hot, the ice turned to a sickly orange syrup within minutes. The sticky plastic wrappers littered the coffee table, where we'd propped up a fan. My mother had taught me that if you filled a bowl with ice and set it in front of a spinning fan, it was almost like an air conditioner.

We were restless.

My mother spent most of the morning on the phone with Margie and Susan, scheduling more auditions with the hopeful caveat that *Midway Girl* might go back into production. Afterward, she joined me on the couch, where we sat and listlessly watched TV. Soap operas were her weakness: *Ryan's Hope* followed by *All My Children*, which I loved, first, because the family shared my name; and second, because it was set in Manhattan. I devoured it; I knew every story line. Every character.

"Maybe I could be on a soap opera," I suggested. "Maybe on *Ryan's Hope*! I could be Ryan Ryan."

My mother had snorted, but not at my joke. "I think you're a little beyond that," she said.

I shrugged. It seemed like a fun job to me, and a lot of the soap operas were shot in New York.

"I really need to get out of here," she said. "This heat is a nightmare."

"We could go see a movie," I said, thinking of the deliciously cool theater. "*New York, New York* is playing at Cinema Village, and we still haven't seen it."

My mother balked. "No thanks. We're done with De Niro," she said.

I fanned myself with my book.

"If we lived in LA, we'd have a swimming pool," she said dreamily. "I think we should really think about relocating after *Midway Girl* is finished."

"Los Angeles?" I said. "But I like it *here*."

Los Angeles might as well have been the Emerald City. In my imagination, it was a technicolor dreamscape of palm trees and blue skies and white sand. It was *Charlie's Angels* and *The Brady Bunch*. "New York is a dying city, Ryan," she said dramatically. "Just look around you, will you? Hookers on every corner, drug dealers, and mobsters. Pollution in the river. Fires everywhere. A murderer on the loose, shooting strangers in the head. The politicians are corrupt. This is where dreams come to *die*," she said, as if this were a monologue she'd memorized for an audition. "They call it *Fear City*, did you know that? It's no place to raise a little girl. I don't know what I was thinking. If the movie falls through, I think we should go to Los Angeles. Before winter comes. Get a nice apartment with a swimming pool and air conditioning."

I nodded silently, but only because I couldn't speak; the words could not make their way past the lump in my throat. I *did* love it here: my Saturday morning ballet classes, the kids at Westbeth, my school. I loved the children's department at the fancy Scribner's Bookstore, where my mother would leave me to read while she went window-shopping on Fifth Avenue. I loved climbing the giant rocks in Central Park and riding the escalator at Macy's. I loved the black-and-white cookies at Rocco's and the anchovy calzone from John's Pizzeria that only Henri and I would eat. *Henri*. I loved making pictures with Henri. My family at Westbeth. I didn't want to leave.

My mother said she was going to Nick's in Brooklyn. He had a window AC unit. She promised she'd be back before dinner to cook for us. Guillermo was rehearsing until late. Gilly wasn't home yet.

Gilly and I pretended there wasn't anything strange between us. He spent most of his days babysitting, and then he and Ben would hang out—Ben lived with his mother, who was a choreographer. She was at her company's studio most of the time, and so they hung out at Ben's, listening to records or watching TV. Gilly had only invited me to come along once, and I had felt like a little kid. I didn't know the bands they were talking about. I hadn't seen the movies they discussed. Ben was from San Francisco, a city in California I only knew from *What's Up, Doc?*, that Barbra Streisand movie. He might as well have been from another planet.

"It's where all the queers go to live happily ever after," my mother said. "Nobody even cares in San Francisco. Two men can walk down the street holding hands, and nobody blinks an eye." San Francisco in my imagination was the Golden Gate Bridge and men dressed in colorful feather boas and platform shoes, like one endless Westbeth Halloween parade.

I wondered if Ben was gay. He didn't seem exciting enough to me to be gay. He was quiet and bookish. He had long, floppy hair and acne. He wore bell-bottom jeans and tight T-shirts. He rode a skateboard in the halls at Westbeth. His favorite band was the Grateful Dead; they were from California too. When Gilly had told me about them, I'd imagined something scary. Like Kiss or Black Sabbath, the bands that the other boys Gilly's age at Westbeth listened to. But when Gilly brought one of the records home and played it on Guillermo's hi-fi, it felt more like the folk and bluegrass music that Serafina listened to at Lost River. Gilly talked excitedly about the fact that Ben had gone to one of their concerts in San Francisco right before he moved here.

"We're going to go see them if they tour in New York next year," Gilly had said. "Dead shows are supposed to be a real trip."

It felt like Gilly had learned another language while I'd been away. A language I didn't speak and couldn't understand.

After that one afternoon, I didn't go back to Ben's, and Gilly seemed to understand that I preferred to hang out with him alone. But he was hardly alone anymore.

I spent most of my time at Henri's. I'd put Fraidy Cat in a little backpack and brought him to Henri's apartment, where I watched him work. I would drag the blue stool into the darkroom and sit there quietly as he made prints. I loved the red glow of the safety lamp and the quiet *tick-tock* of the timer. I even liked the smell of the chemicals that leached his images from the paper. He tasked me with handing him the things he needed—his glasses, the rubber-tipped tongs, the glossy sheets of paper—like a surgeon requesting instruments from a nurse. We took a lot of photos together that summer, as well. Taking long walks and finding interesting places to make pictures.

After my mother took off to Nick's, I went down to Henri's. I had lost Fraidy Cat for most of the morning and finally found him curled up in the cool, empty bathtub. I wanted to check on the mama cat; if it was this hot inside our apartment, it would be super hot up on the roof.

Henri didn't answer, but his door was unlocked, so that meant he was working. I went to his darkroom and knocked.

"Hi, Henri!"

"*Allo!*" he said. "Just one moment, *d'accord?*"

"*No problemo,*" I said, yawning. "I was just hoping I could go check on the mama cat on the roof."

"Go ahead and take the key," he said. "You can bring it to me later. I am so sorry. I am up to my neck in work today."

"Thanks, Henri!" I said, and ran to the card catalog, where I knew he kept the key. I also grabbed a can of sardines from the cupboard.

However, the mama cat didn't come, even when I peeled back the lid of the sardines.

"Here, kitty, kitty!" I tried. Still, nothing.

The sun was blazing down onto the asphalt rooftop. I hoped she had just found a nice cool place to take a nap. I left the open sardine can and went back to the elevator. As I was going down, the door opened on the tenth floor, and Gilly was standing there.

"Hi!" I said as he stepped on. "Are you done babysitting already?"

"The mom came home early."

"That's cool. You going to Ben's?"

Gilly shook his head, but I could tell that he was about to cry.

"What's the matter?" I asked as we reached the ninth floor, but he remained silent. "Gilly, what *happened*?"

When we got inside the apartment, he finally spoke. "Ben doesn't want to hang out with me anymore," he said, followed by a shuddering sob.

My arms opened like those automatic doors at the grocery store, and I let him in. He hugged me so hard, I felt my ribs ache. "He said people will think we're *faggots*," he said, the word like a bitter dandelion on his lips.

I cocked my head, trying to understand.

He lowered his voice and said, "He's embarrassed. About me."

Suddenly, I got it. He hadn't chosen Ben's friendship over mine. He hadn't thought he was cooler or more fun. Gilly *loved* Ben.

"I didn't know you were gay," I said, but it came out angrier than I intended.

"I knew you'd be like that," he said, pulling away. "Henri is the only one who understands. What it's like."

I thought of the moment in the aquarium, when Henri had steered him away from me.

I reached for him and made him look me in the eye. "I'm just sad you didn't tell me. Why didn't you tell me? I don't care whether you're gay or not."

"You don't?" he said.

"No. I swear. But I won't tell anybody, either. If you don't want me to."

I held out my pinky and looped it through his.

★ ★ ★

Even though Gilly was sad, it was nice to have him back. To have him to myself again. We spent that afternoon sucking on the rest of the Fla-Vor-Ice packets in front of the TV, holding bags of frozen vegetables against our hot skin until they thawed, then sticking them back in the freezer. When the sun went down, we figured it might finally cool off, but the heat hung in the air like a memory.

When the knock came at the door, neither of us wanted to answer it. Finally, Gilly rolled off the couch and trudged downstairs. When he came back, his mood had brightened.

"They're getting together a game of manhunt after dinner," he said. "Are you in?"

Manhunt. The game I had successfully avoided since we moved in a year ago. Every time there was a building-wide game, I had come down with a cold or had homework to do. But I felt like I owed it to Gilly. He needed me.

"Sure," I said. "I'm in."

Brooklyn, NY
August 2019

I try to imagine their conversation. My mother met Zev Brenner at Tavern on the Green, my mother coming straight from a meeting with Margie. It was late July, and the renovations on the restaurant were complete. Somehow, he got them a table in the Crystal Room, with walls of glass and sparkling chandeliers, which overlooked the blooming gardens. He told her to choose whatever she liked from the menu, but she was so nervous, she couldn't even imagine eating anything. To be polite, she'd ordered shrimp cocktail and champagne.

"It's touristy as hell, but I know girls like glittery things," he'd said to her, looking up at the dozens of twinkling chandeliers.

She'd pitched him her idea then, like a Hollywood pro. She'd been watching Margie for a while, and even if she wasn't savvy, she could *play* savvy. She'd presented him with a bound copy of the *Midway Girl* script. Told him that De Niro had bailed on the film. "It's taking everything I have not to go tell his father. He's a painter; lives at Westbeth, too."

"Oh, you live at Westbeth?" Brenner had asked then. "Do you happen to know Henri Dubois?"

Her eyes had widened at the simple serendipity of this.

"He's a dear friend," she said. "Actually, he's taken a number of photos of my daughter."

At this, Brenner's curiosity was piqued.

"Speaking of which," she said, "I'm certain Margie talked to you about this already. But Ryan, that's my daughter? She's playing Sadie."

My mother tells me that the shrimp came on crushed ice in a silver bowl, and the champagne tasted like the scent of honeysuckles.

She'd pulled out my modeling book: the oversized portfolio of my brief career. The headshots that Margie had taken. The Baby Love ads. The two local ads I had done since then. Brenner studied the photos, smiling curiously.

"I didn't know," she said to me, setting her teacup down. "You need to trust me on that."

She swore she had no idea about what went on inside his New York penthouse, his Paris apartment, his palatial estate in Key West. She didn't know that Margie had established the juvenile division of Papillon as a favor to Brenner. That these girls—the ones she picked up off the street, the fatherless girls, the ambitious girls, the damaged dreamers—would do anything for fame. Private jet rides and free rent in exchange for spending time with Brenner. She didn't know he was hurting them, she insisted.

"Why did you give him the photo?" I ask her. "I gave it to *you*. It was only for you."

She explains that he had sat back in his seat in the Crystal Room. She was dizzy with champagne, the fat pink shrimp still perched on ice, and he had made his proposition.

He would fund the film. He would write a check to the producers that afternoon.

"I admire your fire," he had said.

"My fire?"

"Your audacity."

She'd bristled at this.

"Oh, no, no," he said. "I don't mean it as an insult. I mean it in the best way. You are audacious. *Tenacious*. A mama bear. Or no, maybe a mother wolf? Wolves are smarter than bears."

At this, my mother nodded.

"You would do anything for her. Your little girl? That's why you are here, right? For your daughter's career."

"Yes, I am," she said.

"You're a good mother."

Four words. Four words that no one had ever said to her.

"I *am*," she said, feeling emboldened by the compliment, by the champagne.

The blackout photo, the one found in the raid, was a gift to him, she says. A thank you. It was also a deal, she explains. She *was* a wolf, but so was he. And wolves do not eat each other.

The rules for manhunt were simple. The group of kids was broken into two; you were either the hunters or the hunted. The hunted, the fugitives, were tasked with hiding, while the hunters sought. It was like a mass game of hide-and-seek. Base was the inner courtyard, but anything beyond the walls of Westbeth was out of bounds. The idea was that the hunted needed to get back to base without being tagged by a hunter within the time limit. Because the building was so huge, and there were so many hiding spaces, the time limit was an hour. If you got tagged before you got back to base, you went to prison.

Until that day, I had watched the manhunt games from a distance, thrilled when I happened upon the hunted lurking in the shadows, hiding in the nooks and crannies, and terrified as I watched a hunter prowl the halls, ready to pounce.

My mother hadn't come home yet, so Gilly and I had eaten leftover cold meat loaf for dinner. It was after seven p.m., the time of day that Henri normally called the Golden Hour, when the light took on a magical quality. But today, despite the heat, there was no sun. The sky was heavy with clouds. Thunder rumbled angrily in the distance.

There were about ten of us; *wild things* was what Liliana called the motley crew. Mostly boys, but a couple of the more tomboyish girls. The littlest kids weren't allowed to play. I was one of the youngest. Charles was the oldest kid—and the one who had lived at Westbeth the longest—which made him the de facto leader of the game. Everyone leaned against the concrete wall, expressions serious, as he explained the rules. I studied all their somber faces, like a police lineup, I thought. Blue jeans and ratty T-shirts. Dirty sneakers and dirty faces. Shaggy hair and Kool-Aid stains. If Henri were here, he might take a photograph. Sometimes, I saw the world through Henri's eyes.

I'd hoped to be on the hunter team; seeking seemed a lot less scary than hiding, but Charles divided us up, and Gilly was a hunter, and I was one of the hunted.

I looked frantically at Gilly.

"Actually, you wanna swap?" he asked a girl named Sky, who nodded.

"We'll stick together," Gilly promised me. "We'll hide together."

Relief washed over me. Maybe this would even be fun.

It was dusk now, and thunder rumbled and then cracked loudly, rain suddenly coming down hard and fast. "Go inside!" Charles said, and we all ran toward the doors, soaked in just the few seconds it took us to get there. Outside, the rain pummeled the pavement, and lightning streaked across the sky.

Charles had a digital watch with a timer, which he made a big show of setting for sixty minutes. At seven-thirty, he pressed the button, and all the hunters sat down on the floor and covered their eyes. I held onto Gilly's rain-splattered shirt.

Charles cupped his hands over his mouth and let out a loud scream: "Go!"

"Where should we go?" I asked.

"Maybe the dance studio?" he said. I tried to think of where we might hide up there. If the door would even be unlocked. And then I remembered something: Henri's key! I'd gotten distracted when I ran into Gilly and forgot to give it back. With the key, we could hide anywhere in the building. We would win the game. And I might really win Gilly back.

I reached into my pocket and pulled out the key.

Gilly smiled with excitement.

"The roof?" I asked. The mama cat always found plenty of places to hide up there. But it probably wasn't safe in the rain. Lightning could strike us.

He shook his head. "I have a better idea."

Together, we ran, the rubber of our wet sneakers squeaking on the linoleum. When we got inside the elevator, he pressed the button for the basement and said, "Take off your shoes."

I obeyed.

"Leave them here," he said. "Nobody will hear us now. Plus, if somebody finds them, they won't know whether we went up or down. We'll come back for them later."

I nodded and set mine down.

The elevator doors opened to the basement. My heart pattered like that hard rain outside, my body a storm.

It was not so hot down here, at least. It had to be ten degrees cooler than the rest of the building.

As we ran through the hallways, I caught glimpses inside the rooms where sculptors worked on giant projects; Liliana had explained that they had staked out the basement rooms because they were large and mostly uninhabited. The welders and metalworkers worked down here, too. A few musicians, the acoustics replicating a grand music hall.

We passed Raymond's apartment door, which was, thankfully, closed. I couldn't imagine what he would do to us if he found out we'd taken Henri's key. I thought of his paddle and felt sick.

As we ran through the labyrinth, I tried the trick of imprinting our path in my memory. I did this in the city, too, so that I wouldn't get lost. I'd learned to use landmarks to navigate: the dry cleaner, the donut shop, the falafel place. But there were no landmarks here, and the map I'd envisioned soon began to dissolve.

When we heard footsteps echoing around the corner, Gilly pressed his palm against my chest, pushing me toward the wall, and put his fingers to his lips to keep me from crying out. Under his hand, my heart slammed against my ribs.

"Shit," he said. Since hanging out with Ben, he'd started saying things like *shit* and *pissed off* and *hell*. I didn't like it. It felt like he'd been pretending to be somebody else, and now he *was* that somebody else.

The footsteps kept coming, the fluorescent lights above us glaring and bright. There were no shadows to hide in. If a hunter came around the corner, we'd both be caught.

"We need to split up," Gilly whispered. "They can't run in two directions at once."

I started to shake my head but then stopped.

I pictured Gilly standing on the other side of the river, waiting for me to swing across. *Come on, Ryan! You can do it!* I remembered the thrill and fear as the earth slipped out from under my feet, and I was flying over the water, and then the terror that overtook me. The way I refused to relinquish the rope until it was too late, and the hard slam of the riverbank against my back. I recalled the panic as my breath was stolen. Gilly had patted me on the back, said not to worry, that we'd try again, but his voice had been tinged with disappointment.

Standing in that corridor, I knew that if I didn't want to lose him again, I needed to be brave. I needed to stop being the girl who couldn't breathe. The girl who was afraid of everything. I needed to prove to him that I could do what he needed me to do. The reason he hadn't told me about his feelings for Ben was because he was worried I would let him down.

And so, as his eyes pleaded with mine, I nodded. We would separate. I would run as fast and far as I could to hide, and he would run in the opposite direction. We would do this so that we wouldn't both be caught.

"Go to the boiler room," he said. "It's straight down that way. Use the key; I'll come find you."

Again, I nodded silently, words no longer forming in my mouth.

In my stocking feet, I ran down the hallway in the direction he'd pointed, peeking into the doorways along the way, searching for the boiler room. I wasn't even sure what that was, though I was pretty certain it was what delivered heat to the radiators in the apartments. The radiators had frightened me that first winter, the way they howled and hissed and breathed steam.

Finally, I spotted the door and, using the master key, unlocked it. On the other side of the door was a cavernous room, the ceilings an interlocking network of pipes. I saw two brick columns, which I figured must be the bottom of the two large chimneys on the rooftop. There were plenty of places to hide in here, but I wanted to make sure that no one found me, that there was no chance I would let Gilly down; and so, I searched for a place where I wouldn't just be hidden by shadows, but where I could be *enclosed*. The overhead fluorescent lights were bright. I needed to get *inside* something. Suddenly, I thought, I could *win* this game. I could be the only fugitive to escape the hunters. I thought about how proud Gilly would be.

I dropped to my knees and crawled around, looking for some cabinet or cubby or closet where I might tuck myself. When I found the metal door at the base of one of the chimneys, I knew this was it. The perfect hiding space, out of the bright buzzing lights.

I pried the door open and immediately sneezed. The bottom of the chimney was filled with ash, at least two feet of it. I looked back toward the door at the sound of heavy footsteps coming closer and closer. Stifling another sneeze, I covered my face with my T-shirt, and I crawled in.

Normally, I hated being enclosed in tight spaces. Even the elevator sometimes made me feel trapped. But inside the chimney, the ash was soft and cool. Inside, I couldn't hear any noises at all except for the distant whirring sounds of the city, traveling from that rooftop down to my ears. Inside, I was safe from the hunters. I hugged my knees to my chest, waiting for the hour to be up.

My Cinderella watch glowed blue. Eight-thirty. No one had found me! I must have won. I couldn't remember how I had gotten here, and so I figured it would be best to just wait for Gilly, and then he and I would make our triumphant return to the rest of the kids. I could already imagine his hand patting my back, his kind words. *I knew you could do it!*

Nine o'clock. I closed my eyes and listened for Gilly. This *was* the boiler room; this was where he had told me to go, where to wait for him. He would be here soon. I looked at my clock again. Almost nine-thirty. Where was he? I felt like I had been sitting here forever.

Now that I knew I had won, I wasn't afraid to give myself away, so I sneezed a loud, satisfying *Achoo*. At the same time, there was a strange sound, like a vacuum cleaner when you turn it off. A loud sucking sound, and then an odd hush, silence. All the sounds of Westbeth, the humming and breathing sounds of the building, were gone. My ears felt like they were filled with water, with ash. I could hear voices, too—screams, it seemed like, but muffled and far away. I scrambled to the doorway that kept me enclosed in the chimney, and pushed it open to complete darkness. It was disorienting. Was I blind?

I thought of the Audrey Hepburn movie my mother loved, *Wait Until Dark*, about a blind woman terrorized by three men in her own apartment. I felt around in the darkness, but for what? This room was not familiar to me. I didn't even remember where the door was that I had come through; I only knew that I had closed it behind me, though I'd left it unlocked so Gilly could come in.

"Help!" I screamed, my voice threaded with shivery terror, but it fell flat, like throwing a leaf to try to break a window.

I sneezed again and tried to brush the ash off my body, but it clung to me. I had been drenched in rain and sweat when I climbed into the chimney, and now the ash had made a sort of paste all over my skin.

I held my arms out, but it was so dark, I couldn't even see them in front of me. I looked at my watch again, and the blue face and Cinderella's arms appeared, thank god. I wasn't blind.

What had happened? Had Russia sent a bomb to kill us all? Had the building collapsed? I thought of those Japanese Godzilla movies that were always on TV on Sundays, and I wondered if New York had been hit by a giant tidal wave. Maybe, like the subway between Manhattan and Brooklyn, we were submerged.

I couldn't breathe. Was I drowning? Was I going to die? I sneezed again and held up my watch, the weak blue glow an ineffective flashlight. I moved slowly across the room. I figured if I could get to one wall, then I could just walk around the room until I found the door. Maybe there would be light on the other side of the door. But what if there wasn't? What would I open the door to? More darkness? Nuclear fallout? The Hudson River?

I was beginning to cry, even as I found the knob to the door. I shook my head. *Be brave*, I said, and I pushed. The door opened slowly, into a black hole.

M y mother talks in circles, her explanations making me dizzy. Brenner saved *Midway Girl*. My career exploded because of that film, and my mother became exactly what Brenner had told her she was that afternoon at Tavern on the Green: a "good mother." She took on this role as the most important of her life. She rehearsed the lines; she wore the costume.

When reporters attacked, she lashed out. She showed them how wholesome I was. How down to earth and unaffected. We did not move to Los Angeles. We did not buy a big house. A fancy car. I went to public school, took ballet. I didn't have boyfriends or even a driver's license. I was a good girl, and she was a good mother. When she was criticized for being overprotective, hovering, controlling, she wore those digs like badges of honor. And she curated my career, allowing me to take edgy roles, ones that would garner attention and publicity, all the while maintaining the reins on what could have been a wild horse.

The ice in my water has melted. I hear music coming from below us.

It wasn't until later, she said, that the pieces of the puzzle had come together, that she understood exactly what it was that Margie and he were doing. But she learned quickly how to turn a blind eye to Margie's business dealings, except when it came to me.

"You knew?" I ask. "You knew how he was abusing those girls? Some of them were only twelve and thirteen, Mom. *My* age back then."

"Did he ever hurt you?" she says.

"No," I say. "I don't even know him."

"Exactly. I kept you safe."

Wolves do not eat each other. I remember the fairy tale, the one I always skipped over in my favorite book. The wolf who disguised himself as Little Red's kindly grandmother, only to devour the little girl whole.

"I gave him the photo as a thank you, because he saved the film. But it came with the understanding that he would never, ever touch you. Never harm you."

I feel as if I have just walked a thousand miles. Fatigue sets into my body, practically narcotic. I am exhausted. Perhaps I have been running away from this moment for forty years.

"Does *Nick* know about all this?" I ask.

"Of course," she says.

So, she shared all of this with an ex-boyfriend before she shared it with me. My skin prickles with her misplaced priorities. Some things *never, ever* change.

"Why don't you just explain this? To the authorities," I say, baffled as to why she would flee rather than simply argue her case as she has here.

She looks toward the window, but the shades are drawn.

"Mom, what else are you hiding?"

She purses her lips together.

"Mom," I plead, and the voice that comes out is that of a child's.

She sits back in the seat, studies a chunky silver bracelet on her wrist. She still won't look at me.

"You know your father never sent me a dime."

My father? My father is a stick man in a child's drawing. An abstract concept. A shadow of a shadow.

"All those years at Lost River, we just scraped by."

I had never thought about money when we were in Vermont. It was not something we had a lot of, but it didn't seem to matter. We had a home, we ate good food, wanted nothing. In the city, Liliana and Guillermo shared their lives with us. Their home. Their food. Serafina took care of us, too.

"You got paid a pittance for the first two films. Hardly enough to feed us."

And then the understanding hits, like a lightning strike. Illuminating everything.

"Did you take *money* from that man?" I ask, the realization that had been a whisper like a full-throated scream now.

My mother's face is blank; I cannot read her. "We had nothing, Ryan. I had a child to care for. I had no way of knowing the future."

"You took *hush* money?" I asked. "Does the FBI know this? Is this why they're after you? Oh my god, did you *sign* something?"

"I was a good mother," she says, but she's not speaking to me.

I shake my head and start to laugh, but tears are filling my eyes. I stand up and grab my purse.

"I need my photos," I say.

Quietly, she shuffles over to a large antique armoire and opens the doors. Inside is a cardboard portfolio, which she hands to me.

I unwind the string from the clasp to make sure she is not tricking me again. Inside, I see the photos—all of them—that Henri took of me: *Illumination, All Hallows' Eve, Little Fish, Independence Day*. The hundreds of pictures we made. And the very last ones in the pile are the imperfect copies of the one she traded with Zev Brenner. The blackout photo.

I pull out one copy and study it. I touch my own face, trace the tracks that run down my cheeks. I touch the soft flannel of Henri's shirt. I note my exposed breast, the tiniest bud. My hair is wet and tangled. Later, Henri would run his comb gently through my hair until every knot was undone. I am a wound in this photo. I am hurt. *Tristesse.*

My heart aches for Henri.

"Henri is dead. Because of what you did," I say.

She is shaking her head.

"He was a good man. And you destroyed him." I rewind the string around the envelope and tuck it under my arm. "I need to go and get my daughter. We're going home."

I walked into the darkness, barefoot and scared. I tried to conjure the twists and turns I'd taken to get here. Should I go right or left? From which direction had I entered the boiler room?

I just needed to find the elevator to bring me back upstairs. But the only light at all was the weak blue glow of my watch, which now said ten o'clock. My mother was sure to be home by now, and she was probably worried. But Gilly knew where I was; why hadn't they come for me?

I remembered a trip we took when I was little, to the neighbor's farm, where they had made an elaborate maze in their cornfield. I had been afraid to go in, but then Gilly had told me that if you just kept your hand against one wall of a maze, and kept following it, eventually you would get out. I figured that if I never stopped touching the wall, and I just stayed to the right, eventually I would walk the perimeter of the basement and find the elevator.

An odd choking sound, a hiccupy sort of sob, escaped from my throat. I took a deep breath and pressed my hand against the wall and began to walk. It was still so hot, but I felt shivery. I wondered how many miles I would have to walk, if the basement would eventually connect to the subway tunnels. The idea that I was underground, beneath the life that surely buzzed and hummed above me, made my heart race. No. A basement was just the bottom of a building. It wasn't endless. It wasn't a cave.

Still, tears welled up in my eyes and then fell down my cheeks. I didn't even bother wiping them away after a while. I just kept moving, slowly feeling my way, my palms identifying doorways. When I came to a door, I would push it open and use the glow of my watch to see if it led to another hallway or if it was just a room.

I was thirsty, and my lips felt parched. I couldn't remember the last time I had anything to drink. The meat loaf I'd had for dinner sat like a rock in my stomach.

"Help!" I cried out, my voice slipping into the darkness and disappearing. "Help me!"

I kept walking and walking and walking. It wasn't until ten-thirty that I realized I should have marked my starting spot. Like Hansel and Gretel, I should have left a trail of crumbs. How would I know when I'd come all the way around again? The idea that I might be circling endlessly filled me with a new dread. What if I never got out of here? And why weren't the lights on? Did they always go off at night? Maybe if I just waited until morning, the lights would come on, and I could find my way home.

I should never have left the boiler room, I thought. That's where Gilly said he would find me. But now, when he came, I would be gone.

At eleven-thirty, I finally stopped walking and just sat down on the floor. It was hard and cold and unyielding. I wanted nothing more than to be in the nest in Gilly's apartment, my mom curled around me, like two slugs in a rug. If she had come home tonight, I wouldn't be here. I would never have played manhunt. I would be safe at home.

At two a.m., I woke with a start. My hand, which had been curled up under my cheek, was damp with drool, my cheek sticky with wet ash.

In the distance, I could hear something. Footsteps? They sounded like boots, like men. I didn't know whether to be relieved or afraid.

I didn't know whether I was about to be saved or on the edge of something far worse.

I curled my knees up and rocked myself back and forth, imagining myself in the cool dark barn, playing hide-and-seek. The smell of hay and the itch of it on my back. The way the light—god, the beautiful sunlight—filtered through the slats in the roof and striped our summer skin. I dreamed of Lost River, conjured home. Then it struck me that Lost River was the only place where I never felt lost.

"Hello!" a man's voice said. It was deep and hollow and sounded far away. "Hello?"

The echo of boots, and I rose to my feet, my legs pins and needles now.

"I'm here!" I screamed, but my voice sounded small. "I'm here!" I cried out again, and then the sound of footsteps got closer and closer and closer, until I saw flashes of light bouncing off the shiny floor and then flooding me.

"Well, would you look at this," the light said. I squinted into the brightness.

When he lowered the flashlight a little, I could finally make out his security uniform, and then his face.

Raymond.

"You found me!" I managed. "I was lost."

"What are you doing down here?" he said.

"It was just a game," I said; then, the realization dawned on me. I'd used Henri's key. Broken the curfew. I remembered: the *paddle*. I felt dizzy, couldn't get enough air.

"What are you covered in? You look like Little Black Sambo. You know that story?"

I shook my head.

"Well, get up," he said, and reached out his hand.

I shook my head, though everything hurt. My head hurt; my heart hurt. The whole center of me felt like it had collapsed.

"I want my mom," I said, the longing for her deeper than any black hole. My yearning for her was bottomless.

"I'll take you to your mom. But you're going to need to get up first," he said, and beckoned with his hand. Reluctantly, I took it and stood up, though my legs felt useless beneath me.

"Where are your shoes?" he asked.

"In the elevator," I said. They were a brand-new pair of tennis shoes. My mother was going to be so mad.

"Elevators aren't working, sweetheart," he said. "Power's out. The whole city's gone dark."

I tensed. "Is there a war?"

Raymond chuckled. "You'd think so. People out there fighting and looting and setting fires."

"What?" I asked.

"It's a blackout," he explained.

I followed behind, his flashlight illuminating our way.

"Did you talk to my mom?" I asked. "Gilly? Did they send you to look for me?"

But he didn't answer.

Suddenly, we were standing at the door to his apartment near the elevators. I'd been this close all along. I couldn't believe it.

"Come on in here," he said, opening the door and holding it for me.

I shook my head. "I really just need to go find my mom."

"You know this is trespassing, right?" he said.

"What?" I asked.

"You've broken a lot of rules here tonight. Go on, right in there."

Inside, I could make out a kitchen table, a single chair. On the table was a bottle of liquor and a half-empty glass. A burning candle in a tall glass cylinder with Jesus on it.

In the low glow of the candle, I focused on the tag on his uniform. SECURITY.

He was supposed to protect us. That was what Liliana said. Security kept people out of the building. Made sure we were safe. Then why did I feel so afraid?

He went to the sink and grabbed a dish rag, running it under the water. He handed it to me and told me to wash my face off. The water was cold, and the rag smelled like mildew. When my whole face was wet, I handed it back to him.

"You're that one in the magazine ad," he said, pointing at me now as if he were seeing me for the first time. "I seen you before, pretty girl."

The way he said this made my skin feel prickly. I furtively glanced around, looking for the paddle. Wondering how many spankings I would get for this. I thought of the master key in my pocket. What would he do if he found out I had it?

"I'm sorry I broke the curfew," I said. "And the trespassing. I didn't do it on purpose. I was just lost. I promise I won't do it again."

He looked at me and smirked. He sat down at the kitchen table, lifted the bottle, and poured some of the amber liquid into his glass; then he took a long swallow. I watched his throat, and it looked like a snake swallowing a live mouse.

I started to back up. Now that I knew where I was, where the elevator was, I could probably find the stairs.

"Are you going to use the paddle on me?" I asked, figuring if I said it aloud, then I could release the fear somehow.

He laughed so hard, it made his chest rumble and wheeze. As he tried to get his breath again, my legs began to move on their own. I backed up slowly toward the door behind me.

He stood up again, and I felt acid rise in my throat.

"I'll tell you what," he said. "Normally, I catch a kid like you down here where you ain't supposed to be, and I'd give you two or three licks. But you seem like a good girl."

I nodded. I was a good girl.

"I think maybe, I could make an exception for you, if you do me a little tiny favor."

He stood up and moved toward me, and suddenly I recognized the slow sway of his body, like my mother's when she'd had too much to drink. The chemical smell of his breath as he leaned close to me. The glassy look in his eyes when he studied my face.

"I am just going to need one little kiss," he said. "Just a nice little kiss."

I felt dizzy with the smell of his breath, dizzy with his words. I had never kissed anyone before. Why would I kiss this old man?

I backed up again, trying to figure out what to say.

"You're an actress, right? Why don't you pretend this is one of your love scenes?" he slurred. And my vision blurred. I was crying. When did I start crying?

When my back hit the door, and my hip hit the knob, I yelped in pain.

He leaned forward then and put his hands on either side of my shoulders, and his face was so close to mine that I could feel his breath on my cheek.

When his lips met my skin, and the sharp bristles of his cheeks scraped against my neck—when his hands grabbed and pushed—I *left*. Just like I did at the photo shoots, when my body stopped belonging to me. I dreamed myself out of my body, rising upward toward the rooftop, clouds surrounding me.

But when I felt his hand go up my jumper, felt his fingernails grazing my skin, and then jabbing inside of me, I came back, crashing from that world into this one. I remembered my mother telling me once that if any man tried to hurt me, to kick him between the legs. With every bit of strength that I had, I kicked hard, and he folded over. The ragged edge of his nail scraping me, sharp and stinging, as I pulled away. And then, I thought of the way she'd spat at that photo of Robert De Niro, and I spat at him.

I don't remember how I got out of the apartment. Out of the basement. I don't remember anything at all except running, my lungs on fire, and finding the stairwell in the dark and racing up the stairs, the way my footsteps and my breath became one. And I remember that the door I pushed led not to the inside of Westbeth, but to the street. And despite the pattering rain, the street was on fire. Shattered glass and oily smoke. My body, a bruise.

I couldn't move forward, and I couldn't turn back, so I sat down and curled into myself, rocking.

"Ryan?" a voice said, and I scurried backward like a crab.

When I opened my eyes, Jackie-O stood there, hands on her bare knees as she looked down at me.

"You okay, sweetheart?" she asked.

I shook my head. My words were gone. I remembered getting the wind knocked out of me, the way my breath had been stolen. Had I lost my voice?

"You stay right here," she said. "I'll be back in two minutes. Don't go anywhere, okay?"

I nodded, wrapping my arms around my knees. The pavement was hard under my bottom, which burned, and for a single moment, I wondered if the fire had gotten inside of me.

I looked up when I saw Jackie-O's pretty red heels standing in front of me, and a shiny pair of black boots. *No, no, no.* But when I looked up, it wasn't Raymond in his security uniform, but rather, a police officer.

"This here is my friend, Officer O'Grady," she said. "He's going to take care of you, okay, hun?"

Before I could respond, before I could resist, he was squatting down and looking at me, his gentle eyes filled with concern.

"Did something happen to you tonight?"

There were no words for what happened. The only words I had belonged to the clouds; my teacher had us label the illustrations: *cumulus, cirrus, cumulonimbus, stratus.*

"What are you doing out here?"

"We were playing manhunt," I said, surprised by my own voice. "I got lost."

"Does your mother know where you are?" he asked, and the clouds turned dark in my mind. Thunderclouds. A sky the color of bruise. My *body* a plum-colored bruise. Everything hurt.

"Can you stand up?" he asked.

I shook my head.

And then he was lifting me up, scooping me into his arms, as if I were a baby. He smelled like cedar, and his arms cradled me. I buried my head into his shirt.

"Thanks, Billy," Jackie-O cooed.

"Well, it sure is nice to be helping somebody out tonight instead of arresting folks. You live in here?" he asked me, pointing his chin toward the building.

I nodded.

As we entered the building, Officer O'Grady said, "Please tell me you live on the first floor." He was breathing heavily with the effort of carrying me, and I wriggled down out of his arms, willing my jelly legs to hold me up.

I thought about telling him that my apartment was on the ninth floor. But then the realization hit me with a jolt. My mother wasn't home. She had no idea that I'd gotten lost in the boiler room. She was not here, and I knew, with a scary certainty, that she was not upstairs, either.

"I just want to go home. I can go myself."

"Sorry, sweetheart. I need to get your mom to sign off."

"Second floor," I croaked.

On the second floor, I led him to Henri's door, and the officer knocked. When Henri answered, his eyes were wild. Frantic.

"Who are you?" the cop asked.

"*Ryan*," Henri said, and I ran into his arms.

"You her dad?" the cop asked.

My breath caught in my throat.

"She is mine," Henri said.

"Her mom home?" the cop asked, looking over Henri's shoulder into the foyer, and I felt like I might vomit.

"Her mother does not live here." Not exactly a lie, but it didn't keep my heart from feeling like it might explode.

"Mind if I come in?" Officer O'Grady was suddenly not so soft-spoken and gentle anymore.

"Of course," Henri said.

There were candles on every surface, the light flickering, casting shadows. The windows were open, and there was the quiet roar of people outside. Alarms going off; laughter and screaming. The sound of glass shattering.

"Where's your room?" the officer asked, his eyebrow rising skeptically.

"I sleep there," I say, pointing at the velvet couch. Also, not quite a lie. So many times, I had curled up on that couch with Fraidy Cat and fallen asleep, only to be woken by Henri's gentle nudge.

"Where did you say her mother lives?" he asked, but then there was a popping sound, so loud it rattled the windows. It sounded like the shooting gallery under the Wonder Wheel at Coney Island. Every time we passed by that summer, I had pressed my palms against my ears.

The radio at the policeman's hip crackled, a female voice speaking in code.

"*Shit.* Pardon my French," he said, and then headed toward the door. "You sure you're okay?"

I nodded.

He gave Henri a hard look, and then the radio squawked again.

"I'll come back to check on you, honey, okay?" the officer said. "Soon as things calm down out there."

When he was finally gone, Henri got on the phone, and I heard him telling Gilly that they'd found me.

"Is Fiona home yet?" he said softly into the phone. "Well, call me when she gets back."

Henri ushered me into the bathroom, and I looked in the mirror, horrified. Despite the wet rag I'd dragged across my face, I was still filthy with soot and ash.

He leaned over the bathtub and started to run the water. "I'm sorry it is cold," he said. "The hot water has run out." He sat down on the toilet seat and reached for my hands. "You must have been very afraid."

I nodded and searched for the words to tell him what had happened to me. *Nimbostratus, rain clouds.*

"Where's my mom?" I asked.

"I'm sure she is just stuck somewhere," he said.

Stuck. I thought of myself stuck in the basement; in the chimney; in Raymond's apartment, pinned against the door. What if she was stuck in the subway? Or in an elevator? Now that I knew the power was out, I thought of all the disasters that could have befallen her. What if, without streetlights, she'd gotten struck by a car? I thought of Son of Sam, the gunshots. Soon, my shoulders were shaking uncontrollably, and Henri was holding me tight. He didn't even care that I was covered with soot. That my body was made of fire, and when he pulled away from me, filthy ash was all over him.

"Your mother can take care of herself," he said. "And I will take care of you."

He went to the linen cupboard and pulled out two clean towels. He disappeared into the hallway, returning with a soft plaid flannel shirt from his closet. "Can you sleep in this tonight? I can have Gilly bring down some pajamas if you want."

"It's okay," I said.

"Take a nice cool bath. There is shampoo right there," he said, pointing at a little shelf over the tub. "Soap and a clean washcloth."

Blackout, 1977

*H*enri closes the door behind him, and I take off my filthy clothes and step into the tub. The candlelight flickers across the surface of the cool water. I study the red line Raymond's fingernail made that travels from my privates all the way to my belly button. Like a jagged lightning bolt. It burns.

As I slip under the surface and the ash lifts from my skin, as the cool water extinguishes the fire, I dream I am swimming at Lost River.

When the water has turned black, I drain the tub and then run fresh cool water over the lingering ash. I dry off and put on Henri's shirt. I find antibiotic ointment in his medicine cabinet and gently spread it across the red scratch.

When I come out, Henri is sitting at his desk, and he motions for me to sit on the couch. He has brought pillows and soft sheets, made it up like the bed I pretended it was.

"Did my mom call?" I ask, though I already know the answer.

"Not yet," he says.

I lie down on the couch and study the melting wax on the candle burning on the coffee table.

I am clean, but I can still smell the soot from the chimney. In the bathroom, I had blown my nose, and black soot came out into my tissue.

"Why did you lie to the police officer?" I ask, and sneeze again.

Henri looks at me and smiles sadly. "Your *maman*. She should not leave you alone, you know?"

I nod.

"You are still just a little girl."

I nod again.

"She could be in trouble. For leaving you alone."

This thought terrifies me. Could she go to jail? What are the rules? The laws?

"If you were hurt while she was gone?" he says.

It feels like he knows. About Raymond kissing me, his bony fingers, his sharp nails.

"I'm not hurt," I say defiantly. "She loves me." But if this is true, then why does my heart feel so hollow? If I ever had a little girl myself, I would never leave her. I would hold her hand and take care of her and be there every night when she went to sleep. I would stroke her hair and kiss her boo-boos and make sure she had breakfast and lunch and dinner. I would never let a bad man find her and touch her like that.

This is what I am thinking as I stare into that small flame. I am thinking that my mother is an ache. In a bone-deep place. That I miss her. And hate her. And love her all at once. I don't have words, but I do have this. I can show her.

"Can we make a picture?" I ask.

Henri shakes his head.

"Please?"

Henri doesn't notice that the flannel shirt has slipped off my shoulders, or that the light illuminates my bare chest. Henri doesn't see what those photographers saw, what Raymond saw—a woman child, a little girl's body with a grown-up's face. He doesn't see anything but the hurt that clings to me, like ash after a fire.

Click.

New York City
August 2019

Sasha and Gilly are already at Westbeth when I get back from Nick's house in Brooklyn.

"How was MoMA?" I ask brightly, trying hard not to reveal that my heart is shattered.

"Oh, Mom," Sasha says, swooning. "I could be totally happy living here. I think I might apply to Pratt for next year. Or maybe NYU."

Sasha's hair is down today, like Rapunzel's. It reaches her waist. Cutoff jeans and a cropped T-shirt. Gladiator sandals that bind her ankles and calves. I think about her driving across country, this girl. This un-worldly girl. I think of the wolves waiting for her in those woods. I have spent eighteen years ensuring that I never comment on her body, on her clothes, on her attractiveness. I have done everything in my power to focus on her intelligence and curiosity and humor. But it is a futile fight, this battle against a world in which girls are still so often in peril. It was true when I was a girl forty years ago, and it's just as true now. Men are the hunters, and girls are always the hunted.

"That's *great*," I say. "I can't wait to hear all about it. But I'm thinking we should get going. Have you packed up your stuff? Where's Gilly?"

"Down at Henri's apartment, I think?" she says.

"Okay," I say, feeling breathless. "We can stop down there on our way out. Say goodbye. Are Liliana and Joaquin with him?"

"They're in the gallery setting up the chairs. You okay, Mom?"

I nod. "We'll see them on our way out, too." I just want to get out of this building. Out of this city. I want to go home.

I gather all my things, putting the photo portfolio in our suitcase before zipping it up. Sasha goes into the bathroom to pack up her toiletries, and I climb up into the loft and start to strip the mattress, tossing the linens down to the floor.

I hear the door downstairs open and heavy footsteps coming up the stairs.

"Ryan?"

"Hey, Gilly," I say as I shake the pillow out of its case, the empty sham fluttering to the floor.

I climb down. He's pacing, running his hand across his head.

"Gill?" I say. "What's the matter?"

He takes a deep breath, pulls his phone out of his pocket, and holds it out as if it's a steaming pile of shit.

God, what now?

"The fucking *City Gazette*," he says.

The *City Gazette* had always been the most critical of my mother. Their "review" of *Midway Girl* was more like a scathing review of my mother's parenting. She had hidden the copy from me, but I had found it and read it anyway. It was full of lies. About the nude scene in the film, the one where Sadie is attacked by one of her father's fellow carnies. That hadn't even been my body, but rather a woman named Mandy's, who was twenty-five. I wasn't even on set when that scene was shot. That September afternoon, the on-set teacher had taken me to the boardwalk for Italian ice, and then we played games at the penny arcade. When the film was released, and we attended the premiere, my mother had made me cover my eyes during that scene. Though, of course, I knew. I knew everything that happened to Sadie.

"This film is gorgeous," my mother had said to me. "And it's important. What they are saying is ugly, but the work you did was beautiful. Anyone worth their salt can see that."

"Gilly, what is it?"

He clicks and clicks and then scrolls. "Here," he says, and passes me the phone.

The *Gazette*'s headlines are meant to incite. To titillate. I remind myself of this, even as I brace myself.

MOTHER OR MADAM? the headline, in all caps, demands.

I close my eyes and take a deep breath.

Who is Fiona Flannigan? A mother who sold her daughter to the highest bidder.

I quickly scan the article, which reiterates much of what was said in the *Times*'s article, though this one focuses a bit more on my mother, pulling info from her autobiography. About growing up in the small border town of Derby Line, Vermont, where her father was a custodian at the Haskell Opera House. It says that her theatrical aspirations likely began here, and then prompted her—at eighteen—to move to the Lost River Playhouse, where she apprenticed and soon became pregnant and gave birth to me. It details our move to Westbeth and explains that Fiona was a failed actress in the Big Apple. Even though this is true, I feel a pang of hurt for my mother. This would kill her. It does not fit the story she has crafted, the narrative of her sacrifice. "It was here," the article continues, "that the precocious beauty was discovered on the street by modeling agent Margaret Schine, who has now been arrested on multiple charges of sex trafficking and abuse of young girls, along with her colleague, billionaire Zev Brenner. The elder Ms. Flannigan is suspected of conspiring in the sexual abuse of minors by Mr. Brenner and is wanted for questioning by the FBI. We have not been able to reach the younger Ms. Flannigan, currently in the city for the memorial of renowned photographer, Henri Dubois, for comment."

Accompanying the article is a slideshow of photos. *Start Slideshow*

Here, a lurid flashing arrow says. So begins a ten-photo chronological pictorial history of my life. A photo of my mother holding a three-year-old me on her lap at Lost River. My mother looks so beautiful in this photo, long hair and flowing peasant dress. I am wearing a pair of Oshkosh overalls and staring right into the camera. This photo is immediately followed by the Baby Love ad. Next come stills from my films. Me leaning my head against Tony's shoulder as we sit on the beach. The famous photo used on the movie poster of me on the Tilt-A-Whirl ride, eyes closed, hands gripping the bar as it spun. Then photos of my mother and me, arm in arm, at movie premieres and Studio 54. Photos of me in an ad for whiskey at thirteen, on teetering heels and wearing makeup; at fourteen and fifteen, in ads with models nearly twice my age. I click and click. Then I stop.

Number nine is a photo of me from *today*. Me, sitting in the Westbeth courtyard, with my head between my knees. And the last photo? Walking up the steps of Nick's brownstone in Brooklyn, glancing back over my shoulder at the sound of the shutter's *click*. I *was* being followed. The photographer tracked me all the way from Westbeth to Brooklyn. My skin crawls.

"It must have been the guy that Liliana saw," I say. "The one loitering around outside."

"What are you going to do?" Gilly says.

"I'm going to take Sasha home," I say to Gilly. "Just like we planned. This is my mother's mess. Let her deal with it."

"Do you think Fiona has seen this yet?" he asks, waving his phone around.

"I don't know," I say, sighing. "I just know that it's time for Sasha and me to go back to Lost River. She's leaving for LA in *two weeks*. I want to spend time with her before she goes. Coming here was a mistake, Gilly. I should never have come back," I whisper.

Gilly goes to the window.

"Shit," he says.

"What *now*?" I ask.

He waves me over to the window in the back of the apartment, the one that faces the Bank Street courtyard. I know before I look down. There are hundreds of people down there. News vans and journalists. Paparazzi and lookie-loos.

I shake my head. "We'll just go out one of the other exits. West Street. Or Bethune."

"You can't," he says, looking out another window. "We're surrounded."

New York City
July 1977

The lights did not come on the next day. I slept until almost noon on Henri's couch. I heard the faint conversations he had in the foyer: with Guillermo, with Gilly.

"She is fine," he said. "Let's just let her get some sleep."

Gilly brought Fraidy Cat down, and he curled up next to me as I flitted in and out of sleep.

I could still smell the burnt ash. It was as if I'd been in a fire; everything was charred. In a sort of exhausted delirium, I thought of that myth of the phoenix, that bird that burst into flames only to be reborn again and again, rising from the ashes into flight. I *did* feel reborn. As if I had died down there in the basement, only to find my wings again. I dreamed of leaping from the rooftop at Westbeth, soaring over the city, searching for my mother. The futility of it.

She did not come home.

At noon, Henri made me creamy mac and cheese from a box, my request, on the gas burner. I ate the whole potful, realizing I had been starving. He kept bringing me water, as well. It was so hot in the apartment, and my throat was parched.

Outside, the rain had stopped, and the city was still on fire.

It wasn't safe to go outside. Henri explained that with the lights out, people had taken to the streets: smashing shop windows and looting. Setting fires and getting in fights. I thought of the broken glass on the sidewalk, smoky air. "*C'est du chaos*. It is not safe."

"Where is my mother?" I asked, feeling emboldened.

"*Je ne sais pas*," he said.

After lunch, I had told Henri that I wanted to go upstairs to see Gilly. He insisted on coming with me, and I didn't argue. I worried each time we turned a corner that Raymond might be there.

When Guillermo answered the door, I set down Fraidy Cat and rushed into his arms. Gilly came barreling down the stairs, slipping on the last few and almost tumbling down. Gilly hugged me, too.

"I'm sorry I made us split up," he said. "I was about to come back down for you, and then the lights went out, and the elevator stopped working. I didn't have a flashlight, and it took me forever to find the stairs to the basement. By the time I got to the boiler room, you were gone." Gilly's eyes were soft and teary. "I was so worried about you, Ry."

"Go on upstairs, you two," Guillermo said to us. "I'll be right behind you."

Guillermo stayed downstairs, talking to Henri. Their voices were hushed, but I knew they were talking about my mother.

"Is my mom home?" I asked Gilly as we reached the top of the stairs.

Gilly shook his head.

"Has she called?"

"Not yet," he said.

Fraidy Cat was crying, and so I went to the cupboard where we kept his food and got out the can opener. But as I was lifting the lid off, the ragged edge sliced my thumb. Blood bubbled to the surface, and I felt woozy. But oddly, I didn't feel any pain. I studied the slice, the way I had studied the one on my belly.

"Oh, no! Ry!" Gilly said when I held up my hand and looked at him in disbelief.

He rushed to the bathroom and came back with Guillermo's first aid kit. He wrapped my thumb in gauze and said, "Raise it up above your heart."

"Why?" I asked, my thumb throbbing in time with my heartbeat.

"It keeps the blood from flowing to the cut," he said.

"Have you been outside?" I asked as he sat down next to me on the couch.

"No. My dad went out this morning for ice, and he said it's crazy. Nothing is open, and people are vandalizing everything. There were people stuck on the subways and in elevators."

"What happened?" I asked.

"They think it was lightning upstate? I don't know; we just heard a little bit on the radio, but then the batteries died."

All afternoon, Gilly and I played war, eating up the food in the house, the stuff from the fridge swimming in melted ice in a Styrofoam cooler.

We waited for my mother to call. For her to come home. Guillermo had tried calling Nick's house, but nobody answered.

Guillermo said he'd been on his way home from the theater when the lights went out; he'd just gotten off his train. He said it was chaos, madness, as people trampled each other to get up the stairs to the street. He'd arrived at Westbeth and found Gilly with the other kids, upset—saying they couldn't find me anywhere. Guillermo had made sure all the kids got home, and then talked to Raymond, who sent Guillermo back to the apartment to wait, saying he'd bring me up once they found me.

As Guillermo talked, I realized I wasn't breathing. I didn't have the words to explain what Raymond had done. I also worried somehow that if I told, if I shared what he had done to me, then not only would Guillermo feel like it was his fault, but that my mom might be in even more trouble. I also didn't tell Guillermo that the cop had asked where my mom was. Or that I'd lied and told them that Henri was my dad. I couldn't explain why I had said any of that. I'd been so delirious and scared, the whole thing felt like a dream now.

But I also couldn't forget Officer O'Grady's promise to come back to check on me. I hadn't thought about it at the time, but now my stomach twisted at the idea of the police coming back here. About what Henri had said about my mom getting in trouble for leaving me alone.

The power still wasn't on at eight p.m. when the sun began to set again. My mother was still gone.

Guillermo had gone out earlier to try to track down something for us to eat. The food in the fridge had started to go bad, and the cupboards were empty. Mrs. Lake gave him a loaf of bread and some peanut butter and jelly, and we made sandwiches.

Every time the phone rang, my nerves were jarred, and I would strain to hear the conversation, trying to fill in the blanks of whatever the caller was saying based on Guillermo's responses.

"Nope. Still not here. She's okay. Kids are resilient . . . Thanks again for last night. I really appreciate it. If you're hungry, come on up. We have PB and J."

Henri.

"Brooklyn? Is that where he lives?" He was talking about Nick now. "Yeah. I called the number. No answer. Anybody know the address?"

I realized that if I could figure out Nick's address, then maybe Guillermo could go there to find my mom. But how? The bus was in Jersey. The subways weren't running.

That would explain why she hadn't come home, at least. I just needed to be patient. She always came home. Always.

I went to bed that night, and I heard Guillermo talking on the phone in a low voice. I quietly leaned over the edge of the loft bed and listened. He was talking to Liliana in Lost River.

"We're okay," he said softly. "Thank god, the police found her. She was terrified. Alone down there in the dark for hours."

There was a long silence, and I thought maybe he'd hung up.

Finally, softly, he responded. "This is *bullshit*, Lil, what she's doing. I know you love her like a sister, but this is neglect. What if something had happened to Ry last night? God forbid, what if they hadn't found her? She wouldn't even *know*."

I thought about everything they didn't know. That I could never tell them.

For a few moments, there was just the quiet sound of Guillermo shuffling about the kitchen.

"Okay. If you hear anything, ask her to please call and check in on her kid. For Christ's sakes. She owes her that much."

I cried silently, my tears soaking my pillow. It was so hot, I couldn't stand anything touching my skin. It was also loud outside: sirens and screaming and blasts from bullhorns.

When the lights buzzed on, I sat up. The entire world seemed to be cheering and whooping. I scurried down out of the loft, and Guillermo, Gilly, and I embraced, dancing around the room. We all ran downstairs and threw open the doors. People were flooding into the hallway in their bathrobes and pajamas, cheering. Music poured out of open apartments. Outside, it was as if a war had ended. Horns honked, and people cheered. The streetlights were on again, and the city was awash in light.

But still, my mother was not home.

It was another hour before I climbed back up into the loft and closed my eyes. I fell asleep as the celebration raged on outside.

In the morning, I awoke to the sound of Guillermo talking to someone in the kitchen. A woman. My heart swung open like a door, and I cried out "Mama!" involuntarily, my body scrambling down the ladder from the loft. But it wasn't my mother standing in the kitchen; instead, it was a lady police officer. She smiled broadly at me, as if she knew me, and said, "You must be Ryan!"

I held my breath.

And I thought, *this is it*. This woman has come to tell me that my mother is dead. Suffocated in the subway, or drowned in the river, or shot in the head by the Son of Sam. I felt every inch of my skin prickly and dizzy, as if the world were spinning like the Tilt-A-Whirl ride at Coney Island. I grabbed onto the edge of the table with one hand and used the other to catch the vomit before it escaped my lips.

The lady's arm was across my back, and she steered me toward the bathroom, where I threw up the peanut-butter sandwiches from the night before. She rubbed my back in slow circles, but this only made it worse. I imagined she was somebody's mother. That this was something she did when her own little girl was sick.

Finally, I sat down on the closed toilet lid, and she handed me a wet washcloth, which I pressed against my head.

"What happened here?" she asked, touching the bandage on my hand.

"Just a cut. On a cat-food can. It's okay."

The bandage was dirty, though, spots of blood having seeped through.

"Can you tell me the last time you saw your mom?" she asked.

My lip trembled, and my hands shook.

"In the morning, on the day of the blackout," I said.

"Your father told the officers that your mother doesn't live here? Did she come for a visit?"

I shook my head. "He said she doesn't live *there*, at his apartment. She lives here. With me. And Henri's not my dad. He's my friend."

"Oh," the lady said, her eyebrow raised. "Well, we're just trying to complete our report. Any time there's a child endangered, we need to follow up with the child's parents. Officer O'Grady was really worried about you; he said you were crying for your mom. It must have been very scary to be all alone like that."

I realized that she didn't know where my mother was, either. She was here because of what Guillermo said. *Neglect*. Mothers weren't supposed to leave their children alone. Weren't supposed to let people hurt them.

"It was just a game," I said. "Manhunt. All the kids play it. I won."
Her mouth smiled, but her eyes didn't.

"So your mom hasn't been home since the morning of the black-out?" she asked, consulting her notepad, as if I hadn't just said this.

"No," I said, wondering if she could hear my heart, because I could. It filled my ears with its drumbeat. "That's not what I meant. I meant that's the last time I saw her before I got lost."

"Oh," she said, looking at me, wary. "So, she came to get you from downstairs that night? To pick you up from your *friend's*?"

I nodded. I thought about the feeling of that cool bathwater enclosing me, the flannel shirt enclosing me, Henri's concern and love enclosing me. I thought about the flickering flame of the candle, the slow-melting wax. About how I still just wanted my mother. I thought about the ache I felt right before Henri clicked the shutter and took my photo, capturing my pain in that photograph.

"She got home late because the subway was shut down. She had to walk all the way home. But then she came and got me. She was here all day today. We played war." The lies cartwheeled out of my mouth.

"Where is she now?" she asked.

"She has an audition," I blurted. "She's an actress."

The police officer flipped her notepad to a blank page. She scribbled something on it and tore the page out. She squatted down then, so she was looking me right in the eyes.

"You are a very lucky little girl."

Her words felt like a bite. I thought of what happened in the basement and didn't feel lucky at all.

Tears spilled out of my eyes, despite my best efforts at keeping them inside. She pressed the paper into my hand. She had written her name, Officer Leslie, and her phone number. "You call me anytime you need help. You got that?"

I wiped at the tears and jutted my chin out.

"My mom will be home any minute," I said. "But thank you for checking on me. I won't need this." I handed the paper back to her.

She frowned and shook her head, refusing to take it. Then she stood up and opened the bathroom door.

In the kitchen, as if I'd conjured her, my mother was sitting at the table with Guillermo. She popped up as we came out, her face ashen.

"Mama," I said, running to her, clinging to her as if I were five instead of eleven.

"Hey, baby," she said.

"How was your *audition*?" I asked. Trying to communicate how important it was that she went along.

She looked at me and then at Officer Leslie.

"Oh! It was *amazing*," she said with a smile and a hard squeeze of my wrist. "I think I got the part."

That night, Guillermo and Gilly went to the living room to watch the Yankees vs. Kansas City Royals game. I climbed up into the loft with a book. From up there, I could hear the muffled sound of the game, a sound I fell asleep to many nights. The Yankees were on a roll that summer, and Guillermo was a huge fan. But I could also hear my mother in the kitchen, talking to Liliana over the phone.

"So, Nick and I had decided to try to get into Studio Fifty-Four to go dancing, but the line was too long. We were just dying of the heat and wanted a cold drink," my mother said. "So Nick took me to this club on Forty-Third Street, Jouissance? It used to be Le Jardin. A discotheque. They had real palm trees and hammocks inside. Beautiful people. Celebrities *everywhere*. But much more intimate than Studio Fifty-Four and those other warehouse-style discos. It was early, so we had the dance floor to ourselves."

As she spoke, I petted Fraidy Cat, who had climbed up to be with me in the loft.

"So anyway, we were sitting with this other couple," she said. "And they told us that over at the *Daily News*, they were filming the *Superman* movie. With Christopher Reeve? That dreamy guy on *Love of Life*? He plays Ben."

Silence.

"Yes! Him. And suddenly, the guy we were with suggested we go down to Forty-Second Street and watch them filming. It was still early, only about nine o'clock, so we figured why not?"

I remembered the blue glow of my watch. At nine o'clock, I had been curled up in the ash pile in the basement, heart pounding.

Fraidy Cat purred.

"There were hundreds of people outside; it was just so hot. Even with the rain," she continued. "And then! Oh my god, it doesn't even feel real," she gushed. "Some person with the film comes up and asks us if we want to actually be in the crowd scene. So of course, we said *yes*. They gathered us all together, and we had to look up and pretend that we were looking at a helicopter overhead. I guess Lois Lane is supposed to be dangling from it. Nick and I were right there, in front. But then, all of a sudden, we were in complete darkness. I can't even describe it. It was like the whole world went blind."

I thought about the moment I'd crawled out of the ashes, terrified that I'd lost my vision.

"But the show must go on, as they say. The *Daily News* had a generator, and so they hooked it up to the crew's lights so they could keep filming. They even gave each of us extras fifty bucks!"

She was quiet then for a while as Liliana spoke.

"I was getting to that," she said, a tinge of something in her voice. "So, we were going to try to go back to Westbeth. But it was madness. People were smashing windows, looting shops. Police were everywhere, trying to keep things under control. It was crazy. We just needed to get somewhere safe, out of the city, so we decided to walk to Nick's place." She paused. "Yes, in Brooklyn."

She went on to describe the two-and-a-half-hour walk down to the Brooklyn Bridge. The throngs of people moving together. People directing traffic in the dark. The view of the city behind them, on fire, as they got to the other side.

I squeezed my eyes shut, but when I did, I could feel Raymond's hot breath on my neck, his fingers on me. Inside me. I shook my head.

"When we finally got there, we were exhausted. And so sweaty. I swear, my dress was completely drenched. I called the apartment to let everyone know where I was, but nobody answered."

A few moments.

"No. I didn't call Henri. Why would she have been at Henri's?" she asked. "It was her bedtime. She knew she was supposed to be in bed at nine o'clock. I told her that under no circumstances when I was gone was she to leave the apartment. But with Guillermo gone, apparently, she and Gilly decided it was okay to play in the basement."

My eyes stung. She was blaming this on Gilly? On me?

"Yesterday?" she asked. "Oh, you know. The power had come back on. Also, Guillermo had Nick's number. I figured if anything was wrong, he would have called. How was I supposed to know the freaking cops were going to come? My god. Seriously. The city is literally burning, and they're worried about a game of hide-and-seek."

"Manhunt," I said, and then bit my tongue.

"No, everything's fine. I explained, and they left. Clearly, it was a mistake. I think we need to have a sit-down with the kids. Lay down some ground rules about what is acceptable and what is not. I just wanted to check before I talked to Gilly. Didn't want to overstep my bounds."

Silence.

"That's exactly what I was thinking, too. They're old enough to know better."

When she hung up, I heard her opening the cupboard and the sound of something being poured into a glass, probably wine. Then her footsteps across the floor and into the living room, where she said, "So who's winning?"

New York City
August 2019

I look out the window and see the crowds gathered below. There's no way we'll get past them.

"Mom?" Sasha says, as she comes out of the bathroom.

"Hi baby," I say, and force a smile. "Almost ready to head home?"

She's holding her phone. *Damn it.* I must have been a fool to think that I could keep this from her for even a second.

"Mama," she says. "Why didn't you tell me any of this? She's a suspect? The *FBI*?" Her face is open and hurt.

"It all looks much worse than it is. Because she and Margie were friends. I'm sure she'll get it straightened out. Her lawyers will help her figure it out."

I think about Fiona, hiding in the attic of Nick's apartment. The things she told me. Her complicity.

"You went to see her today?" she asks, looking at me with something like pity in her eyes.

I nod.

"Mom," she says. "Maybe she *deserves* to go to jail."

I am stunned by the anger threaded through her words.

"What kind of mother does something like that? Those photos of you, the movies. How could she let them *sexualize* you like that? You were just a little girl."

I smile sadly. I have raised her to be a feminist. To feel empowered by her intellect. I have taught her that a woman's body is merely

SUCH A PRETTY GIRL

a vehicle for all that it carries: humor, compassion, empathy, and grace. But those lessons feel meaningless as she looks at the photos of me as a child, dressed like a whore. Someone who could sell their own daughter out would have no problem turning a blind eye to the other girls. My mother could be bought. It doesn't even matter if she's telling the truth and had nothing to do with Margie and Zev Brenner's scheme. That she was merely guilty of keeping their secret, of accepting a payment for her silence. The journalists, with their sharp words, are right. She was a monster.

"Mama," Sasha says. "She's your *mom*. She was supposed to protect you."

My phone buzzes. An unfamiliar number. I worry that it will be one of those reporters; the feeding frenzy has clearly begun. Still, something compels me to answer.

"Ryan," she says.

"Mom?"

"I can't believe you'd betray me like this. After everything."

"What are you talking about? I didn't do anything."

Her voice is panicked, desperate. "You led them right to my doorstep, Ryan. The photo they printed, it shows Nick's *address*."

I grab Sasha's phone and study the picture. There it is. They're going to find her. It won't take long now.

"I really need to go, Mom," I say.

Sasha is holding my free hand, squeezing it.

My mother is quiet on the other end of the line. "I need you to bring me to Lost River with you. They won't expect me to be there. They all think you'd *love* to see me fry. They think you hate me."

The ancient feeling rises, the pain and anguish and hurt that has been living somewhere beneath my heart. The dam I have built to keep it back is cracking, and there is nothing I can do to keep it from tearing through, flooding me with so much sorrow. The sob that escapes me is not a sound I ever wanted my child to hear. The keening of a wounded animal.

New York City
Fall 1977

After the blackout, my mother and Nick broke up. I wouldn't have known except that my mother stopped going out at night. She was restless but not sad. A nervous bundle of energy. She took the stairs at Westbeth rather than the elevators, and always seemed to be breathless. But she was happy, and she was home. That was all I had wanted.

They'd also finally caught Son of Sam, at his apartment in Yonkers. I studied his photo in the paper. I couldn't make sense of the fact that this normal-looking man, David Berkowitz, had managed to terrorize an entire city for over a year. He didn't look like a monster; he looked like the guy who worked at the bodega down the street. I found that terrifying and felt more afraid than I had when he was on the loose. If a monster could look like this, then there could be monsters all around us.

I avoided Raymond and never went anywhere in the building alone. I was so glad when Mr. Moretti finally called and said that we would be finishing up the film. We returned to Coney Island in late August for the final three weeks of shooting. This time, we stayed at a much nicer hotel on the boardwalk, though I felt a little sad each time we walked past the Terminal Hotel, where the rest of the cast stayed. We still met them at night for dinner at Meng's, but I could tell they were a little put out that my mom and I were not sharing a bathroom with a bunch of strangers, like they were. Only Tony acted as though nothing had changed.

"I can't believe we're really going to get this flick made," he said, our first day back on set. "I kept telling my wife that it would be a damn shame if we didn't get to tell this story. You're one fine actress, Ryan."

I'd forgotten, in the brief time we were back in the city, how much I enjoyed being on set. How much I loved slipping into the imaginary world of *Midway Girl*. How much I loved being Sadie.

We only had a few scenes left to shoot. The first was the one right before Sadie was attacked by Kurt, the carny who operated the Tilt-A-Whirl. That scene was shot in the little apartment where Sadie and her dad lived. That night, Sadie and her father got in an argument. He didn't like that she'd been flirting with Kurt. He said Kurt was bad news: a former convict at Sing Sing. But Tony was a single dad. He couldn't keep his eye on her all the time. He was working two jobs: his day job at the amusement park, and his night job driving a taxi. He had rules to keep her safe. She was not to leave the apartment after the sun went down. She was not to talk to men like Kurt. She was not to talk to any boys. Period. She was to use the telephone and call the dispatch center if she ever found herself feeling unsafe. They had a secret code. If she was ever in trouble, she was to say, "Can you tell my dad he needs to bring home cannoli?" When the dispatcher relayed the message, he would know to come right home. Each night, he'd kiss her goodbye before his shift and say, "No cannoli tonight."

One weekend, Tony had even brought me some cannoli his wife made so I would know what Sadie and her dad were talking about. A crisp golden pastry stuffed with sweet creamy ricotta filling with little chocolate chips, it was one of the most delicious things I'd ever tasted.

In the apartment, Sadie's dad confronted her. Someone had seen her talking to the Tilt-A-Whirl guy again. He was furious. She yelled at him that she was not a baby, and that this life wasn't normal. She wanted to live in a real house; she wanted a dog, siblings, a *mom*. At this, he went silent. His wife had walked out on them when Sadie wasn't even a year old. Her words hurt him. But she didn't care.

"Well, you're welcome to go find her, then," he said. "I'm sure she'll be real happy to see you." Then he left. He didn't say *No cannoli tonight*. He didn't give her a kiss on her head.

Angry, she got dressed, in the shorts and tube top that Kurt said he liked, and went to the Midway. He let her ride the Tilt-A-Whirl for free and gave her money to go buy cotton candy. But then when he got a break, he took her with him to the funhouse, said that because he worked for the park, he got to go on all the rides for free. But inside the funhouse, he attacked her.

Because I wasn't in the scene of the attack—Mandy, my body double, stepping in for me—Mr. Moretti had to explain everything that happened to Sadie. He didn't go into detail, only that her dad was right about Kurt. That he was a violent man, and that he hurt Sadie and left her cowering in the hall of mirrors when he was done, looking at her own reflection, the reflection of her reflection. When we filmed this scene, I thought about the shattered glass on the street where Jackie-O found me after I'd gotten away from Raymond during the blackout, my reflection in the mirror before I slipped into the cool water in Henri's tub.

We spent a full day shooting the scene where I returned to the apartment after the attack, staggering down the boardwalk, my clothes torn. Cotton candy in my tangled hair. Using the key I kept on a ribbon around my neck to go inside and finding my father there, on the phone with the police, out of his mind with worry. Him, hanging up the phone and embracing me, and then dropping to his knees to apologize, saying, *"La mia bambina."* My little girl.

In this scene, I had to be angry and sad all at once. It was easy. I just dreamed myself back into that boiler room in the basement at Westbeth. I thought of Officer O'Grady, who had taken me upstairs to Henri's apartment. And the kindness Henri showed me as he ran the bathwater and then offered me his soft flannel shirt. I remembered exactly how I had felt when the shutter on his camera clicked. Somehow both safe and in danger. Both loved and ignored. How my love for Henri was so big, it felt almost swollen inside me, while my love for my mother felt like the love you have for the stars. For something you can never really have. A longing for something beautiful but too far away, untouchable.

My mother became Sadie's mother, a shadow. A flickering star. I'd learned at school that the stars we see in the sky are more than ten thousand light-years away, and so that starlight we see left the star ten thousand years ago. Starlight is only the memory of a star. This is what I thought of in that scene. Of a girl mistaking the bright shimmering light she thought of as her mother as something real.

New York City
August 2019

Outside, the crowd is oddly peaceful. We watch as they continue to gather: the news ladies with their hair spray and hose, the male reporters with their clean white shirts and teeth. And the paparazzi, too, their cameras like weapons slung across their shoulders. I can't tell if they are waiting for me to leave or for my mother to arrive. One thing is clear: There is no way I am going to get out of the building unnoticed.

I had gathered myself together, assured Sasha I was okay, just worried about my mother. Then I sent her downstairs to the gallery with Liliana. Now Gilly and I are in the apartment alone.

"Stay for the memorial," Gilly pleads. "It's why you came. Security is going to keep them out. They'll get bored eventually and go home."

"She wants to come to Lost River," I say.

"What?"

"She's hiding out in Nick's attic in Brooklyn. The paparazzi photo shows the house number; it's just a matter of time before they find her. She wants me to bring her to Lost River."

"Jesus Christ," Gilly says.

The enormity of this hits me. My mother has done something terrible, something that has put not one, but hundreds, if not *thousands,* of little girls in harm's way. In Brenner's way. Her complicity is egregious and selfish and awful. Now, she is running away, just like she has always run away. My mother has been a fugitive for most of my life. This realization fills me with anger, but then the anger is swallowed by sorrow.

"What do I do, Gilly?" I ask. "She says she wasn't involved. She knew what was going on, but it's not like she brought the girls to him herself. Margie was the mastermind. My mother just looked the other way." I swallow hard. "She accepted money for keeping quiet."

"That's called *conspiracy*," Gilly says. "And if she's not cooperating, that's *obstruction*. These are the *feds*. She could go to prison."

It feels unreal, as if he is talking about a movie he saw or a podcast he listened to.

"What would you do?" I ask him. "If this was your mom?"

"Liliana?" he says in disbelief. "It would never be Liliana."

He's right. His mother would never have found herself in this situation, and if she had, she would have told someone. She would have gone to the police. She would have protected those girls, not taken his filthy money to shut her eyes to it.

"She said Brenner is the one who saved the film. *Midway Girl*. That he invested. She gave him the photo as a *thank you*."

"And the inscription?"

"It was an understanding. That he would never hurt me. She said she was protecting me."

Gilly takes my hand and seems to study it, tracing the scar from the cut I got from the can of cat food with his thumb. He's never known about the other scar I got during the blackout.

"Ry," he says, his face filled with pity, and he doesn't have to say anything more, because I know what he is thinking. That my mother didn't protect anyone but herself.

I remember the way my mother looked that night. Forty years later, it is her I recall. She wore a white silk halter dress that spilled down her body, her bare, sharp shoulders sprinkled with sparkling gold dust. Gold earrings and strappy gold sandals to match. I remember sitting in the back of the limousine in my own white dress, though mine had a high collar and long sleeves, and it was itchy and hot. My mother's hair was done in an elaborate updo, but mine fell loose, with just a simple set of sparkly barrettes holding it out of my face. I remember her playing with the diamond bracelet on her tiny wrist: one we'd spied through glass at Tiffany's, when we first got to the city. It had appeared as if by magic tonight.

The nominations were a surprise to everyone. Best Director for Mr. Moretti. Best Actor for Tony. Up against Robert De Niro himself. My mother had delighted in that, though she grumbled that it would have been nice if there was a Best Supporting Actress nomination for me. "Next time," Susan had said when we met with her in her office. She was already getting bombarded with scripts, she said.

We'd flown to Los Angeles for the weekend to join the rest of the cast. No Terminal Hotel this time, either. This was the fanciest place I'd ever been. The soaps were shaped like seashells, and with a simple phone call, we could order anything we liked from the room service menu.

We arrived on Saturday morning and would stay through Wednesday, when we'd return to New York. Susan had arranged for a half dozen meetings with Hollywood casting agents. She said that *Midway Girl* being acknowledged by the Academy meant everything was about to change for me. Margie had a full week of appointments set up for when I returned. There was an up-and-coming designer looking for a fresh face for his ad campaign. She'd told him to go watch *Midway Girl* and he'd come back "obsessed," though that word made me feel prickly.

My shoes gave me blisters. I had wanted to wear heels like my mother, but she'd said that they'd make me too tall, and insisted I wear a modest pair of ballet flats instead. But the leather bit angrily into my heels, and I was grateful that my dress was floor-length, because I was able to slip them off during the awards.

I watched my mother scanning the audience, and every time she spotted a new movie star, she would pinch me and whisper. *That's Jane Fonda! Ingrid Bergman. Oh my god, that's Sir Laurence Olivier.* She might have just spied Jesus Christ himself.

I was jet-lagged, and so my body was ahead by three hours. I found myself stifling yawns throughout the whole show. At one point, I caught a photographer snapping a photo just as I was pressing my fingers against my lips to try to keep the yawn in. He winked at me, and I felt my face flush red.

I was sitting next to Tony, who leaned over and said, "I'm pooped, too. Wake me up if I start to nod off?"

When Audrey Hepburn walked onto the stage in her burgundy gown to present an honorary award, my mother gripped my fingers so hard my bones ached. There was no way I could fall asleep now.

Best Director and Best Actor were some of the last awards announced before the Best Picture award. Luckily, I got some sort of second wind. Or maybe I just could feel the excitement in our row as Johnny Carson introduced Ali MacGraw and Francis Coppola, who would be announcing Best Director. I leaned over so I could look down our row at Mr. Moretti, who smiled and gave me a thumbs-up. They named the nominees, and when they announced *The Deer Hunter*, I felt my mother stiffen. When Michael Cimino won for Robert De Niro's film, she let out a long, slow breath from her nose. I whispered, "It's okay, Mama." I don't know why she was still mad. We'd made the movie without him, and here we were.

Ginger Rogers and Diana Ross announced the winner of Best Actor, and we all sighed with disappointment when Tony didn't win. But he just smiled and squeezed my hand. "We had fun, though, didn't we?"

I nodded.

The Best Picture announcement was a blur. John Wayne, from those old cowboy movies, was the presenter, and when he walked slowly down the staircase on the stage, everyone stood up. I had to slip my shoes on underneath my gown.

"And the winner is . . . *The Deer Hunter.*"

When *The Deer Hunter* cast made their way to the stage to accept the award, Robert De Niro walked right past us, and I could practically feel my mother's rage simmering in her skin. It filled me with a familiar unease, a sort of electricity.

Here we were, at the Oscars. In Hollywood. A place she'd only ever dreamed of, and it still wasn't enough.

I was feeling sour and angry as we left the theater that night, taking the limousine to some party, where people fawned over me and asked me questions about what it was like to work with Mr. Moretti and when they could expect my next film. I was sullen and exhausted as my mother turned on her charm, as if there were a switch that illuminated her from the inside. I, however, found a spot on a lovely sofa, slipped off my shoes, and curled my knees up. As the crowd swirled around me in a cloud of champagne bubbles and diamonds and heady perfume, my eyelids grew heavy, and soon I was slipping away.

"Ryan," my mother said sweetly. She was squatting down, gently shaking my shoulder. For a moment, I thought I was in the cabin back at Lost River. When I opened my eyes, I expected to see the sunlight streaming through the window, to feel the warm body of one of my cats. I could feel my heavy patchwork quilt covering my body. But when I came to, I realized someone had draped their fur coat over me.

I sat up, rubbing my eyes. I heard cameras clicking as my mother reached for my hand and helped me up.

"Ryan, honey," she said. "I want you to meet someone."

There was a man standing with her, and his arm was draped over the shoulder of a girl I recognized as one of Margie's models. A girl named Hannah I had done a shoot with after we got back from Coney Island. She was not too much older than me. Maybe sixteen? I wondered if this was her dad.

I reached out my hand to him, the way I had at least a hundred times that night. But instead of shaking it, he bent over and kissed it.

"It's really uncanny," he said, shaking his head. "You two could be sisters."

My mother swatted at his arm and flushed pink.

"You," he said, pointing at me, his gaze fixed on my face, "are such a pretty girl. Just *magic*. Best investment I've made in years."

My mother lowered her voice and said, "Mr. Brenner is the one who gave us the funding so we could finish the film."

"Oh," I said. "Thanks."

Camera bulbs went off, and I stifled another yawn.

"You should get her back to the hotel to get some sleep," he said to my mother. "And I'll see you back in the city?"

"Yes. Terrific," she said.

He leaned over and kissed her cheek, slung his arm across Hannah's shoulders again, and walked away.

The photo that appeared in the papers the next morning was of me asleep on the bench at the party, my hands resting under my cheek. *Even angels need sleep*, one caption said.

New York City
August 2019

This is why we came to New York, I remind myself. For Henri. To honor his memory. To say goodbye. And as we find our seats in the row of folding chairs in the gallery, and we are surrounded by his friends, his Westbeth family, by his art, a wave of grief rolls through me.

It has been a long time since I lost someone. I have forgotten the cruelty of it. The way grief feels like music: a soft melancholy melody building to a heartbreaking crescendo. It is deafening, too loud, overwhelming.

I close my eyes and try to breathe slowly.

I feel Gilly's hand enclosing mine in my lap. Sasha leans against my shoulder. I turn and kiss her, smelling the green apple scent of her hair. It recalls a thousand baths, a thousand times she sat on the floor before me as I spritzed her hair with detangler and gently coaxed a comb through her curls. The grief I am feeling over Henri conflates with the grief I am feeling about Sasha leaving. About her childhood. About the little girl she was. And the little girl that *I* was.

Breathe.

Henri's neighbors stand up and tell their stories about Henri, and as I listen, I am astonished that he meant so much to so many people. I knew his art meant the world to many people, that the images he made would live on long after he was gone. That is why we make art, after all; even me. Those films I made so long ago, the ones I can barely watch anymore, are my legacy. My mother's autobiography, her paintings. Her inclination was always to leave something behind. Everyone in this room knows this. That art and memories are human beings' only true bequests.

I remember the afternoon Henri and I stood together in the darkroom. It had been a week since the blackout; that night spent in the basement felt like a dream. A dream of a dream. My mother had diminished it, as she did so many things, making me wonder if I had made it larger in my mind than it actually was. "You weren't *lost*," she had said with a chuckle. "You never left Westbeth." She didn't know that I had floated above the clouds, above the rooftop, the city completely dark below me. Like Superman.

The hours that I had sat in the ashes, and the hours that I waited to be found, and the hours that I worried I might never see the light of day again, became minutes as she retold the story. The day after, when she didn't come home, disappeared in her retelling. In her version of events, she walked back across the Brooklyn Bridge the next day, through the wreckage of a city on fire, like a mother separated from her child during an act of war. "There was nothing but rubble," she said. "People had turned into animals, scavengers."

As she spun her web, the shimmery filaments of her new truth, I imagined her, holding her high heels by the straps, walking barefoot across the shattered glass to find me. I imagined her trying to hail a taxi to bring her home to me, but none of them stopping. She told me she had never been separated from me for so long. Since the day I was born, we had never spent a night apart. That I was a *part* of her. She said that as she walked through the rubble to get home to me, she felt the pain of someone who had lost a limb. She told me that when she found me at home, she made a vow that she would never leave me again. That she would always be there to protect me.

But as the image emerged from the paper, I realized that this photo was the only evidence I had. The girl in the photo, wet hair and a man's shirt, was wide-eyed with fear. With a sadness so deep, just looking at her hurt. This motherless girl.

I remember studying the image from the blue stool in Henri's darkroom.

My god, Henri had said as he lifted the paper from the stop bath and clipped it to the wire strung across the wall like a clothesline. I had nodded. We knew it was dangerous. But not for the reasons one might think. Not for the reason that my mother offered the photo to Zev Brenner. She could never see herself in this photo. She could never see this as a photo of her damage. She was incapable of hearing the secret this photograph told.

It was then that Henri had asked me—again—what had happened in the basement. He knew; it was written all over that photograph. My secret. And so, I stood on my tiptoes in the darkroom and whispered to him everything.

By the time we got back from Coney Island in September, Raymond was gone. The kids said he got fired for being drunk on the job. But I knew that Henri was responsible. "You're safe here now," he said to me. "He won't ever hurt you again."

Gilly nudges me. "Do you want to go up and say something?" he whispers.

There is rustling around me. People are waiting for me to speak. Sasha looks at me expectantly.

I have prepared nothing. I'd thought that I would be on my way back to Lost River by now, retreating as I retreated so many years ago to the place *before*. Before the city. Before the movies. Before my mother left me.

Still, I rise. Despite myself, I stand and walk to the podium.

I look out at the expectant faces, the people who loved and were loved by Henri. What can I offer them now that will act as a levee for the surge of sorrow each of them feels? What can I do to keep my own dam from breaking?

Strangely, I am transported back to the set of *Midway Girl*. It was an early scene that was shot before we ran out of money and were sent home, a scene between Sadie and her father as he put her to bed at night, before locking her inside the house and going to his job driving the taxi. When we watched the premiere, I remember feeling my throat close when I saw the scene. Tony leaning over me, torn between staying and protecting Sadie and going out to make a living. The anguish of the decision is threaded through his words. But Sadie is oblivious.

"Love you, Daddy," she says. "More than ice cream."

"More than whipped cream," he says.

"More than nuts." She giggles.

"More than cherries on top. Listen," he says, his voice breaking, "no cannoli tonight." And then the lights go out, leaving the room in complete darkness, and we hear only his footsteps and then the loud crack of the deadbolt sliding into the lock. It made me jump every time I saw the film.

"Henri was like a father to me," I say to the crowd. "He took care of me. He loved me. He protected me." I keep talking, but my words feel like smoke.

Henri did not want to leave me in the dark place that was life with my mother, but what were his options? He could only tuck me in tight, and lock the door.

Young Dancer, 1981

*B*allet class is the one place where I am in complete control. Every muscle in my body. Every joint. The hush, hush of my slippered feet in a rond de jambe, the precision of bone. Acting is a collaborative project: so many people involved; the actress is just one tiny cog in a giant machine. But ballet is solitary. There is no one but myself to depend on or to blame.

I live for my Saturday classes. Even at fifteen, I'm too tall to be a professional dancer. I'll never perform at Lincoln Center, my mother says. But performance is not why I love to dance. It is the opposite. I love how inward ballet makes me feel. How I am never more inside myself than when I'm doing a combination at the barre.

The other girls in my class have aspirations. They are so hungry: starving for the teacher's attention, for corrections, for love. Ballet, for them, is about denial. Refusing the body's needs in pursuit of some elusive thing. My mother should have been a dancer, I think. I see her need in these girls' eyes. I feel her yearning in their eager giggles after class, in their every breath.

But ballet, for me, is freedom. Joy. And so, after class, while they huddle together outside the studio, smoking cigarettes to squash their appetites, I walk the three blocks to Disco Donut, where I order two jelly donuts (one raspberry, one lemon) and eat them both at my favorite table by the window, the one under the painting of the butterflies. A scene in Taxi Driver was filmed here, right in this very spot. I know this would make my mother angry.

On Saturdays, I take a taxi to class, but I often walk home, lying to my mother that class ran late or that I was hanging out with the other girls after class so that I can walk. I love imagining that I am a real ballerina, a professional from American Ballet Theatre or New York City Ballet. I keep my hair in its bun and wear a skirt over my tights. My mother and I went to see The Turning Point a couple of years ago, and I feel just like Leslie Browne's character, walking duck-footed down the city streets.

This Saturday in April, I am running later than usual, and so I grab my donuts to go, the little greasy paper sack in hand as I head west on 14th Street. It's a long walk, about half an hour, but a straight shot. It's one of those glorious spring days in New York when the bite of winter is just a memory, and the air is filled with promise.

I have a new ballet-pink wrap sweater that I've thrown on over my leotard. I kept my leg warmers on, a pair of crinkly trash-bag pants over my tights. The sun is warm and so are the donuts, fresh out of the fryer.

I don't realize I am being followed until I'm about to turn off 14th Street onto 7th.

Every now and then, someone recognizes me from Midway Girl or one of the other films I've made. But it's New York, a place where far bigger celebrities than me walk around and get coffee and go shopping all the time. I figure he's probably just someone who wants an autograph.

Outside a pawn shop, I stop dead in my tracks and turn around. The man is close on my heels, his camera a dead giveaway. And so, I do what I always do. I smile sweetly and say, "Have a good day." I even think how cool it would be for there to be a photo in the tabloids of me in my ballet clothes.

But as I turn the corner onto 7th, I sense that he is still following me, and fear creeps into my throat, constricting it.

I remember that day my mother and I had gotten lost in Times Square, and I quickly dash down the subway stairs, praying that I might find a Guardian Angel, but as I descend the filthy steps, there is no one but a man playing a plaintive version of "Send in the Clowns" on the clarinet.

I look at my watch. I promised my mother I would be home by noon. She wants to run some lines with me for an upcoming audition. I have about ten minutes.

None of these trains will take me closer to Westbeth. The only way to get there now is to go back up and hop in a taxi or walk. I used the last of my allowance on donuts, and so I hurry back up the stairs and onto the street, and then I run the rest of the way home, my lungs on fire as I make it to the court-yard. I glance around frantically, hoping I've lost him. But across Bank Street, I see him, and he gives me a smug little smile and points, as if to say, "I got you."

The photo Henri and I make that afternoon might look like a portrait of any other aspiring ballet dancer. I am sitting on the windowsill in his apart-ment, the backlighting making me a bun-headed silhouette. You can't see the stain from the lemon donut I pressed so tightly against myself as I raced home. You can't see the tremor in my hand as I searched the streets below for the man who had followed me home. Or the others who might eventually try to hunt me down. To someone who didn't know, you might think I was gazing out at the world, at the future.

The next year, I will get my own apartment. I will begin to wear sun-glasses and hats, only going out when I need to. I will keep making movies and modeling, but my mother and I will begin to argue. Over everything. Her drinking while we are on location for a film will lose me the role that I worked so hard for. She will garner a reputation in the industry as a drunk. A bitch. And, if you believe the papers, a monster. And when her book comes out, I will be sickened by the lies. It will make me angry, red-faced and clenched-fist furious, but then, just as suddenly, it will make me sad. And I will pity her.

When Serafina gets too sick to run Lost River alone anymore, I will see an opportunity to go home. To leave my mother behind. To leave everything behind. I will tell her one night when she arrives at my apartment, falling down and mumbling apologies, that I don't want her in my life anymore. That she stole my childhood from me. That she is a horrible mother. And then I will buy a one-way ticket home.

Serafina and I will run Lost River Playhouse together for three seasons. It is here that I will meet Andy, when we choose his play, his debut, to stage. It is also at Lost River where he will propose after only three months, and where we will say our vows in the barn, on the stage, where my mother's dream began.

But for now, in this photo, I am just a girl at the edge of everything.

"What do you think?" Howard beams as Sasha devours his lemon tart. It is, as promised, delicious, but it sits heavy in my stomach. We balance our plates on our knees and pretend there isn't a media circus outside. I hear the whispers slither, though, winding their way through the room.

But mostly, there is grief. Henri was *beloved*. He came to the US in 1960, a young man who had been spurned by his family, ostracized and alone. Before Westbeth, he had lived with a lover, but the young man had died of cancer. When Westbeth opened, Henri had moved in and created a family out of thin air. A family who embraced him. I wonder how many considered him, as I did, like a father. I study the mournful faces and feel a pang of jealousy. As people steal glances at us, I feel angry. I loved him. I deserve to be here. I didn't do anything wrong. It's my mother who has stolen this moment. Who has created chaos where there should only be peace.

We are waiting until after the sun goes down to leave. Hoping that the press just gives up and goes home. My mother has texted from the unknown number ten times, becoming increasingly more terse, more desperate.

Is the memorial over?
Is the media still there?

If I don't hear from you by seven, I guess I'll just assume you're leaving me here.

Liliana is putting together doggy bags for the trip home. I have asked Sasha several times if she's sure she can drive at night, and she has assured me that she'll be fine.

I make one last trip around the room, studying Henri's photos and offering and receiving condolences from his friends. I stop when I get to the far half-wall, where a small, framed print is hanging alone.

It appears to be a picture from the first time we went to Henri's apartment together, my mother and me. When she went to get her headshots taken. I have never seen it before.

In the photo, my mother is sitting on the blue stool in Henri's studio, wearing Guillermo's shirt and that beret. She is barefoot, and I am sitting on her lap; I'm too big for this, my long legs dangling to the floor. I'm wearing mismatched tube socks and that T-shirt that says, ANYTHING BOYS CAN DO GIRLS CAN DO BETTER! with a little girl swinging a bat at a ball.

I am leaning back against her, her thin arms wrapped around my waist. Her eyes are closed as she kisses my hair, and for a moment, I can feel this. I can feel the sharp corners of her as she held me, the whisper of a kiss. I can smell the orange blossom smell of her, feel her long hair tickle my arms.

"She was the best mother she knew how to be," Liliana says softly. "And she was so proud of you. I don't think you know that, but she was. *Is.*"

I turn to her, and she's holding the bags with food for us.

"What's going to happen to her?" I ask.

Liliana smiles sadly. "I don't know. But she can't run forever."

Lost River
July 1981

We'd been in Los Angeles since May, filming a teen romance. My mother loved California and was reluctant to leave. While I was on set, she'd spent most of her summer working on her tan by the pool, flirting with the bartender who manned the tiki bar. But she had promised we could go to Lost River and stay for a month before we went back to the city, and I held her to it.

Guillermo, Liliana, and the kids had been there since June. The Playhouse was putting on a production of *Of Mice and Men*, and Guillermo was George. I missed Gilly, and I couldn't stop thinking about the rope swing. The river.

I was fifteen now. A teenager. Practically grown-up. Margie had started sending me on assignments with adults. I was auditioning for parts that were much older than I was. In the film we'd just shot in LA, I played a seventeen-year-old.

Gilly greeted us at the train station. He'd gotten his license that summer. It felt so strange to be chauffeured by him on the long road to the compound. We hadn't been back for more than a weekend since we left, and we hadn't gone at all the prior summer.

The road turned to dirt, and we bumped along, the leaves almost blindingly green. My mother sat in the front seat, and I sat behind Gilly, my chin resting on his shoulder.

We had talked, of course, when I was in LA. But long distance was expensive, and so our conversations were short, hurried. I could tell he was keeping something from me, but I wasn't sure what it was. But I knew the moment I saw him, his flushed cheeks and bright eyes. He was in love again.

The boy's name was Marcus. He was eighteen, an actor himself, from somewhere in the Midwest. He'd been cast as Slim. He was soft-spoken and kind.

"He's nice, Gilly," I said as we walked along the well-worn path to the river.

"Isn't he?" he said, beaming.

I missed the easiness of us, the way I could just be myself around Gilly. It was easy to forget who I really was sometimes, when someone was telling me who I should be.

"I'm going to come back and live here someday," I said, articulating for the first time something I hadn't said out loud before. "When I have a family."

"Yeah?" he asked.

"Yeah. It's safe here," I said. "And peaceful."

"You wanna have kids?"

I nodded. "Just one. A daughter."

"And a husband?" he asked, wiggling his eyebrows.

I rolled my eyes. "I guess, if I *have* to."

What I didn't tell him was that the only guy I could ever have imagined myself married to was him.

It was one of those hot summer days in Vermont, humid and thick. Everything felt sluggish, even the river that churned below us. I slapped at a mosquito on my arm, and Gilly tugged my hand, and we ran to the oak with the rope swing.

We were surrounded by green. The cacophony of birds in the trees, the hum of insects, and the sloshing river felt so strange after the absence of sound in Los Angeles and the oppressive city noise in New York.

We'd told Liliana and my mother we were going for a walk, maybe a swim. My mother had put her hands on her hips and said, "Don't do anything dangerous. You *cannot* get hurt right now. No broken bones. No scratches. 'Kay?"

"I'll go first," he said, slipping off his sneakers and tearing off his shirt.

It still took my breath away when I saw his concave chest.

"You never told me why," I said, motioning to that hollow place, "it's like that?"

"My mom used to say that it was because I always gave my heart away," he said, laughing. "It was a nice way of making me feel better. It's just a malformation of my bones."

"I think she was right, Gilly," I said, teasing. "And now *Marcus* has it."

"Maybe you're right," he said, and grinned, and then grabbed hold of the rope and backed up before running ahead and howling as he swung across the river.

After he'd reached the other side, he cupped his hands together and said, "Now you!"

I had to climb up the oak a bit to retrieve the rope and pull it back to my side. The end had dragged in the water and was cool and wet.

The last time I stood here, I'd been terrified. But the desire to fly was the same. I wanted to prove to Gilly and to myself that I could do this. That I was brave. I was taller now, nearly fully grown, but I still felt as scared as I had been when I was ten years old.

"You can do it, Ryan!" Gilly said, and I was transported back to that other afternoon. The day we learned we were leaving Lost River for the city. The day that everything changed.

I gripped the rope in my shaking hands.

"Run really fast!" he said, and I thought about the way I had run away from Raymond, and then just last month, from the man who was following me. But this time, I wasn't running away. I wasn't fleeing.

I backed up as far as the rope would let me, took a deep breath, and began to run. When the earth fell away from me, I kept my eyes open and watched the sky appear from behind the canopy of leaves. I didn't look down.

And when Gilly said, "Now let go!" I did.

I released the rope and felt myself flying, then falling, then landing. On my feet. On the other side. Safe.

New York City
August 2019

At nine o'clock, when the floors have been swept and the trash bags filled with punch-stained cups and paper plates have been taken out, when no one remains in the gallery except for Gilly, Liliana, and me, I go to the window and look out at the empty street. They've finally given up, gone home.

I wonder how long it will be until the FBI descends on Nick's house. How long before they take my mother. Will they handcuff her? Bend her over to fit into their back seat? The idea feels ludicrous. Awful. My body is hot with both guilt and shame.

From everything Liliana has told me, and my mother's explanations, it is possible, it seems, that her involvement in Brenner's business was peripheral. It's not as though she were out on the streets, recruiting girls. It's not as though she were the one making them promises of fame, only to turn them into Brenner's playthings. It's not as if she ever put me in harm's way, with Brenner, anyway. If she's telling the truth, then she did the opposite. She kept me *safe*.

I try not to think of his victims. Of all those other girls. The girl on his arm at the Oscars. The ones in the photos in the news articles. The ones with the hungry eyes. My throat aches at the thought of a girl like Sasha, at the beginning of her life, wanting so much. I think of those ballet dancers, the longing and yearning in every sinew and breath. Why must so many women be made of need?

I had sworn I would never be one of those lovesick girls, those pining ones. But when I'd met Andy, all my determination went out the window. It wasn't his fault. No one could fill the empty spaces my mother had left inside me.

My mother.

"Call me when you get home, okay?" Gilly says. "Drive safe. And I'll be up for a visit before school starts and bring the things from Henri's. Would you like the card catalog? I'd take it, but our apartment is already so full of Howard's antiques. I can get a trailer and bring it up."

I nod.

"Can I have this?" I ask, pointing to the small portrait of me and my mother.

"Of course," he says, and lifts it from its hanger.

I hold it to my chest.

Gilly hugs Sasha and then embraces me. "You'll make the right choice," he says.

Together, Sasha and I exit the building and walk briskly across the street. There's no one out, but still my heart is pounding in my throat, in time with the rolling of the suitcase wheels. We enter the garage, and I feel disoriented, almost dizzy.

"Where did we park?" I ask, trying not to let on how anxious I am.

I hear footsteps echoing heavily somewhere behind us.

"I took a picture with my phone," Sasha says. "Hold on one sec."

As the footsteps come closer, I clutch the handle of the suitcase and whip my head around, trying to determine where the footsteps are coming from.

"Third floor," Sasha says finally, and then looks up and around, trying to locate the elevators.

"Let's just take the stairs," I say, locating the sign.

"You sure? That suitcase is super heavy."

"Yes," I insist, and lead the way.

As we enter the stairwell, I can hear someone running toward us, breathing heavily.

"Miss Flannigan," a male voice says.

I stop on the landing, the smell of urine and cigarette smoke almost overwhelming. I back down the steps, putting myself between the man and my daughter.

"What do you want?" I ask.

"I'm so sorry," he says. "I didn't mean to startle you." He puts up his hands in surrender. He's older. Distinguished-looking. No camera in sight. "I didn't know how else to reach you."

"Well, following two women into a dark parking garage is probably not the best way," Sasha chimes in.

"I am truly sorry. I just wanted to catch you before you left the city."

"Who are you?" I ask.

"I wanted to talk to you about the Dubois photo," he says. "*Blackout, 1977.*"

A reporter.

"I have no comment."

"No, no. I'm sorry," he says, pressing a weathered hand to his chest. "I am a collector," he says. "A completist." At this, he chuckles. "I have nearly every photograph that Mr. Dubois has ever published, and many unpublished, as well."

I sigh. "You want me to *sell* you that photo?" I ask. "Because I don't even have it. It's probably in police custody."

"Actually," he says, "*I* have it."

"What?"

"I was able to procure it from the authorities."

As he says this, I realize that the FBI must know about the payment. The hush money. The photo enabled them to connect Brenner to my mother, but the *money* is the real evidence. Bank records. Whatever it is that she signed. The photo hardly matters anymore.

Suddenly, I am filled with rage. These rich men, able to purchase or steal whatever it is they desire. To sate themselves, their sick obsessions.

"So what do you *want* from me then?" I ask. "What more do you need?" I reach over then and unzip the outer pocket of the suitcase, suddenly wanting nothing to do with the photos, wanting nothing to do with whatever sort of twisted exchange this was. My entire career had been based on my face and body as currency. My mother had capitalized on my beauty as a child, and perhaps even Henri had, as well. Maybe this is all I ever was to anyone.

I push the stuffed portfolio at him, press it against him.

Sasha grabs my arm. "Mama, what are you doing?"

"Just take it," I say. "Take them all. I don't even care anymore."

The man gently takes the portfolio from me and hands it to Sasha, who clings to it. He reaches into his briefcase and pulls out his own envelope.

"No. You misunderstand. I just wanted to return this to you. I am a collector, but I also understand that some images are not for consumption. I have spent forty years studying his work, appreciating his art. This image is different," he says, and smiles at me sadly. "Some pictures ask a question. Others make an argument. But this one, this one. Sweet girl, this one is a *plea*. It does not belong to me."

With that, he hands me the photograph. The print I had given my mother after the blackout, the one she'd handed over to a monster. I realized when she looked at me, she never saw *me*. She only saw her own dreams, and she would do anything to make them come true.

I give Sasha directions to Nick's in Brooklyn. There is an open spot in front of his brownstone, a light on in the attic. They haven't found her yet.

"There's a hydrant, Mom," Sasha says. "I can't park here."

"It's okay. Leave the car running," I say, and open the door. "But lock up."

When I close the passenger door, I hear the electronic locks engage.

I open the wrought iron gate, still gazing up at the illuminated window. I think I see movement, a shadow pass. I take the steps and feel my phone buzz in my pocket.

Are you here? she texts.

I think about calling her, telling her to come down. I imagine her climbing into the back seat, the car filling with her orange blossom scent. I imagine bringing her back to Lost River, where she might live in one of the cabins, maybe the one where she and I used to stay. I remember the way she carefully brushed the tangles out of my hair, me nestled into the crook between her knees.

The doorbell glows a weak orange. The mailbox's lid is open.

I pull my phone out again and think about what I could say. *I love you? I hate you? I'm still so afraid?* I am at a loss for words, just as I was the day she finally came home after the blackout. And so, I offer her, again, what I tried to give her back then.

I put the envelope with the photograph in the mailbox and shut the lid.

Lost River
September 2019

On the morning of Sasha's departure, her friends have gathered again.

Zu-Zu has been in the kitchen, helping me make Sasha's favorite pumpkin muffins, while Sasha and Luca load up her car.

"I used to do ballet, too," I say, as she hands me the brown sugar. "Never like you, of course. But in the city. When I was a girl."

"Sasha never told me that," Zu-Zu says. "I mean, I know you were an actress. I've seen *Midway Girl* about a hundred times."

I smile. "You know what I loved most?" I ask, stirring a bright yellow egg yolk into the batter. "About dancing?"

"The blisters and corns?" Zu-Zu laughs.

"No." I smile. "I loved my point shoes. The way that something so delicate and fragile could support me. Just paper and glue. It always felt like a miracle."

Zu-Zu stops what she's doing. "People always think that. They always assume there must be something about the box. But it's not the shoe. It's the dancer. Her strength. She holds herself up. You were holding *yourself* up."

Sasha comes barreling into the kitchen, and through the window, I see Luca's old Volkswagen tearing down the road away from the house.

"Where's he going?" I ask. "I thought he was helping you load up the car."

"I broke up with him," she says, and her sigh is the happiest sigh I've ever heard. I find myself feeling a swell of pride.

"Finally," Zu-Zu says. "Only took a year."

"You okay?" I ask Sasha.

"I am," she says, and nods. "I feel free."

I smile.

When Gilly texted the article about my mother turning herself in, I'd expected to *feel* more. To second-guess my decision. To feel guilty about leaving her to fend for herself. To feel sad. But instead, I felt like this. Liberated. *Free.*

Sasha had said she would delay her road trip. Stay with me. She could go in a month or two, she said. LA wasn't going anywhere. But as much as I wanted to say yes, to hold her close, to hold on tight, I knew this was not my job. Not anymore.

And so instead, I took her to the used car lot and helped her pick out a car we'd researched. I offered to pay half, which she balked at. She'd been saving all summer for this. I made the calls to ensure that her health insurance would work in California. I helped her apply for a credit card.

Last night, I found her in her ravaged room and handed her the gift-wrapped box. Her going-away gift. She loves presents, and her eyes were alight as she tore away the striped paper and ribbons.

"It was Henri's," I said as she lifted the Rolleiflex out of the box.

It had been with a whole carful of Henri's things that Gilly and Howard had delivered the week before.

"I love it, Mama," she said. "But are you sure you don't want to keep it?"

"You're the photographer," I said, and laughed. "You will make beautiful pictures with it, I'm sure."

At ten o'clock, her friends crowd around her, enclosing her like a swarm of bees. She is nectar, I think—attracting everyone, but nurturing them, too. When they finally disperse, every one of them is blubbering. Mascara running. Shoulders shaking. She is so very loved. When they have all gotten in one last hug, I go to her, and she falls into my arms.

"Hey," I say when I feel her body shuddering.

"I'm scared, Mom," she whispers.

"There is *nothing* to be afraid of," I say. We separate, and I smile. "You've got a cell phone and Triple-A. A credit card. I can Venmo you in an emergency. Just keep your phone charged."

"I'm not afraid about *that*," she says, and I'm confused.

She looks at me, her eyes fixed on mine. "I need to know *you* are going to be okay."

And for the first time in her whole life, I see myself in her eyes. Me, always worrying about my mother. Taking care of her when she should have been taking care of me.

"*That* is not your job," I say firmly. "Your job is to grow up and be amazing."

She releases me and opens her car door. It dings and dings, impatient for her to just get in already.

"I'm already amazing," she says as she gets into the driver's seat.

She shuts the door, but her window is rolled down.

"Yes, you are," I say.

Acknowledgments

This novel would not have been written, and certainly would never have been published, if not for the generous guidance of many people.

For sharing the stories of their lives at Westbeth Artists Housing, I am tremendously indebted to Christina Maile and Rachel Williams. I hope that the Westbeth of my imagination does justice to the real thing.

Thank you to my astute and talented editor, Wendy McCurdy, and the rest of my Kensington family for the warm welcome home: Steve and Adam Zacharius, Elizabeth Trout, Carly Sommerstein, Alexandra Nicolajsen, Kristin McLaughlin, Matt Johnson, Lauren Jernigan, Vida Engstrand, and Lynn Cully. To Scott Helm for the meticulous read, and, for the evocative and achingly beautiful cover, my heartfelt thanks to Kris Noble.

David Forrer, thank you for taking a chance on me and this story. Your insights and patience and kindness during the whole process (from first draft to first pass pages) are unparalleled. Thank you for believing in this world I created as well as the characters who live there. It is my pleasure and privilege to work with you.

Thank you to Jillian Cantor and Amy Hatvany for reading the early drafts and helping me navigate the dark labyrinth of my imagination. And my appreciation, as always, to Patrick for being a reliable bit of light in that darkness.

Lastly, all the love in the world to my daughters, Mikaela and Esmée, who continue to inspire me to be both the best writer and mother I can be. You are both, already, amazing.

SUCH A PRETTY GIRL

ABOUT THIS GUIDE

The suggested questions are included to enhance
your group's reading of T. Greenwood's
Such a Pretty Girl.

Discussion Questions

1. *Such a Pretty Girl,* like many of T. Greenwood's novels, is about the relationships between mothers and daughters. Discuss how Ryan's relationship with Fiona changes over time. And how is Ryan's parenting of Sasha a response to her own mother's failures?

2. Fiona is an aspiring actress when we meet her, yet her dreams are ultimately unfulfilled. How does this affect her relationship with her daughter? Do you think she is both proud of her and jealous as well?

3. Fiona explains that she was protecting Ryan by making the deal she made with Zev Brenner. Do you think this is true, and if not, what do you think she was doing?

4. Do you believe that Fiona should be punished for her complicity in Brenner's schemes? Is what she did on par with what Margie did?

5. Do you blame Fiona for Henri's suicide? Why do you think he took his own life?

6. There are two major settings in the novel: Lost River in Vermont and Westbeth in the West Village in New York City. Think about the contrast between these two places, and what each represents to Ryan. Why does she flee to Vermont when she leaves her career behind?

7. The 1970s was a dark time for New York City: it was both morally and financially bankrupt. However, for Ryan and the other children at Westbeth, it is *magical.* Discuss the depiction of childhood in this novel.

8. If you were also a child in the 1970s, what do you recall about your own childhood? How does Ryan's childhood differ from Sasha's? If you have children, how does yours compare to theirs?

9. As an adult, Ryan is forced to revisit her childhood through a contemporary lens. As an adult, she is able to see how the adults in childhood both failed and exploited her. Is there anything from your own life that you now see through a different filter?

10. The modeling industry and the film industry clearly exploit Ryan's innocence and beauty. She argues that Henri really saw her—and that his photos were not exploitative at all. Do you think this is true? Or is it possible that Ryan was wrong about his intentions?

11. On that note, in the last few years, many women have reexamined past experiences thanks to the #metoo movement. Behavior that was once tolerated or dismissed or even *expected* from men has come under new scrutiny. How do you think the #metoo movement liberates Ryan?

12. Gilly is Ryan's best friend and the single consistent presence in her life for decades. What role does he play in their lives as children and how does this carry over into their adult lives?

13. Ryan has kept the secret of what happened on the night of the blackout for decades. Why do you think she does not reveal what Raymond did to her to anyone but Henri?

14. Ryan's anxiety begins as a child and is something she contends with her whole life. How does this manifest in the way she parents Sasha?

15. If Ryan had not been "discovered" by Margie, what do you think she would have done with her life? Have you had any moments in your own life that changed its trajectory?

16. Discuss the photo that Henri took on the night of the blackout and what it means to each of the characters: Ryan, Fiona, Henri, and Zev Brenner. What does it "prove" to the media?

17. This book is also about family—the families we are born into and the ones we make. Discuss Ryan's "family."

Visit our website at
KensingtonBooks.com
to sign up for our newsletters, read
more from your favorite authors, see
books by series, view reading group
guides, and more!

Become a Part of Our
Between the Chapters Book Club
Community and Join the Conversation